A beautiful reporter and a charming rancher are caught in a web of mayhem, murder...and lust.

Reporter Sawyer Cahill returns home to Cheyenne, Texas to report for the local television station. But leaving behind the coverage of San Antonio's gangland murders only lands her in the middle of a wave of realistic animal mutilations. Harassed and threatened by Hunter Kane, the freak behind the bizarre mutilations, Sawyer plunges into her investigation.

A former attorney turned rancher, Jake Spooner lost his wife to the man he believes is now tormenting Sawyer. Torn between his desire for Sawyer and his need to keep her safe, Jake's mission is to bring Hunter down before the murderer strikes again.

Winterkill

By P.H. Turner

*For Keela,
So good to see you
at RWA '14*

P.H. Turner

KENSINGTON BOOKS
Kensington Publishing Corp.
www.kensingtonbooks.com

LYRICAL PRESS
An imprint of Kensington Publishing Corp.

First Electronic Edition: June 2014
eISBN-13: 978-1-61650-55-6
eISBN-10: 1-61650-551-6

First Print Edition: June 2014
ISBN-13: 978-1-61650-633-9
ISBN-10: 1-61650-633-4

Printed in the United States of America

Chapter 1

I met him for happy hour at the Yella Feather bar over on the south side about 5:30 on a hot August evening. He was dead by 6:15. Ours was a short relationship.

Lieutenant Deaver was one of the old guys with the San Antonio PD. He strolled in with the coroner, finding me where the first responder had put me. Over in a corner holding up a yellowed wall that reeked with years of stale nicotine.

"You okay?" Deaver asked.

"Yeah, think so." I took a weak swallow of warm Coke.

"What happened?" He pulled out a rickety chair and sat down.

I slumped into a seat beside him. "I didn't see the killer. My back was to the door when I heard the sound of a round chambered. Right in front me—Rodriguez was talking to me—a small, round hole drilled into his forehead. I heard the door bang shut and a car squeal off, but by the time I made it outside there was nothing to see and only cordite to smell."

I looked around the bar, broken-down scarred tabletops, wobbly chairs, flaking vinyl floors with duct tape covering the cracks. The stink of disinfectant and stale grease mingled with gun smoke. *Helluva place for a kid to die.*

"How long you known him, Cahill?" Deaver asked softly.

"I'd say about forty-five minutes, give or take."

He scratched his left armpit, his face screwed into thought. "What were you doing with Rodriguez? Source of yours?"

"Yeah, for a Latin Kings story. I've been trying to get in front of him for weeks."

"Looks like your time with him is over. You get much

outta him?"

"Not much more than I already knew."

"Which is?" Lt. Deaver probed.

"He and his older brother live two blocks down in the Oleander Projects with their mom. No dad around. He denied he was a King. Claimed he was twenty-one and an unemployed high school dropout. Just another guy from the south side."

"Hell, that's a lie," Lt. Deaver grunted. "He's a King just like his brother. Rodriguez isn't—wasn't— eighteen. Let me know if you come up with anything else." He shifted his bulk in the chair. "Why don't you get a job fitting a woman, Ms. Cahill?"

"What job would that be?" I tossed over my shoulder watching Deaver zeroing in on the bartender. I stepped out of the grimy bar into the oppressive heat, popping the lock on my Laredo.

Rodriguez was just a kid, with scarcely a twist of beard masquerading as a goatee. My hands began to shake. I pulled over to the side of the curb, wrenched opened the door and puked on the street. When my head quit spinning, I slammed the door shut and hit the automatic lock. Air conditioning cooled the sweat on my upper lip. Easing •the Jeep back into the San Antonio traffic, I headed toward the station. Maybe Deaver was right. *Sawyer Cahill, you need to look at that job offer you have sitting on your desk.*

Chapter 2

I pushed open the barn doors to the studio area of NBC7. The news director Andy shouted over the bedlam of two electricians hanging metal lights on the grid. "Hey, look who just blew in. Did you get any footage of the Rodriguez shooting? We need it to cut in under Manuel's lead. We don't even have a body bag shot."

"I'm fine, thank you."

"You know the drill," he barked. "Cryin' babies, dead bodies. Great footage. Your job is to bring me, the news director, what I need—news." Andy's hands were on his hips.

"No footage, Andy. I didn't take a camera. I just went for background. I got damned little of that."

"Next time take some gear, Cahill. Amateur's mistake," he sniped.

"Like hell, Andy. Rodriguez woulda split the second he saw a camera. How long since you were in the field?"

I stepped over the cables snaked on the floor. Andy's news rundown was on the desk. The lead story was Rodriguez's killing.

Andy walked up behind me. "You got a source to replace Rodriguez on the Kings story?"

"Jesus, Andy! Rodriguez's body is barely cold. What the hell's wrong with you? All he was to you was a south side banger?" I threw the rundown on the desk. "He's got a mother for Christ's sake. You think she isn't bawling her eyes out over her dead son? You have no compassion—none. He was a kid for god's sake, not just one hundred-fifty pounds of dead meat in a body bag! Screw you, Andy. I'm done here."

"Get a source," Andy called after me. "Soon, Cahill. Or I'll pull you. I'll get a reporter in there who knows how to get the job done."

A threat from Andy. All I need to cap my day.

Exhaustion seeped into every pore. The adrenaline rush ended before I could get out of the station. In its wake, I felt lethargic. What a loss! A kid who would never get the opportunity to turn his life around. Rodriguez's killer would probably never be found, leaving his mother to cry for justice.

I made it home and threw my keys on the counter. Thumbing the mail, I dropped most of it in the trash. All I wanted was a long soak in my favorite lavender bath salts. I kicked off my shoes, leaving a trail of clothes on the way to the tub.

My second glass of wine took the edge off. I had most of my right leg shaved when my mom called to ask about my love life. Since my dad died, she'd made her life's work to get me presentable, paired and pregnant—in exactly that order. "Sawyer, honey. How're you doing? I don't get nearly enough time with you. I've been worrying about you." I took a sip of wine and stuck my big toe in the spigot to catch the drips. This was going to take awhile. "All this running around down there on the bad side of San Antonio talking to gang members. I just want what's best for you."

I shifted the razor to my left leg. "Yes, Mom…"

"You know, you work too hard at that job. Crime reporting really doesn't suit you. You know that, don't you honey?"

"Mom, I like my job and I'm damned good at it." I immediately regretted the *damned*.

"But Sawyer," she wheedled, "a man wouldn't want his wife to interview criminals. Think of your children. You couldn't very well tell them what you did all day, could you?"

The imaginary zygotes drove me nuts. "I'll think about it," I said. "Can I call you later and catch up with you?"

"Sure. You call me now. Love you."

"Love you, too. Take care." I slipped deeper into the lavender scented water letting the warmth work on the kinks in my neck.

* * * *

By seven AM, I was editing video, listening to a social worker talk about the forty-seven percent dropout rate of Hispanic students in the south side high schools. Gang membership was surging. My cell rang.

"Ms. Cahill? It's Clay Watkins." His deep voice boomed out of my speaker.

"Good morning Mr. Watkins. How are you?"

"Fine. Sorry I missed your call. I'm hoping you're gonna tell me you're coming on up here to join us at CBS3. I need a reporter like you. Am I right?"

The offer letter was staring up at me from the desk. I fingered the paper, lingering over the clauses. Sure, I could stay right here. Find Rodriguez's killer. Probably the kid's best shot at justice. Might even win another Emmy. Why should I stay? Just to see a new kid try to ace the gang initiation and get his head blown off?

"Absolutely. Shall I sign and fax it and then put the hard copy in the mail?"

"Whew! Yes." He cheered. "We're happy to have you. When can you start?"

"Two weeks."

* * * *

I stood outside Andy's office waiting for him to get off the phone.

"Yeah, yeah," he barked impatiently into the phone. "Go to hell, Frankie. I'm not doing it." He slammed the receiver down. "Yeah? What do you want, Cahill? Better be good. Better brighten my day. Had my fill of assholes already."

"Me too, Andy. I'm resigning." I laid the letter on his desk.

"What the hell do you mean you're resigning? You wanna tank your career, fine by me. You haven't worked here two years. Two years. You got clauses in that contract of yours. Read it and weep. You aren't going anywhere without a lawsuit."

I sat in his hard plastic chair. "I've read my contract. There's no clause saying I have to work here for two years. It says I can't take a job at an NBC affiliate within five hundred miles of San Antonio and I'm going to CBS3 in Cheyenne." I dropped the letter of notice on his cluttered desk.

He didn't touch it. He fumbled in his file drawer, pulled out a file and started to read, flipping pages noisily. "Got your contract right here." He peered at me over his cheaters. "So, there's no clause in it." He looked up with a nasty smile. "Big shit! News business is a small world. I call that news director and tell him you're some flighty bitch who jumps from job to job and you'll be out of a gig. I'll do it too."

"I've signed the contract in Cheyenne, Andy. We haven't always gotten along, but I *have not* broken my contract with you."

"Then turn in your keys and get the hell out," he snarled. "Turn your crap you're working on over to Manuel. He'll do a good job on that story of yours."

"Consider it done."

* * * *

I put my Press Award plaques in the single box—all that was needed to carry out my personal things. I called Lt. Deaver and he had nothing on the Rodriguez killing. He did wish me well. The gangs were silent, but so was the gunfire on the south side. Let Manuel chase it. I pulled my station keys from the ring and stared at them in my hand. Andy was right about one thing; news directors were a tight bunch. What if he called Clay Watkins and tried to screw me at CBS?

I dialed Clay's number. "CBS3. This is Margery. How may I help you?"

"Sawyer Cahill, here. Could I speak to Mr. Watkins, please?"

"Oh, hello Ms. Cahill. Mr. Watkins is in a staff meeting. Would you like to leave a message?"

"No, I'll call back later," I said. "But would you tell him I called?"

How fast could Andy make that call?

Chapter 3

Cheyenne was my hometown until the end of my seventh grade year. I cried for three weeks that first summer in Denver, missing Julia Graham every day. She answered on the second ring.

"I hope you're calling to tell me you're coming home after fifteen years. You're taking that job you told me about, right?"

"I'll be there in a week, give or take a day or so!"

"It'll be like old times, Sawyer. Where are you going to be living?" she asked.

"I'm hoping you can help with that. Got any recommendations?"

"Ohh, Sawyer. Rentals are scarce what with the oil boom. Some oil workers are bunking in Laramie and driving back and forth to the fields. I'll get on Craigslist and see if anything decent is available," Julia said.

"Thanks, you're the best."

* * * *

I left San Antonio in a red-streaked dawn. I was officially homeless. So far, Julia had struck out on finding me a rental.

I-25 skirted the mountains around Raton, New Mexico. I'd make Denver late tomorrow and spend the night with mom. Dad died last spring and she was having a terrible time being alone.

She opened the door before I could get my key in the lock, looking perfect in her pearls and deftly applied makeup. Her cashmere twinset matched the shade of her long skirt. "Sawyer, so good to see you, dear." She kissed my cheek. Hands on my shoulders, she stepped back looking me over. "You look scruffy, honey." She scrutinized me. "I'm not sure that shirt color does much for your red hair. Maybe a different shade, blue to accent your eyes."

"Mom, I didn't dress up to drive ten hours." *God, she brings the petulance out in me.*

"Well." Her eyes welled up. "I'm just saying…"

"No problem, Mom." I hugged her. "Let's get this stuff up to my room." Thirty seconds together before I hurt her feelings and tears spilled. I wanted to do better. I *would* do better.

I followed her out to the deck. She precisely dusted off her chair, arranging her skirt around her knees. I enjoyed a cold Dos Equis. She had her favored merlot.

"Tell me about your new job, sweetheart."

"It's what I always wanted. I'll be a special projects reporter at CBS. I'm excited, Mom."

She sighed, rolling her eyes. "I can't believe you haven't gotten this journalism stuff out of your system by now. It's just not right Sawyer. You need a job fitting the type of young woman you are." She slammed her glass down, sloshing merlot, staining a red ring on the table.

"Mom, *this* is the type of woman I am. I love my job and I've worked hard to get where I am." I remembered Andy's threat to call Watkins and sour my prospects. Andy wasn't going to screw this for me.

"I just worry about you dear." She patted my hand. "I want you to be happy, that's all your Dad and I ever wanted. With a nice young man and a life together."

"My life is good."

"But Sawyer, you've let some good opportunities for marriage pass you by. Remember that orthodontist in Boulder? He offered you such a promising life. Then there was Connor. Connor's so accomplished and he was such a lovely young man. From a good family, too. I really enjoyed him. You broke off with both of them. Honey, do you know what you're looking for in a man?"

"I guess not, Mom."

The tears formed in her eyes again. Guilt rolled over me. She's my mother, for god's sake. Why can't she let me be the adult woman I am?

"Mom." I pulled her into my arms. "I want you to stop worrying. I'm fine. My life is not a mirror of yours, but I'm happy."

She pulled a Kleenex out of her skirt pocket and dabbed at the corners of both eyes. "You're my only child and I just want what's best for you. Your dad's gone now." The tears rolled down her cheeks. "He would know what's best."

"Mom…" I warned.

She sat up in her chair until her back was ramrod straight. Raised her chin and tugged at her twinset. "So. You're going back to Cheyenne. Where are you going to live? You haven't told me."

"I don't know." I laughed. "Julia's looking for place."

She clasped her hands on her knees. "Sawyer, you have no home?"

"Mom, I have a job. The worst that could happen is that I have to stay in a hotel and store my stuff for awhile."

She worried at a miniscule piece of lint on her sleeve. "But Julia is helping you. Right?"

"She is. She and Dave got married, remember?"

"That boy she was dating when you two were in college?"

"Yes, they moved from Boulder to Cheyenne after they graduated." The crinkled worry lines on her face relaxed. "Julia looked at a rental for me today. I may hear from her tonight." I gave her hope.

We cleared the dishes. I hugged her goodnight and climbed the stairs to my old room. I opened a window to let in fresh air. She had left my room as it was the day I left for CU. A dry, brittle corsage was pinned to my sagging bulletin board. The ribbon hung in limp dusty streamers. I was ten years older than this room.

* * * *

At nine sharp, I called Clay Watkins.

"What can I do for you?" His distinctive voice boomed out of the radio speakers.

"I'll be at work tomorrow. I'm looking forward to it." I paused. "The news director at NBC and I didn't part on the best of terms…"

"I know." Clay's voice was louder. "Heard an earful from him."

"I left under the terms of my contract. I changed networks and moved over five hundred miles."

"Didn't get the particulars from Andy. I know him, you know. Couple of us go drinkin' every year at the convention."

"I assumed you knew each other. The important thing is that you understand that I fulfilled my contract and I gave two weeks' notice."

"Tell you what's important to me. You get here and do a helluva professional job for me and this station. And don't be an asshole while you're doin' it. See you tomorrow." The line went dead.

I tapped my phone off. I could work with that.

Chapter 4

I drove into the wide-open spaces of Wyoming deciding to quit rehashing my old relationships. I wasn't missing any of them. Or Andy either.

What I needed was a house.

I picked up the phone and called my go-to person. "Julia, did that guy call you back about the house?"

"Finally. I hope you're gonna like this place. It's a restored farmhouse ten miles north of Cheyenne. Probably bigger than you need, but it's nice and it's available. He's offering a twelve-month lease and the price is good." I sensed her excitement and pictured her flushed face and bright eyes.

"Great! Tell him I'll take it. I'm excited about seeing you. I'll call the movers now to give them my new address so they won't put my stuff in storage."

"When are you getting here? I can meet you out at the place after four."

"I should be in town by then. I don't mind waiting at the house for you. Give me the directions again."

"Head north on I-25. Take exit 233 for Horse Creek Road. It's about nine miles from town. Turn right at the exit and then turn right again. Keep going until you see the first stone house on the right. You can't miss it. See ya."

A couple of hours later, I turned into the drive. A rural mailbox decorated with horseshoes sat sentinel at the entrance. *Great. Yard art.* The house was set at the end of a small well-kept green yard. I took the three steps up the broad porch. "Hello?" I called into the screen door. No answer. I peered into the dimly lit house. Nails scratched and clattered on the hardwood floors. I jumped back as the screen banged open. A big black and tan dog planted his feet in front of me, barking furiously. I backed cautiously down two steps, the dog matching me step by step. Behind me, I heard a male voice ask, "Can I help you?"

"Yeah, call your dog off." I didn't take my eyes off the madly barking animal.

"Chet! Come!" he commanded in a deep baritone.

Chet brushed past me and ran down the steps. Only when he was behind me did I turn around.

A tall man with longish dark hair and a good set of cheekbones looked mildly amused.

"Sit, Chet," he said. "Good boy. You're a good boy aren't you?" He ruffled the head of the fawning dog. "May I help you? I'm Jake Spooner and that's my porch you're standing on."

"Sawyer Cahill," I said, extending my hand. The touch of his firm handshake sent a frisson of warmth up my arm. We stared at each other for a nanosecond too long. I loosened my hand. "Thanks for calling your dog off. I've rented a house out here somewhere. Supposedly, it's the first stone house on Horse Creek Road. Obviously not. Sorry for the intrusion."

"No problem." He flashed a warm smile. "Yours would be the second stone house about a half mile from here on the right side. If you like, I can show you the way. I heard Sam had rented the place. Met him?"

"Not yet. I'll take you up on the offer to lead the way. Thanks."

Chet's tail was thumping and he was wriggling his way closer to me. I showed him the flat of my palm. He sniffed, woofed his approval and sat on my foot.

"No problem." This guy had some seriously gorgeous gray eyes. He stepped aside for me to join him. "Sam Jordan is the local vet. Where are you moving from?"

"San Antonio."

Chet jumped in the back of Jake's truck.

"I hope you'll be happy here."

"I will be. I grew up here."

"Really? We might have met. I used to come up from Denver to spend the summers with my grandparents when I was a kid."

His hand grazed my forearm when we walked to my Jeep. *I wouldn't have forgotten that face.* "We moved away when I was twelve and I don't think we've met."

He flashed a great smile. "We'll have time to get know each other. Is Sam meeting you at the house?"

"I don't know. Julia's meeting me."

He opened the door of my Jeep. "Who's Julia?"

"Julia Graham. My childhood friend."

"I know them. I've done some business with her husband, Dave, at the bank. You're lucky to get anything to rent in Cheyenne right now. Follow me down the drive and we'll turn right."

When I got into my car, I called Julia. "You there at the house?"

"Yeah, I just got here. Sam's here too. You'll see my blue Toyota from the road," Julia said.

I followed Jake's truck into the drive, parking my dusty black Jeep by Julia's car. The house had a welcoming wrap-around front porch running across the front and down the east side.

"Welcome home." Julia ran down the steps grabbing me in tight hug. "Jake, good to see you, too." She looked at me quizzically.

"I found my way to Jake's house and he was kind enough to lead me over."

An older, heavyset man stepped through the front door. "Hi there, you ready for the tour?"

"Yes." I extended my hand. "I'm Sawyer Cahill."

He took my hand and it disappeared into his meaty paw. "Good to meet you. Julia has some fine things to say about you." His eyes crinkled with his grin. "I hope you'll like the place. I'm sure glad to have you renting it."

He turned to Jake. "Afternoon, Jake. See you met your new neighbor."

"I've had the pleasure." Jake grasped Sam's hand.

"Come on in." He held the screen door open. "This was my grandparents' home. They ranched out here in the 1930s. When I was a kid, I used to shoot my twenty-two back in those pastures. You got Jake's place across the back fence from you.

The house had creamy plaster walls set off by yellow pine floors. A huge brick fireplace with a raised hearth anchored one end of the room. There was a modern kitchen with what looked like the original farm sink. Down the hall were two good-sized bedrooms and a bath.

"Nice restoration Sam. I saw lots of workmen coming down here for months," Jake said.

Sam nodded to Jake. "Took longer than I thought. I added that insulated garage out back. You can get in and out without getting wet."

"Is that your cattle herd on the east side of the house, Sam?" I pointed at cattle grazing along the side fence line.

"No, I leased the land to Jake. I lost my herd about three weeks ago now." Sam's face was hard. "Jake's running cattle over there now. Damn glad he leased it."

"You lost them?" I asked

"The government boys slaughtered them. A couple of my heifers tested positive for brucellosis." Sam's fists were opening and closing. "All of them, wiped out in a single afternoon."

Behind Sam, I saw Julia give a little warning shake of her head.

"I'm sorry. I didn't know."

"You couldn't have known. Lost my whole breeding operation in one afternoon. The genetics of my herd went back years to my grandfather's time. Anyway, I got the land leased to Jake and the house rented to you. That'll help me some. I can rebuild me a herd." Sam's clenched hands had stilled at his sides.

Jake clamped his hand on his shoulder. "Soon you won't need to lease me that land. I got just the bull to stand for stud when you get some heifers."

"I'll take you up on that bull of yours." Sam punched Jake's shoulder.

"Deal," he said to Sam. "Sawyer, I'm about a half a mile from you. Let me know if you need anything. See you all later."

"Jake's a good man," Sam said as he watched Jake get in his truck. "He inherited his place from his granddad. He's got fine herds—he's ranching cattle and buffalo. His buffalo are out of the 1880s Charlie Goodnight herd from down in Texas."

"I worked a news story about the Goodnight herd in the Panhandle of Texas."

He grunted. "Yeah, not many of 'em left. He shuffled out the door. "You call me if anything in the place needs fixing."

Julia sat on the hearth. "No way you could have known about Sam's herd. Word around town is he's really hurting for money."

"Why were they slaughtered? Just a couple heifers were positive."

"That's the law. Helps contain the disease, I guess."

"So, does the rancher get any money for his herd?"

"A pittance. The government comes onto your ranch,

loads 'em up and hauls them to slaughter. Once brucellosis is found in a herd, it's out of the rancher's hands."

"So is it catching? Jake put cattle in the same pasture where's Sam's infected herd was."

"I don't know how it spreads, but it must not be in the dirt or Jake would never have put a herd over there. I just know what I read in the paper and what little I picked up from Sam."

"Bad for Sam." Interesting. A possibility for my first story.

Julia changed the subject. "What do you think about the house? The quiet out here will do you some good after seeing that guy murdered in San Antonio. And you have a very handsome neighbor." Her eyes twinkled.

The rumble of the mover's truck as he downshifted into the drive sent us both to the porch.

Chapter 5

I awoke and stretched sore muscles that screamed for a good work out in the gym. Julia and I had unpacked most of the boxes and many old memories. Although I lived light, owning and moving only the stuff I used and loved, my aching muscles reminded me that I still had plenty of household goods.

I dressed for what I hoped was success for my first day on the job. Navy pants, good cream cashmere sweater and small gold hoop earrings. With my current wardrobe, dressing for success couldn't happen too many sequential mornings, but this was the first day.

I found the news director's office behind the studio's soundstage. I stopped outside his door. My heart pounded nervously in my ears. *At least he's not Andy.*

Clay Watkins's office was a dusty cave stacked high with old news scripts and a Betamax recorder. In one corner, an ancient pile of three-quarter inch tape mounded in a precarious heap. Clay lived in a historical display of the last forty years of broadcasting.

He peered over his bifocals, waving a hand at the junk. "Hey, Sawyer. Don't look too close. Clear off a place and sit down. You get squared away with the HR people?" I nodded. "Good. HR's such a pain in the butt."

I perched on the corner of a dusty chair unable to get a word in edgewise. He was filling all the airtime.

"Took you long enough to make your mind up about the job. We talked about it at the convention nearly two months ago. Don't know what finally tripped your trigger, but I'm damn glad you're here."

I could feel the tension in my shoulders relax. "I'm ready for new challenges."

"I got plenty of that. What I need is the hard-ass reporting I saw on your DVD resume—that corruption business where your story got that guy indicted. I'm not saying we've got a witch-hunt. But we got some important beats and you're the reporter to cover it. Go find a story." He challenged.

"I've found my story. The government slaughtered a cattle herd infected with brucellosis," I answered.

His booted feet hit the floor. "Heard something about that. Make it good." He stood. "Now let's go meet the talent around this place."

* * * *

I sat at my desk off the news bullpen researching cattle and brucellosis. The weathercaster was at work on the green screen. "And ah rain storm will cool the air bringin'much needed relief by thuh end of thuh week."

"Graduate of Georgia Tech. Just sounds like a dumbass. Can't seem to lose the twang. Sometimes his accent is so thick his weather report won't stick to tape." The smirk and the retreating swagger belonged to the sports anchor, Dwayne Hamilton. *Lucky me, I won't be working with him.*

I closed the browser and picked up the phone. I wanted to score an interview with one of the owners of Cattleman's Auction.

"Hello, this is Sawyer Cahill with CBS3. Could I speak with George Carlisle about a story I'm working on?" A click and a pause.

"This is George Carlisle," he rasped.

"I'd like the benefit of your expertise for a story I'm working on."

"Not this afternoon. No, not today. You call Hunter Kane, my partner." Carlisle hung up.

No western hospitality there or even good judgment. Most business owners jumped at the opportunity to be on camera. He didn't even suggest another time. Why was he so sure his partner would talk with the press? I called Hunter Kane. He was pleased to represent his company.

* * * *

My camera operator turned out to be an attractive thirtyish woman named Benita Lopez. She was already loading a tripod, sound mixer, and camera into the station's SUV when I arrived. I double-checked the number of extra batteries and cables. On the ride over to the auction house, I got to know Benita. She was a Cheyenne native who had worked at the station for five years.

Pickups and stock trailers hogged all the parking spaces. Benita finally weaved between two cattle haulers. Swearing cowboys were coaxing animals into squeeze chutes. I had seen a headshot of Hunter Kane, but before I could find him in the crowd, Benita called out, "He's over there by the loading pens." I gave the back end of a horse plenty of room. A cowboy stopped putting on a bridle to appreciate the view of Benita's ass. "Mr. Kane, Mr. Kane," I called over bawling cattle and clanging gates. Hunter Kane turned. He was a tall, well-built blond man. Topping a crisp Brooks Brothers shirt was a beautifully tailored navy cashmere jacket. His Lucchese brown boots—boots that you wear to impress, not to cut cattle, were clean and shiny. Mine were dusty and manure-stained with a layer of red dust and part of a cow patty I had tromped through.

I looked up from my stinking shoe in time to catch his smile. He nodded down at my wet boot. "Have to be careful where you step here…Ms.?"

"Sawyer Cahill, Mr. Kane. CBS3. Thanks for talking to me today."

"Of course. We'll go upstairs in the arena. Our offices and conference room are there. You're new, aren't you? Or I haven't had the pleasure of meeting you."

Slick. "I just moved here from San Antonio."

"Come this way." He led us into the reception area of a small stucco building. The woman seated at the information desk greeted him effusively. He gestured to the stairs. "I moved here eight years ago from Montana to raise Angus cattle. Best decision I ever made." He motioned us into a large conference room with floor to ceiling windows giving a view of the mountains. "Got into the auction business with George Carlisle a couple of years ago."

Benita set up for a two-shot. "We're going to shoot the interview parallel to the windows," I told her. "Just a few questions, Mr. Kane. Then we'll go down to the auction and get some footage."

"Unbutton you shirt and pull your microphone up to attach it to the front, right below your chin," Benita said to Hunter. He fumbled the tiny alligator clip. "No, it's still crooked. Here let me fix it for you." Benita straightened his microphone and smoothed the front of his shirt across his shoulders. Kane looked over my way and caught me watching. A lazy smile played at his lips.

Benita counted down, cueing me for the first question.

"Thanks for having us at Cattleman's Auction today, Mr. Kane."

"Thanks. I'm happy to be of service."

"How important is the cattle industry to Wyoming's economy?"

"We're called the Cowboy State for a reason. Agriculture is a billion-dollar industry in this state. Cattle ranching makes the money here. Hay is the second largest money maker in our state."

"Tell us about today's cattle auction."

"We have a load of prime breeding bulls. We're live streaming this auction. Taking bids over the Internet, too. Should be real interesting."

"How much does a top bull go for at auction?"

"These bulls sell for around ten thousand dollars each." He rose suddenly, dragging the microphone wire with him, creating crackles and pops that would require more editing.

"Auction's about to start. We need to get down to the arena."

Usually the interviewee didn't end the interview. "Thank you Mr. Kane for taking the time to talk to CBS3."

Hunter pulled off his microphone. "Would you care to join me in my box for the breeder's auction? You could meet some of the other local ranchers."

Benita looked up from packing her camera. "I'll shoot cover footage from ringside if you want."

Amusement crinkled Hunter's brown eyes. "Settled."

We had a good view of the dusty arena. Snorting bulls lumbered out of the chute. The stick man tapped the legs of each bull, urging them to the center of the arena.

"Hey yebba de yebba de yebba de yebba. Whadda ya gemma me? Whadda ya gemma me?"

The stick man tapped on the legs of a massive black bull and after a flurry of bids, he guided the bull to the new owner's stock trailer.

"Why did that bull go for more than average?" I asked Hunter.

"That bull's bloodline has some fine stock behind it," Hunter explained, bringing his mouth down to my ear. I caught a whiff of spicy cologne. "Mike Wiley bought him. He needs a new bloodline on his ranch." He shifted in his chair. "A month ago Wiley paid sixteen hundred dollars apiece for about twenty heifers. Breeders wait a lifetime for a chance at bloodlines like this. That bull is going to sire a lot of calves for the Iron Horse. Each of those heifers will drop seven calves in their lifetime. Count that up! Wiley'll make money putting him out to stud too. Not a bad life for the bull either." He smiled.

The auctioneer called the last bid and closed the auction. Hunter leaned over briefly and touched my forearm. "Would you join me for a glass of wine and dinner? I don't often get to spend an afternoon with a lovely and intelligent woman."

I just met him. Just a casual drink, no dinner. "I'll be at the station until around seven. I could meet you then for a drink."

"Perfect." He had even white teeth when he smiled. "I'll meet you at the station and we'll walk across the square and have a drink at the Plains Hotel. Beautiful old bar built in 1911 when the ranchers began staking their claims."

We joined Benita near the door of the arena. A slender young man called, "Mr. Kane, can I have a word with you."

"Sure Walker, you need something?" Hunter asked.

A skinny kid wiped his hands on his dirty jeans and stuck it out to Hunter. "I want to thank you, Mr. Kane, for all you done for me. Takin' a chance on me and givin' me this job. I—I got me a new job. Gonna be a cowhand over to the Wildcat with Mr. Rogers's outfit. I wanted to tell you myself."

Hunter gingerly took Walker's grimy hand. "I'm wishing you the best, Tom. Nate runs a good outfit. I want to hear how you get on."

Walker turned on his boot heel with a silent nod and walked away.

Hunter puffed out his chest and thrust his chin up. "A little protégé of mine."

"What do you mean?"

"Kid was in foster care when I met him. Came by the auction house and wanted to work after school. I gave him a chance. Foster care is a terrible place to be. By god, he learned what hard work is. Without me teaching him, he wouldn't have been hired by Nate."

"He finish school?"

"Naw, he dropped out. I taught him what he needed. Just my little way of helping people. I really enjoy guiding people, you know? I live my life to be an example for others. Damn proud I could help him." Hunter tilted his head back, clasped his hands behind his back and smiled down at me.

I heard someone clear his throat. I turned and caught Jake

Spooner's intense gaze. His lips turned up in amusement.

Hunter caught Jake's glance, too. "Hello Spooner."

"Kane," Jake said, striding past him.

"Met Jake Spooner?" Hunter asked. We stepped out of the arena into the afternoon sunlight.

"Yes, briefly. He's a neighbor of mine."

"You'll get to know him. Cheyenne's not that big."

Chapter 6

Hunter was at the station at exactly seven PM. We walked out into the crisp night, to his recitation of the virtues of the Plains hotel. "It's early Twentieth century. They brought the wood and stone by wagon from Colorado. Look at that veranda topped by five stories of gables and windows. Grand isn't it?"

Hunter opened the double glass doors into the wood paneled bar. He pointed up. "Original tin ceilings." Our images reflected from a leaded glass mirror hung behind the bartender.

"I love this place" Hunter ran his hand over the smooth wood. "A hundred years of cattle and land deals were done here. Some of them were mine. I want to be a success for my late wife, Emily. I still miss her after all these years." He trailed off.

I was shocked. Young for a widower. "I'm sorry. I didn't know."

"Thanks. Took some time to get used to going on without her."

We slipped into a booth at the end of the bar. The bartender cocked his head at Hunter who answered, "Bourbon neat. What do you want?"

"Vodka martini, please."

Hunter covered my hand with his. "Did I do okay today?"

"Yes, you gave me a good interview." I slipped my hand out from under his.

"What other stories are you working on?" He asked.

"Sam Jordan lost his herd to brucellosis."

He thrust his face so close to mine that I could smell the bourbon on his breath. "Terrible loss for Sam. He'd been breeding that herd for years. Good thing he has his vet practice to support him. He's been trying to rent out his place."

"He did. I am the renter. How do cattle get brucellosis?"

He took a long slow drink of bourbon. "Buffalo," he spat out. "Jake Spooner runs a couple of hundred head of buffalo right across the back fence line from you." Hunter's shoulders bunched up under his ears.

"You angry about that?" I asked.

"Hell yes. My ranch shares a fence line with Spooner's goddamn buffalo herd. His buffalo better not spread disease to my cattle. Sam lost six hundred head of Angus cattle. Years of work gone in one afternoon."

"Is the infection in the dirt? Because Jake leased that land from Sam and is raising cattle on it."

"That irony is rich! Spooner profits from Sam's loss. No, a cow can't get brucellosis from dirt. Brucellosis is spread from body fluids." Hunter bit out his words. "Let me give you something for your story, Sawyer. This is cattle country." He was stabbing the air between us with his forefinger. "People in America eat beef, not buffalo." His shoulders lowered. "I can teach you the cattle business." His fingers curled around mine. "Could be fun, too."

He'd be a good source. Side benefit—he was easy to look at. "Why is Jake ranching buffalo?"

"Spooner's trying to put buffalo meat in every grocery store. He'll fail." Hunter slammed his empty glass on the table. He released a pent up breath and smiled, but the smile never reached his eyes. "I came to this bar to share a drink with an interesting woman. Let's talk about something else."

"Okay. Tell me about your ranch."

"The Bar-A is my favorite subject. I have four sections of the most beautiful grazing land you ever saw. Up on the north end is a ridgeline with a good view of the high country. We ought to ride up there sometime. You can see all the way out east onto the plains." He gave my hand a quick squeeze. "You know why it's called the Bar-A?"

"No..." His hand felt warm and solid. He twined his fingers with mine.

"After my wife, Emily. Her maiden name was Alston. She would've been so happy there on the ranch. Emily died before I bought the place, but she would have loved this land."

"I'm sorry for your pain."

He gently ran his fingertips down my jaw. "Hope you never have to feel it. You bring out a man's thoughts. Not many women make a warm place where a man can bare his soul." He leaned back into the leather bench. "I've got a thousand head of Angus on the ranch. That's my main business. But, I'm trying my hand with producing cashmere."

Wow, the guy put the *e* in ego. "I didn't think cattle ranchers did much sheep ranching."

"That's *goats,* city slicker, not sheep." He laughed. He had a great smile that lit up his face. "Cashmere goats produce your cashmere sweaters. He's a hardy little animal from the steppes of Mongolia, so our winters are no problem for them. They do real well on the tufts of dry grass in the winter until spring rains come."

"Have you sheared them yet?"

"Yeah, my shearers come up from Mexico every spring. They're a family business, traveling around the west shearing. I made a nice little bundle off the fiber."

"I've never seen a cashmere goat."

"I can fix that." He smiled again showing those attractive crinkles around his mouth. "You grow up on a ranch?"

"No, I'm a city girl. But my Dad taught me to ride and how to shoot a .22 rifle by pinging cans in a pasture. When I got good enough, he bought me a .410 shotgun and took me dove hunting."

"I got a windmill tank that draws the dove on fall evenings. We could hunt out there. I marinate the breasts, then grill them. Does your whole family hunt?"

"I'm an only child. My parents lost two sons, each when they were a few days old. Both were named after my dad. By the time they got pregnant with me, they were both knocking on the door of forty. Growing up, I believed that Dad had hoped I'd be a boy. He took me deer and dove hunting and bought me a mare. I loved the time I spent with him and I'm grateful to him for teaching me to love the outdoors."

"You still ride?"

"Not lately. Dad gave me a mare when I was eight. Piggles was a beautiful paint. My heart broke when I found out we were moving to Denver and I couldn't take her."

"I'll take you riding. Get you back in shape." He smiled.

The restaurant was filling with diners and customers. I could tell the bartender was itching to turn the table. I finished my martini. "I'd like that." I gestured to the waiting group. "We need to give some of these people an opportunity to enjoy the bar."

Hunter slid a few bills on the table. He slipped his arm under my elbow. We ambled across the square full of dog walkers and kids on bikes to my car in the station lot.

"Thank you for interesting evening, Sawyer."

"The pleasure was mine, Hunter. I look forward to sitting a horse again."

He took my key and popped the lock on the Jeep. He put both hands on my shoulders and gave me soft kiss. I lightly touched the back of his neck. "Good night, Hunter." I loved that he was tall. My head was only inches shorter than his. God, at nearly five-foot-eight, by the time I was thirteen, I was the tallest girl in middle school, making dance lessons a nightmare of stooping to hold little guys. Driving home, I relived his soft kiss lingering on my mouth. A tingle of anticipation kept me company.

When I turned into my drive, I was happy to see Julia parked in the drive. "Surprise," Julia called, getting out of her car. "I brought my favorite takeout lasagna from the best pizza place in town."

"Have you been here long?"

'Nope, just got here." She held out a white bag. "And in here—" She paused dramatically. "—are two perfect chocolate éclairs. I tried to call, but got your voice mail." She cocked her head. "I hope this is all right. I can take my éclairs and go home." She tantalized me by shaking the white bakery bag.

"Absolutely not!"

We plated up the lasagna. Julia snagged a bottle of wine off the counter and followed me out to two comfortable chairs on the back porch.

"You happy at the station?"

"Definitely. It was good move for me to come home. Look at that sky full of stars and a crescent moon."

"Yeah, hard to get that view in the city." Julia handed me an éclair.

"What do you know about Hunter Kane?" I hoped I sounded casual.

She cocked her head with an amused smile. "Is he the reason your lip gloss is smeared?"

"You never did miss much."

"So, give. Obviously you met him?"

"Yeah, I had a drink with him this evening."

"Wow! You're moving fast."

"I wouldn't call a drink at the Plains moving fast."

"I don't know much but the gossip around town. He's got a nice size ranch, not far from you. Moved here from Montana I think," Julia offered.

"He told me his wife died. Do you know anything about her?"

"All I know is he moved here after she died. Sorry I don't know more. I don't get out of the second grade much. Tell me about having a drink with him."

"He talked about raising cattle … Oh god, I started talking about Piggles. You remember her, don't you?"

"Of course, I remember Piggles. We spent a lot time on that mare. Remember how your mom wanted you in dressage?" She laughed. "All you wanted to do was gallop like a wild child. I hadn't thought about Piggles in years."

"He got angry talking about Sam's herd. He blames buffalo ranchers for spreading brucellosis to cattle. You know anything about hard feelings between cattle and buffalo ranchers?"

"I know when brucellosis breaks out, people lose a lot of money. I bet everyone who is involved in the cattle business is talking about Sam's herd. I can't help you much. Really, if it's not about addition and crayons, I'm out of the loop. You're the journalist. I'm betting you'll find out."

She refilled our wine glasses licking the drop that hung from the rim of the bottle. She tucked her legs under her. "You leave any guy behind in San Antonio?"

I wasn't sure I wanted to go there. "Nobody left behind."

She sipped her wine. "You ever think you have trouble trusting a guy enough to make a commitment?"

"Well, there's a leap in the conversation. I guess you think I do. Failure to trust? I don't know." I fiddled with my glass.

Julia hesitated. "I don't think it's trust in the sexual sense like 'I don't trust you not to two-time me.' But you do have more than a few broken relationships. Ones you've left." She held up her hand to ward off my interruption. "I'm not saying you didn't have reasons. I'm just asking about the trust thing."

"I don't know. Most of the time I feel like I'm marking time with a guy. He fills the basic needs of a woman, his yang to my yin, but we never develop a deeply intimate relationship. I feel like a kid licking a lollypop, hoping to get to the soft center. Only I never find the center, and after I while I don't want the lollypop."

"You picking the wrong sort of man?" Julia asked.

I laughed. "Mom probably thinks so." I looked out at the moonlit night, buying time. "I wonder if Katharine Hepburn had it right. A man and woman should never marry. Just enjoy each other while living in adjoining houses. Sure minimizes the potential for the misery index."

Julia tilted her head back and took the last drink of her wine in one gulp. "Sounds real lonely to me. You're a striking woman. You're whip smart, athletic..."

"Next comes the part about how you don't want me to end up alone?"

"I do want more for you."

I sighed. "I'm not doomed to the single life."

"I just want you to find a good guy." She poured the rest of the wine into our empty glasses. "So, let's be who we are— practical girls. We always made plans nursing a beer in our favorite bar in Boulder. You've met Hunter Kane. I'll even the field by telling you what I know about your neighbor, Jake Spooner. If you want, you can pretend either of them is Spencer Tracy. Or you could try a new approach. Relax. Open yourself up to possibilities."

"Sure, tell me about Jake."

"Jake was an assistant in the DA's office in Denver. When his grandpa died, he took over the ranch. His grandpa was a Huddleston. Remember them? They had that funky little grocery in town with the bakery. Anyway, the ranch was rundown, probably not making a dime when Jake took it over. He's worked on the house and bred a good herd. He's also ranching buffalo over there."

"I'm stuck on my suspected 'failure to trust.' Do I at least get points for having always dated within my species?"

Julia followed me into the kitchen, putting her wine glass down in the kitchen sink. She slung her bag on her shoulder and fished out her keys. "No. Remember that strange orthodontist you dated for a while in Boulder? I gotta go. Early day with the second graders tomorrow. Love you. Think about it."

"Love you, too."

Julia hadn't changed much since our college days spent drinking beer on Pearl Street. She had always wanted to work with children, have the house with the picket fence, the husband and a family. Her plan was in place. My plan was less structured and involved fewer people. Julia's was an interesting question that I would have to consider. Could I trust a guy? And if I couldn't, what did I do about it? Or maybe I didn't trust because I didn't want to. Existentialism was such a bitch.

Chapter 7

The smell of acrid dust roused me from a deep sleep. I blearily looked out my bedroom window at great clouds of dirt rolling across the backyard. Men's voices, the sounds of animals moving and creaking leather filled the air. I slammed the window shut, hurriedly pulling on jeans and a tee. I grabbed my camera on the way out the back door.

I stood about a yard from the fence fiddling with the aperture control. I shot bracketed exposures in a rapid sequence of lumbering buffalo, shaking their massive heads. The earth shuddered with their passing. I attached the flash, squatting to shoot a rapid series of hooves. Dust sifted onto the lens from their hooves kicking up the loose dirt.

A rider broke away from the group of men. Jake pulled his horse to a stop opposite the fence from me. "A couple of strings of barbed wire won't slow a buffalo charge, much less stop him." He soothed the skittish black gelding. "Sawyer! Turn the flash off. You could spook the herd." Chet ran out of the dust thumping his tail in recognition.

Chet looked friendlier than Jake. I stood up. "Sorry, I didn't think. Got carried away."

He eased back in the saddle. "You need to be careful near the fence line." A ghost of smile flitted across his face. "You settled in over there?"

"Yeah, just about. Thanks."

His smile reached his eyes. "Maybe you'd like to see the herd when we get them down in their new pasture. Until then, if you need anything, I'm one mailbox down the road from you. Come on Chet. You've got work to do." He turned the horse to join his men.

I replied to his back. "Thanks. Count on it." He lifted his hand in a silent wave, disappearing into the herd.

My cell phone vibrated in my pocket. "Sawyer, where are you?"

"Still at home, Clay. What's up?"

"Sherriff's office has an animal mutilation up at the Shadow Mountain Ranch. You know where that is?"

"No. Give me directions. I've got GPS in the Jeep." I was back in the kitchen scribbling. "Got it. Tell me what you know."

"Ray Foster called the sheriff this morning saying he found a mutilated buffalo. Sheriff's name is Wolfe Barton. Benita will meet you out there. It's only fifteen minutes north of your place near mile marker forty-seven"

"On my way. Call me if you get any more news."

"Keep in touch."

I followed the ruts of the sheriff's truck across the Shadow Mountain pasture. Tall grass whipped my legs as I walked to join them standing around the carcass. The ID around my neck was my entry into the conversation. Ray Foster was answering Sheriff Barton. "I saw the vultures circling over in this east pasture and found him like this. I was out dropping salt lick blocks this morning." He looked dazed, shook his head and stared nervously at the bloody animal.

A young bull lay in the center of a perfect ring of trampled grass. A dark stain circled around his head. Brown fur matted in the bloody wound on his neck. Flies lazily buzzed his left eye. His slack mouth was gray with dried blood and his tongue lolled out, parching in the morning sun.

"I hoped I was gonna find a hurt animal, but I found him like this, all cut up. I never had no trouble like this before." Foster turned and pointed at the high outcrop of rock to the east. "Took me a bit to find him. You can't see him from the rest of the pasture. Look at this trampled grass around him," he said, toeing the dried grass. "Took some time to do this. See that rock cairn there? By his head? Them rocks were gathered up from over east there and stacked up by his head after the grass was flattened." He took his hat off, wiping the morning sweat from his brow on the sleeve of his shirt.

"We'll find this guy, Ray," Sheriff Barton said.

"You better," Ray shot back. "I ain't got no more stock to lose."

The sound of a heavy diesel truck throbbed to a stop. Sam

Jordan slammed the door and shambled our way.

"Morning Wolfe. Deputy." He nodded at me. "Sorry to hear about your troubles, Ray." He knelt by the dead bull, grabbed his horns and pulled back to expose a gaping wound in his neck. Neck slash is what killed him." The buffalo head thudded back on the dry grass.

Wolfe Barton turned to Ray. "You got any new hands, Ray?"

"No. Same boys I've had for nearly thirty years. Never had no trouble."

Benita was shooting the scene. "I want to talk to Ray a minute," I whispered to her. She nodded her understanding and panned the camera to Ray.

"I'm Sawyer Cahill from CBS3. Sorry for your loss. Did you see or hear anything unusual last night or early this morning?"

"No, I already said we saw nothing this morning. We ain't seen any strangers around either. But we was working over on the other side of the ranch. Haven't been over this way 'til this morning." Ray snapped his dirty hat on his jeans

"Was this an expensive animal?" I pointed down at the carcass.

"Hell yes, breeding bulls are expensive," he shouted. Can't get no calves without a bull. Going to have to put my cows out to a stud now. That's gonna cost a pretty penny." Foster shifted his weight forward on his toes. Dust plumes rose over his dirty boots.

"Are you worried about the safety of the rest of your herd?"

"What do you think? Course I am. We'll be watching. My boys and me, we'll be watching real close."

I had no doubt he would. Who had a bull to put out to stud?

Foster started to walk away. I called after him softly. "Who do you think did this, Mr. Foster?"

He whirled around. "How the hell would I know? Some crazy bastard. If he comes back on my land, I'll kill the son-of-bitch."

Barton's authoritarian voice broke the uneasy silence. "Foster, don't. You have any problems out here, leave 'em to me. That bull's important, but not worth a murder charge. You hear me, Ray?"

"You better git him soon. Before somebody else gits to

him." Foster glared.

Sam interrupted the tension. "Neck wound cut the artery. That's post mortem damage to his eyes, probably birds." He pulled up a hind leg. "Look here. Someone cut his balls off. See the wound under there?"

"What?" Barton shouted. "His balls are missing?"

"Yeah, and that's not all. Tail's gone. I'm guessing that peace sign painted on his side was done with the tail. He coulda dipped the tail in the blood from the throat slash. See the incision here?" Sam pulled back on the groin wound. "This guy had some skill and knowledge. It's sure no hack job. He used a surgical knife to take those balls." Sam pushed his bulk awkwardly off the grass. Sick SOB. I'm going to take a blood sample."

"You think he was tranqed?" Barton asked.

"I'll know soon enough. But you couldn't do this without rope and sedation," Sam said.

"How long you think he's been dead?" Barton bent over the carcass for a better look.

"I'd say no more than two days. Long enough for the vultures to get to his eyes."

I bent over the legs of the dead bull. I picked through the hair above his hooves. Something was matted in the dirt-encrusted fur. "Sheriff, look at these strands of fiber caught around the hoof." Barton grimaced, his knee popping when he squatted by me. "His hair is broken off and his hide is chafed. He was hog tied," I said.

"Deputy, get over here with that damn kit," Barton hollered. "Hand me the tweezers and a bag." He grunted at me. "Don't touch nothing else at my crime scene."

Benita and I walked the area. There were no tire tracks other than our vehicles. Hoof prints dug into the dirt under the bull's legs where he had struggled to stand at one point. His carcass was about a mile from the main road giving someone privacy for their work.

* * * *

I headed home to shower. Standing under the steaming water, I sifted through motives. Who mutilates an animal? Why cut an animal up if you just wanted to eliminate the competition for stud service? I knew a psychologist back in San Antonio. He liked strange puzzles.

I was drying my hair when my phone buzzed. Hunter had a sexy low baritone. "Sawyer, I was thinking of you. Wondered if you'd like to join me for dinner tonight at the Little Bear Inn. I promise you a memorable steak."

I'd been having some pretty vivid thoughts about him, too. But he's a news source so I hesitated.

"Come on. You have to eat. By eight, you're long finished with the evening news. Give us some time together."

"I may have to cancel if the day gets crazy," I warned.

"See ya at eight."

Immediately my phone rang again. Without even a hello Clay asked, "What have you got on the mutilation story, kiddo? You got enough to lead at 6 o'clock?"

"Count on it. Start teasing the story now. I'm on my way."

I slipped into my office balancing the first of many coffees, ready to call George Carlisle.

"Hello, I'm Sawyer Cahill. I'd like to speak with Mr. Carlisle," I said to his secretary.

"I'll see if he can speak with you now," she said, putting me on hold.

I heard the click. "Carlisle, here."

"Mr. Carlisle, Sawyer Cahill. Good morning. Thank you for putting me in touch with Hunter Kane."

"How can I help you today, Ms. Cahill?" He barked.

"Ray Foster had a bull mutilated…"

"I know. News gets around fast. What do you want?"

"You are one of the most respected ranchers in the area and the owner of the local auction house. I need the value of your expertise in an on-camera interview. Your opinion is pivotal." That ought to grease the wheels of his vanity.

"I'll give you fifteen minutes. Set it up with my secretary."

Click. I recalled his secretary and booked the time.

* * * *

Barton might have a lab report on Foster's bull back. I googled large animal tranquilizers. A wildlife vet suggested Ketamine/Xylazine at a rate of 1 mL/8lbs, claiming the dose would tranquilize the most agitated animal.

I searched online news stories of animal mutilations. Cattle were most often the target. Idaho and Montana had a couple of occurrences. Wyoming had two instances in the last decade. No cases of buffalo mutilation. Something else to ask Barton.

"Sheriff Barton, Sawyer here. Did you get the lab report?"

"Hell, I'm not talking to the press."

"Did you find anything specific about those rope fibers?"

"What about 'hell no' do you not get?" Barton sniped.

"Our viewers would appreciate a comment, Sheriff Barton." Give me something, buddy. I found the rope fibers while you were diddling around the corpse.

"I am speaking off the record. You screw me and I'll be looking to book you for obstruction. Got it?" Barton asked.

"Got it. What'd the lab report show?"

"Can't take a buffalo down by hog tying him."

"Did he use Ketamine and Xylazine?" I asked.

"No, just Xylazine," he answered.

"Any burglaries of vet clinics?" I asked.

Barton grumbled, "Drug's not hard to come by. You can get in on the Internet. Ranchers use the stuff. Hunters use Xylazine illegally."

"So there are a lot of suspects?"

"Yeah. You'll damn well share with me if you get anything, or your ass will be cooling in jail."

"Got it. What physical evidence did you find?"

"Damn little. Fibers came from common rope. Can't lift footprints off dried grass. Some sick fuck was damned careful." He stopped short. "Remember, that's off the record. People around here are going to get real uneasy about their stock soon enough."

"Why Foster's ranch? Was it personal?"

"When a man's prize bull gets his balls cut off, it's personal. Hurts Foster's bottom line."

"You talk to the men who work for him?"

"Yeah, I know my job. He only has three men. Two of them have worked for him nearly twenty years. Other guy is the son of one of them. Nothing there. We got some sick bastard with a sharp knife."

"This wasn't an impulsive act. Someone brought rope, drugs and a surgical knife."

Barton clammed up. I called Sam. "Tell me about the drugs, Sam."

"How the hell you know about that?"

"My job. We can be off the record if you want."

"You quote me and I'll deny it. Bastard used Xylazine. It's a common large animal sedative. I use it for minor procedures like dental work and dehorning and before surgical anesthesia if I think my patient's going to be difficult to anesthetize."

"So was the buffalo anesthetized, Sam?"

"No, he wasn't. Not the same. The bastard didn't know to add Ketamine to the mix. Son-of-bitch tortured that animal."

Chapter 8

I hadn't joined a gym yet, but I did get in a two-mile run before meeting Hunter. By eight, I was showered and presentable in my one go-everywhere-but-to-work outfit of a black cashmere dress and heels. Mom would find Hunter a suitable date. I had a few minutes so I called and let her tell me about the charity auction she was working on. Finally, she asked about my job and my house. I assured her the house was safe. "I'm working on a story about a mutilated buffalo bull."

"Sawyer, honey, I thought you were going to cover environmental stories up there or economic stories, whichever."

"I am Mom. Ray Foster raises buffalo for profit."

"Are you safe? Are you going to be okay? You're not out there by yourself are you?"

"No, Mom. I'm fine. Really it's okay."

I closed my cell.

* * * *

"You look great." Hunter gave me a quick hello kiss. I gave him the short tour of the house. "I like what you've done with the place." He slipped his arm around my waist. I felt warm and protected with that big arm around me. "The ten miles into Cheyenne won't be too much for you in the winter? The county does a pretty good job on clearing the road but sometimes it'll be a tough commute."

"I learned to drive in Denver. I'll be fine."

Hunter held the door for me. I slid into his Tahoe. "You need better tires than whatever you were using in San Antonio. That tire place on Main will make you a good deal on crossover tires. I run them on all my vehicles."

"You ever been to the Little Bear?" he asked as he buckled up.

"No, I don't remember ever going there." I said.

"Probably wasn't open back when you were a kid. Used to be an old Inn and stage stop. When they started the remodel, they found a hundred-foot tunnel connecting the Inn to the stable. When a posse was after an outlaw, he could just drop in the trap door and make it to his horse."

"Can we see the tunnel?"

"Tunnel's still there, but it's crumbling so badly no one can go in it. You'll like what they did in the old saloon. They kept the old mahogany bar. The food is topnotch and I'll make sure you get fine service from the staff."

A grove of trees sheltered the low-slung log building. A wide porch led to hobnail double doors. We crossed the distressed pine floors to a table set in front of a stone fireplace.

Over a rich merlot and great ribeye that would have fed two, Hunter mentioned the mutilation on Shadow Mountain. "I heard around town Ray Foster lost a buffalo. You working on this story? I apologize. I don't see the local news too often."

"Yeah, heck of a scene."

"What happened out there?" Hunter sipped his wine.

I was careful to tell the edited version of the story.

"Bad business." He drummed his fingers on the table. "Foster's got a small operation out there. What's he going to do?"

"I asked him that. He's worried. I don't know how you babysit stock out on the range. Foster only has three hands and a lot of acres to watch."

"Yeah, that's the problem. Stock mutilation is a form of terrorism. You'd have to have an army to watch your whole ranch. You either round up your stock, feed 'em and babysit them, which costs a fortune, or you turn 'em out and hope for the best. Either way, it doesn't help a man sleep."

"What are you going to do?"

"I told all my hands to be on the lookout for strangers, tire tracks, signs of anyone camping—anything out the ordinary. Not much else to do." He rubbed his hand across the back of his neck.

"I researched stories of stock mutilation. Found a couple in Montana. Do you remember anything from when you lived there?"

Hunter wrinkled his forehead. "I remember some trouble

around Missoula. I had a client at the bank who ranched. He had a cow mutilated on his place. It's been awhile. I don't remember all the particulars, but I do remember there weren't any arrests."

"I didn't see any arrests. The mutilations just stopped."

"You find any cases in Wyoming?" he asked.

"A couple out of around Laramie, but that was seven years ago," I said.

"Not much of a pattern. I hope this is an isolated case out on Foster's ranch, but it may not be."

The waiter was hovering. "Will you be having dessert this evening?"

"Sawyer?"

"Nothing more for me, thank you."

He ordered two brandies. "We'll have our brandy before the fire."

Hunter slipped his arm around my shoulders, tucking me close. I enjoyed his embrace, the scent of his cologne and the rasp of his beard when he leaned close.

"I'm happy around you. I can be open with you. Almost like I've known you for a long time. I don't share Emily's story with too many people."

I put my brandy on the side table. I was getting too relaxed.

"Do I make you feel that way? I mean—I know we've only to begun to see each other, but do you think I can?" he asked.

Before I could answer, Hunter's focus shifted to the door of the restaurant. His fingers tapped out a rhythm on my shoulder. Jake entered the dining room with a tall, willowy blonde who was laughing at something he'd said.

Hunter snapped his attention back to me. "Know her? The woman with Spooner?"

"No, I've never seen her before."

"Morgan Hall. She owns a successful public relations firm over on Main and Third." Hunter drained his brandy. He took his arm from around my shoulders, motioning the waiter for a second.

Jake and Morgan stopped by the fire. "Good evening. Sawyer, this is Morgan Hall. Morgan, Sawyer Cahill. Sawyer recently moved here from Texas." I flushed, remembering the way Jake sat a horse.

Morgan and I smiled our hellos.

Hunter dipped his head to Morgan. Without looking at Jake, he said, "Spooner."

The waiter showed Jake and Morgan to a table. "What's with you two?" I asked.

"You could say we have nothing in common."

Chapter 9

I was on the phone early to catch my friend in San Antonio before his morning caseload began. Logan Matthews was a clinical psychologist at the University of Texas Med School. I'd gotten to know him when he was a source on a child abuse case I covered. We had a favorite cafe in Alamo Square where we met to share a drink when he was working with me.

"Good morning Logan. Sawyer here. Hope I caught you before your day cranks up. How are you?"

"Quite well, Sawyer. I haven't heard from you in awhile. You must be working on a story." He sounded curious. I pictured him sitting in his cluttered office with his mane of unruly white hair sticking up in tufts.

"I'm working on an animal mutilation. I'd buy you a drink in the Square tonight, but I moved to Cheyenne a couple of weeks ago."

"Cheyenne! I'll miss our little gatherings." I heard his chair creak. "Tell me what you've got going."

I summarized the facts. "The testes and tail were taken. What do you think?"

For a while, I only heard his quiet breathing. Finally, he cleared his throat. "He took the symbol of manhood while enjoying the bull's suffering. Inflicting the pain makes him feel in control and the mutilation is a catharsis for his rage."

"You sure he's a man?" I nudged.

"Almost certainly it's a man. A very angry man with a dangerous psychopathology. He thinks very little of the consequences of what he's doing and views the animal as existing only to serve his needs."

"Have you treated any patients like this?"

"I've treated a couple of cases, but with very little success. FBI profiles indicate that animal abuse is one of the early traits of serial murderers."

"Do they all become serial murders?"

"No, not always. What triggers the human mind to act out its thoughts remains a mystery."

"If taking the testes made him feel in control, what was cutting off the tail about?"

"My dear, some hunters in Africa take the tail and horns from their trophy animals. I don't put much significance in his taking the animal's tail. Drawing the peace sign in blood on the side of the animal may have been a sardonic gesture. He may be just thumbing his nose at the police."

"Could you give me a quick profile of this guy?"

"He's probably between twenty and fifty, in good shape, and probably knows something about stock ranching. These men can be bright, successful—charismatic even. Then there is the economic angle of killing a rancher's prize bull. You have a very interesting case. I want you to let me know what happens."

"I will."

"One more thing, he'll mutilate again. Rarely are they able to act out just one time. The rage builds until he's desperate for release. Be careful following the story, my dear."

I finished my notes, scribbling a reminder to send a bottle of Chivas to Logan when Clay stuck his head in my office. "Hey, great work covering that mutilation, kiddo. Have you seen the comments on the website? Viewers are guessing about what kind of sick person we got and what's going to happen next. One guy wants to know who the new good looking reporter is!"

"Thanks. I'll check the website. I talked to Hunter Kane about Sam's losing his herd to brucellosis…"

"Tell me about it." He settled into the one comfortable chair in my office.

"You know much about the disease?"

"Nah." Clay scratched his head. "Never been around ranching much. I know what happened out at Jordan's place is standard operating procedure by the government to keep the disease from spreading."

"I didn't know much either until I researched it on the web. Brucellosis infects the cow causing her to abort her fetus. Any animal that comes in contact with infected birth fluids gets the disease." I began to sell my next story. "Buffalo ranchers compete with cattle ranchers to be the meat on the dinner table. You know who else brucellosis slams financially? The hunting business. The elk and big horn sheep are infected, too."

"Where you goin' with this? You tossed a bunch of stories on the table."

"I'll follow the money. Brucellosis is an economic story affecting ranchers and the hunting business."

"I like where your head's at. Keep me in the loop. Anything new on that mutilation? I don't want to lose viewer interest in Foster's bull." He stretched out in his chair. "Hell, it's even a human interest story. Another guy loses his livelihood. Play that angle, kiddo."

I was irritated, but ignored the kiddo reference. "I called a source of mine in San Antonio. He's a psychologist. Logan gave me a profile of a mutilator."

Clay bit. "What makes a guy do this stuff?"

"The short answer is he's raging on the inside and needs to control and dominate. Power and money are what this story is about. Who gets to make the most money selling their meat?"

"I like the way your mind works, kiddo, but don't say it until you have some proof." He slapped my desk on the way out of the office. "Good hire on my part." He winked at me over his shoulder. "Hey, update the web story with that psychologist guy's opinions. We'll give the audience something new to chew on."

Kiddo. What the hell does kiddo mean to him? I'm sure no kid.

I tapped into the station's server with my password and updated Foster's story. Just the high points to keep the audience interested. I didn't share Logan's statement that animal abuse was a trait of serial murderers. I scrolled the comments posted after my story. Herdman05 worried about protecting his herd. Several others hoped the incident was a one-time event.

I logged out of the server and called Ray Foster, waiting a few minutes for him to pick up his phone and drawl out his answers. Talking to Ray was a dead end. Time to talk to Spooner.

After four rings, he answered. "Jake, it's Sawyer Cahill. I'd like to talk with you about a couple of stories I'm working on."

"I heard about Foster's bull."

"Why don't we meet? I'll buy you coffee in the morning and we can talk a few minutes," I proposed.

"We're cutting herd and I don't have any time to meet this week."

"That's fine. The offer of coffee stands. I'll be in touch."

My email chimed. I looked at the subject line: *news for your Foster Ranch story.* One click and the message opened. *Stay out of it.* I recoiled from the monitor. I clicked back to the inbox. Anonymous. Sweat popped out on my forehead and my hands turned to ice. I didn't want gossip until I could find out a bit more. I called our tech guy. "Mark, I got an anonymous email from an unhappy viewer. Is there any way you can get me the IP address?"

"Yeah, sure. Everyone has an internet address, but if your guy sent it from a public computer, the machine's address isn't going to help. Do we need to call the police, Sawyer?"

"Not yet. But can you see if you are able to pull the IP address?"

"Sure. Forward the email to me and I'll give it a go this afternoon."

"Email me what you find out."

I saved the email and printed a copy for my file. Who was this guy? Was he just trying to scare me?

* * * *

Mark's answer came right before five. My email had come from a computer at the Cheyenne County Library. Dead end. My desk phone rang while I was reading his email. "Hi Sawyer, it's Mark. I sent you the search results for the IP address. No way to tell who used a public computer over at the library. I'm not real comfortable with that message you got. Sure you don't want to make it official and call the police?"

"Not yet, Mark. Could be just someone letting off steam."

"Call me if you need me."

Dwayne was loafing in my doorway. I stifled a sigh of exasperation. I hadn't seen much in this guy that made me want to hear from him.

"Heard you had some unhappy viewers. I might be able to help you with that." He smirked.

How did Dwayne know about the email? "We're journalists, Dwayne. We don't broadcast the news to make people happy. We cover the news the public needs to know to make informed decisions. Remember learning that in J-school?"

"I'm the sports director. J-school isn't in my past. My viewers love my stories." He simpered. "Check my Facebook page. Friend me if you like."

"Happy for you, Dwayne." I loaded up my laptop and grabbed my bag. "I'll get in touch if I need your help." I scooted by him and out into the hall.

Chapter 10

At four in the morning, my cell jigged out its happy tune. No caller ID. "Hello... Hello?"

No one there.

I was wide awake now thinking about the anonymous email and the blocked call. No coincidences. I pulled on some ratty sweat pants. I needed coffee. Rummaging through the kitchen cabinet turned up an empty coffee bag. I shrank from drinking the cold dregs of coffee in the pot from yesterday morning knowing Starbucks was on my way to work. I decided to run. Nothing cleared my head like loping though the cold dawn. I ran a couple of miles, walked a half mile, and jogged the rest of the way home. By the time I'd showered and driven to town, I just needed coffee to help me write a follow-up story.

Through the drive-through window, I could see Jake and Morgan Hall enjoying their morning brew together. She looked beautiful and like she had slept well. I flipped down the visor mirror looking at the bags under my eyes.

"Ma'am? Ma'am? Here's your coffee." The window jockey interrupted my self inspection.

"Thanks." I fumbled in my bag for the money. I coasted out to the street. Jake and Morgan. Were they an item? Friends? Lovers?

My cell danced. I sloshed coffee trying to put the cup back in the cup holder. "Good morning," Hunter said. "Hope I caught you before you were too involved with the news business. I want us to go riding on my ranch. How about Saturday afternoon? We'll picnic up on the ridgeline. What do you say?"

"I haven't been on a horse in a couple of years," was my

knee-jerk response.

"You'll be fine." He laughed. "Sitting a horse is like riding a bike. You never quite forget. I've a great little mare for you. Interested?"

"You got me with the words 'great little mare.'"

"I'll show you a good time. Pick you up around two on Saturday."

"I'll just drive over to your place. No need to come by for me."

The station was humming with activity when I pushed open the back doors. The lighting techs were setting up for Tobin's morning shot and Dwayne was shouting at a photog. Clay called out when I rounded the corner by our offices, "Hey kiddo." *There's that kiddo, again.* "Whatcha got on the story from Foster's place? I gotta plan the six o'clock rundown."

"Give me a minute for the follow-up story. I'll have it finished by the time Benita and I leave to interview George Carlisle this afternoon."

"I thought Carlisle wouldn't talk to you. How'd you get him to sit for an interview?" Clay asked.

"I appealed to his vanity. Suggested to him that he didn't want to see this story run without his expert opinion."

"You on a fishing trip with Carlisle, or you got something?" Clay looked up at me.

"Fishing."

"He's an important businessman in the community. I don't want the station lawyers having to defend a defamation suit."

"Got it," I answered, walking out. I turned and called his name softly. "Clay, I'm a professional. No proof. No story." The tension eased in his face. "And Clay, cut the kiddo, will you?"

He knitted his brows and cocked his head to one side, "Sorry Sawyer. Just a habit. I call everyone kiddo. You don't like it, I'll stop."

"Thanks."

Benita was standing in the edit bay with two coffees. Bless her. "Thought you might need some extra this morning."

"Definitely."

"Clay calls me kiddo, too. I don't like it either. I keep wondering if he thinks I'm still a kid."

"It means what it means. Kiddo. An adult-to-child form of address. I haven't been a kiddo in many years and neither have you. Clay's a good guy. He'll deal with it."

"I hope so."

"I've got about thirty minutes of work here before the Carlisle shoot," I said.

"I'll be ready in thirty," she murmured, engrossed in her editing.

I took my coffee to my office, got comfy and started working the phone. "Hi Sam. Got a minute?"

"One," he said abruptly. I'm on my way to a cow that has been in breach labor all night. Whatcha need?"

"Did you work any of those old cases of mutilations around here?"

"No. Foster's bull was my first. I hoping it's my last, but I don't believe it."

"Why do you think it wasn't a one-time event?"

"Young lady, I can do some research too, you know. Folks that cut up animals for fun don't just do it one time."

"Had some aspects of ritual with that tamped down grass and rock cairn," I said.

"Don't forget his balls were cut off. And are missing."

"Hard to overlook that. How many people you think have the skills and tools to do that?"

"That's Barton's job. Talk to him," he growled.

"What message is he sending by taking the testes?"

"I'm a vet. Only message I see is, you aren't getting calves this year. I do know the asshole doesn't know how to figure a dose of anesthetic. I got work to do. Just drove through the ranch gate."

Sam had the tools and the skills. A vet tech might have access to the tools and witnessed lots of castrations. Nurse? Doctor? Surgical tech? Rancher who castrates his own bulls? There were too many people who could get their hands on a good knife and have some knowledge. But who had the most to gain?

I called Jake. No answer. Damn it! Why couldn't he answer his cell phone! "Jake, it's Sawyer. That offer for coffee still stands. I'm on my way to interview George Carlisle. I need your perspective to balance this story. Give me a call."

* * * *

Carlisle's office was dark and stuffy. Benita set up an auxiliary light and the dust motes danced through the stale air. "Ready for a sound check?" Benita called out from behind her camera. Carlisle was rubbing the two fingers of his left hand across his forehead. I asked Carlisle about the picture of him and his dogs while Benita checked his audio level. He quit fidgeting and picked up the picture.

"These two bitches are my prize cattle dogs. Work a herd all day without a whimper." Benita gauged his voice levels, giving me a thumbs up. "Whelped some great pups out of these two."

He looked less antsy. Nothing worse than an interviewee who stares straight into the camera lens, nods, and answers stiffly "Yes" or "No" to every question. Hard to make those interviews stick to tape.

Benita counted me down and cued me. After the standard request that he agreed to be interviewed and the thank you's, I pitched him an easy first question. "How did you get started in the cattle business?"

Carlisle leaned into the camera, hanging his hands between his spread knees. "I came back from Nam in '69 with a little money in my pocket. I didn't want to move back onto the family ranch with my dad. I wanted my own place so I used my stake from the Army to start Cattleman's Auction in '70. Had my first cow-calf auction that spring. Cow-calf pairs went for under twenty dollars back then. Yesterday we sold five cow-calf pairs for twelve hundred a pair." He shook a leonine white head. "Business has improved." A satisfied smile split his craggy face.

"Tell me some of the changes you've made."

He jerked his jaw up and expanded his chest. "My feedlots are open twenty-four hours a day. We have our regular weekly sales and our special quarterly sales like the one you saw the other day. We live stream our auctions. Come a long way from the two squeeze shoots and a couple of holding pens I started with."

"Does Cattleman's Auction handle the sale of buffalo for the local ranchers?"

Carlisle swung his weight forward in the chair, his booted feet thudding on the floor. "Absolutely not. Buffalo are a menace to cattle. Heard of brucellosis? Threatens the cattlemen's way of life." Carlisle's knarled finger was jabbing the air in front of my face. Spittle sprayed on my cheek. "Brucellosis can destroy an entire cattle herd. Ask Wayne Johnston or Sam Jordan. They lost years of breeding. They'll never build a herd like the ones destroyed. You know what happens to an infected heifer? Abortion and sterility. Heifer's worthless if she can't be bred."

"Why do you think buffalo are the problem?"

Carlisle leaned forward gripping the rough wooden desk top. "Buffalo are the host animal for the infection. Why do you think the government regulates those wild bison in Yellowstone? To keep them away from domestic cattle. I won't help buffalo ranchers make a dime off their herds by slaughtering their meat."

"How does the infection spread to cattle?"

"Disease spreads through a healthy animal eating the infected animal's placenta or licking the cord blood after the birth. Animals are attracted to the rich blood in the birth fluids—good protein source for them. Animals seek out birth sites. Can't keep 'em away from it."

"Why aren't ranchers fencing their cattle away from the buffalo?"

"You listening, Ms. Cahill?" He rubbed his fist in the palm of his hand. "Buffalo pass the disease to the elk, the deer and even the big horn sheep. You can't fence elk and deer out of a cow pasture. Buffalo are the original hosts who pass the infection to the wildlife who jump fences and get in the pastures infecting cattle. Gotta stop this cycle by getting buffalo out of cattle country." The ghost of a smirk passed over his face.

"But one way to protect cattle herds is to vaccinate them for brucellosis, isn't it, Mr. Carlisle?"

Carlisle waved his hand irritably. "That vaccine isn't proven effective. Plus, it costs cattlemen money. Won't be needed if you eradicate the host animal." Carlisle tapped his steepled fingertips together.

"So cattlemen risk the infection to save vaccination costs?"

"It's a business, Ms. Cahill."

"You compete with buffalo meat for space on the family dinner table and also with feedlot operators, who don't have roundups, pay extra hands and don't have losses to predator animals which make the animal cheaper to bring to market. How do you compete with a cheaper beef product?"

"Americans like the sweet taste of grass-fed beef. No comparison to inferior beef fed out in a lot. Don't ever underestimate the consumer, Ms. Cahill. They know good beef."

"Your solution is to get buffalo out of Wyoming's cattle country. How would you suggest that be done?"

Carlisle narrowed his eyes. "I'd like Wyoming to follow the example set by Montana's Governor Schwarz. Montana just prohibited the importation of any buffalo into the state. Wyoming should do the same and all Wyoming slaughterhouses should be prohibited from slaughtering buffalo." He held up three fingers and jabbed them at the camera. "Third, Wyoming counties should have the right to prohibit buffalo ranches in their counties. The cattle industry must be preserved for our children and grandchildren."

"One last question. There was a buffalo mutilation over on Ray Foster's ranch a couple of nights ago. Do you have any comment?"

"Yes, I do." He set up straighter looking directly into the camera. "Animal mutilation is sick behavior. I support Sheriff Barton's efforts and urge all the ranchers in the county to be alert and to support the authorities."

"I appreciate your time today, Mr. Carlisle."

We did the shake hands and thanks so much and we were out and off camera. I called Clay and verified a minute thirty-second package for tonight's news.

Benita asked me what I thought about Carlisle's interview on the drive back to the station.

"I think he's angry, maybe defensive, certainly entrenched in his beliefs. But is he angry enough to indulge in a little terrorism in a pasture to protect his share of the meat market?"

"I don't know," Benita said

"At least, with all that emotion, Carlisle's interview will play well on TV," I said.

I got a local phone book from the station's receptionist. Sometimes research was just that simple. Wyoming Big Game Guide was located on I-80 on the edge of town. His yellow page ad claimed Javier Contreras could help you bag a trophy elk.

Chapter 11

I vacillated between editing Carlisle's interview video and thinking about Jake. Why the hell doesn't he call? You've got about fifteen minutes until I finish this story and then it's answer time, buddy.

Satisfied, I sent the story to the server. I scrolled through my contacts and tapped Jake's name.

"Spooner, here."

"Jake, it's Sawyer."

"You want an interview, right?"

"I do. I talked with George Carlisle today. You've probably seen the story with Hunter Kane. I want your viewpoint. It's to your benefit, Jake, and to Ray Foster's and all the other buffalo ranchers in the county. Why don't you meet me at the Drover Bar a little after seven tonight? I hear it has good food and if you like it, a little country music."

"I know where it is. I'll meet you at seven. You're persistent Cahill, I'll give you that."

"Look for you then."

* * * *

I was enjoying myself at the Drover savoring a Dos Equis with a huge wedge of lime perched on the frosty rim of the glass. The music was pretty good too, with Chesney singing about Tequila.

Jakes' low sexy voice vibrated in my ear. "You're looking pretty content there."

I jumped, then turned my head to look into a pair of dark gray eyes right off the tip of my nose. "Hello Jake," I said, cocking my head back to look at him.

Jake pulled out a chair by me and sat down.

I caught the waiter's attention. "What are you having?"

"The same." He pointed to my beer.

"And we'll have the beef sliders, too." I told the waiter.

"Did you have to wait long? Sorry if I held you up."

"No, I've been here about half hour. Thanks for meeting with me."

"Okay," he said guardedly over the rim of his beer.

"Why the hesitation, Jake? Bad experience with the media?"

He smiled. "I was an Assistant District Attorney in Denver for a couple of years. Goes with the territory. First rule in the DA's office is ADAs do not give interviews."

"Ah, well you're not an ADA any more. You're an expert in a different field. Let's approach the interview that way. Deal?"

"Before we seal the deal over beer and sliders, I've seen your interviews. You're good. But you don't have the facts straight and you won't get them from the likes of Hunter and George."

"That's why I'm here. Talk to me, Jake."

Jake took a slow drink from his beer. I watched his long fingers tidily square up the coaster with the edge of the table. "Running buffalo and cattle on the same ranch is safe. On the Eagle Canyon I run a conservation program for the preservation of the American bison, raise hybrid buffalo for meat and Angus cattle. I've never had a problem. You won't get that story from cattlemen. Some cattle ranchers find it real inconvenient to accept the facts."

"What's in it for the cattlemen to lie about the facts?"

"Buffalo meat competes with beef for a place on the American table. Buffalo is leaner and healthier. Every time buffalo meat is served for dinner, beef isn't. Heard of market protection?" He pushed his chair back crossing his long legs. He grabbed his beer off the table and cocked an eyebrow.

"You think Hunter and George are lying to protect their market."

"Yeah. Six months ago, the Wyoming State Parks Department asked for a small herd of Yellowstone buffalo to be moved over here to the Guernsey State Park for a breeding program. The Montana Parks Department guaranteed those animals were brucellosis free. Hunter and George starting howling to their congressmen. Now both states are involved in conducting a new environmental assessments study."

"Tell me why you think it's safe to ranch both animals."

"It's my job to know how to keep my herds safe. The best brucellosis research is done down at Texas A&M's vet school by Dr. Kent Henderson who also maintains the database of the DNA of every buffalo who is a descendent Goodnight's herd, including mine."

"How do you prevent infection on your ranch?"

"I vaccinate all my animals, cattle and buffalo with the RB51 vaccine. Vaccination is your first line of defense. Open range cattlemen should vaccinate their animals. Second, I have strong fences that keep my buffalo herds in separate pastures from the cattle. Buffalo aren't jumpers. Elk pass at will over all fences. Elk infect the cattle." He motioned to the waiter for a beer. "There are tens of thousands of infected elk in Wyoming and Montana."

"If elk are the vector for disease, why are you separating your cattle from your buffalo? Fencing adds costs, doesn't it?" I asked.

"Because cattle and buffalo will breed with each other creating a cattalo. I keep all three herds separated. Most buffalo have a few cattle genes, but you don't want to add to the animal's cattle heritage."

I took a swig of beer. "Why aren't open-range cattle ranchers vaccinating their herds and passing along the cost of the vaccine to the buyers?"

"They compete with feedlot beef—herds of animals closely contained in their own filth. Animals in feedlots are not intermingling with elk so they don't need vaccinations. A feedlot operation can sell a cow more cheaply to slaughter."

"But Americans love the taste of grass-fed beef." I quoted Carlisle's line.

"Ranchers with grass fed cattle are threatened by the price competition from feedlot beef and buffalo meat. Feeling the squeeze like that makes them do anything to keep their costs down, including not vaccinating their animals." He shrugged. "When their cattle get infected, it becomes the classic ploy of 'never lose the opportunity of a disaster to twist it to your advantage.'"

I stayed still and silent, letting him talk.

"You've heard a lot by Hunter Kane. I'm telling you Sawyer, there's more there than you might want to know about him. Keep your eyes open when you deal with him."

"You have any specifics you want to add to that?"

"You're a journalist. I bet you can find out." Jake tapped the coaster under his beer.

Hunter was a bit controlling and a braggart, but what else? It was obvious Jake wasn't going to be the one to relieve my curiosity and I wasn't going to beg. My cell phone buzzed.

"Excuse me, this might be the station." The caller ID read *Caller blocked.*

"You need to go?"

"No, some robo-call probably. What I didn't mention was the other blocked call in the wee hours of the morning. "How many head are you running?"

"You mean for meat production or total head?" Jake asked.

"Both."

Jake was finishing the last of the beef sliders and motioned for the waiter.

"Another beer, sir?"

"No thank you, but I would like some coffee. You, Sawyer?"

I nodded yes, and Jake ordered two coffees.

"You seem a bit more relaxed now, Mr. Spooner," I teased. "I guess this interview went better than you anticipated."

"Obviously, you've done your research. I'm impressed with you, Ms Cahill. I have eight hundred-fifty head of buffalo that I'm ranching for meat. They have some cattle genes. Not a bad thing. Makes a fine meat animal. They're just not the American bison. I've got fifty genetically pure buffalo, descendents of the original Charlie Goodnight herd." Jake added cream to his coffee and sat back. "You know the way Goodnight started his herd?"

"Yeah." I surprised him. "His wife nagged him into roping five wild buffalo calves to save the species."

"There's three herds up here out of Goodnight's. One in Yellowstone, the Shoshone's and mine."

"I've only seen the herd in Quitaque in the Texas panhandle."

"They are the iconic image of the untamed west," Jake said softly. "They deserve to be bred and cherished like the land. Come to the ranch. I'll take you to see them."

"I'll be there." I had one last question for Jake. "Buffalo haven't been the target of a mutilator before. What do you think?"

"I haven't prosecuted a mutilation case, though there were

a couple of cattle mutilated in Colorado out on the eastern plains. But I'm a rancher so I'm angry. No one can really protect stock. A mutilator does his work alone and in a lonely place." He toyed with his coffee cup, idly stirring in more cream. "I saw your story. You didn't go into a lot of detail about how the animal died, but I hope he had an individual signature that copycats can be identified."

"He did."

"Good. Get to the bottom of this, Ms. Cahill."

"I intend to. Thanks, Jake. I appreciate the time you took tonight." I enjoyed my time with him.

"I'll give you a call next week and we'll pull a time together to see the ranch." He smiled scooting his chair back on the scratched wood floor. "Now, let's see if you can dance," he said, pulling out my chair. "I'll buy you more coffee if yours gets cool."

Jake proved to be good dancer who knew how to lead a woman around a dance floor. I was acutely aware of just how close his chin was to my shoulder. If I cocked my head back a little, my mouth would be right below his. His hand was burning my back. He deftly steered us to the left, narrowly missing a middle-aged cowboy who was vigorously pumping his arms while turning the missus in big galloping circles.

Jake leaned in closer. "You've danced a country song before."

"I have. You dance pretty well yourself."

"I got a lot of practice in Denver."

Another tight turn drew us closer. He held me there to his chest in the turn. "Was it hard to leave Denver?" I asked.

"It was. I lived and worked down in Lodo where there're lots of good restaurants and bars. Plus, the DA was a great mentor. I was young and green. Learned a lot."

"Why did you give up law?"

"After my granddad's funeral, Dad and I walked the ranch. He told me Granddad had left it to me because he knew I loved the land. He was right. I flew back to Denver composing my resignation letter in my head on the plane."

The music slowed and the band drawled out the "Remind Me" duet. Jake pulled me closer. I rested my head on his shoulder while we swayed to the music. The band hung onto the last note, ending with a flourish. Jake said, "Let's step outside and get some air."

We stood on the front porch of the Drover in the starlit

night. "I missed the big western sky when I was in San Antonio."

Jake shifted his gaze from the starlit sky to me. "I went to school in Austin. Did you ever get used to the heat and the humidity in the summer down there?"

"No, summers were ugly. Why did you pick UT?"

"UT was far enough away from home for me to do some real growing up, but close enough for me to come home. I ended up staying for law school. You happy to be back in Cheyenne?"

"Absolutely. I knew your Grandfather Huddleston. Julia and I used to trick-or-treat at their place in town. They always gave us doughnuts and ladyfingers from the bakery of their little grocery store. Best place to go to on Halloween."

He laughed. "I remember that hole in the wall store my grandparents had in town. My grandmother always had something for me. The sugar doughnuts were the best. You kept up with Julia all these years?"

"Yes, we went to CU together. Dave was there, too."

He leaned his elbows on the railing, crossing one booted leg behind the other. Long lean stretch of leg right up to a great ass. "I'd stay at the ranch every summer. Some of my best memories are working with my granddad. When I was fifteen, Dad started working me in his law office. I stopped coming up here for long visits. But I always loved this place." He took my hand. "Glad you came home, Sawyer."

"Me, too…" My cell phone vibrated in my pocket and the caller ID was the station. "Jake, it's work. Excuse me."

Jake's phone began to ring. I turned my back to him and heard him answer "Spooner," before I stuck my finger in my ear.

I pocketed my phone, waiting until he slipped his into his pocket. His face was grim.

"You heard, too." I raised my phone. "That was Clay from the station. I'm so sorry Jake. I can't imagine how this feels for you."

Jake grabbed my hand and we ran to the cars. When he jerked open the door of his Ford 250, he yelled, "Follow me over to the county road. It's faster." I scrambled into my Laredo.

Eighteen minutes later, we parked in the high, greasy grass off the side of the county road on Jake's ranch. The pasture was artificially lit, full of dark shadows thrown from a single halogen bulb mounted on a rickety tripod. A small Honda generator hummed in the darkness. In the center of the unnaturally white light, lay a bloodied buffalo carcass. Jake looked down on the carnage and swore softly. "Look at her. Hell of a thing to do to an animal."

We joined Barton and a short middle-aged man crouching by the carcass. "Jake, I called you right after I called the sheriff."

"You did the right thing. Sawyer this is my foreman, Brad. What happened?"

"You're seeing all I know." Brad removed his cap and scrubbed his hand over his face. "I got up from the TV to fix myself a bite to eat. Thought I saw vehicle lights out here in the pasture. Told myself no, it's nothing, just dang fool kids messing around. Then I got to thinking about what happened over at Ray's place and got out here quick. I lost sight of this high ground in that little valley between the ranch house and this rise. By the time I regained the high ground, I couldn't see the headlights anymore. I found her this way. This look like the one over at Foster's place?"

"Similar," Barton mumbled. His shoulders sagged. "I don't have much Jake. I can't run around chasing ghosts. I got one deputy. Hell, I can't be all over the county watching for this asshole to kill somewhere new."

Jake placed his hand on the buffalo's shoulder. "She's not cooled much. He hasn't been gone long." He stood looking at Barton. "Any tire tracks? Foot prints?"

"Grass is beat down where he drove in. Can't get prints off grass. Brad may have interrupted him coming out like he did. He wouldn't have seen him if he went out north on the county road with his headlights off. You two pass anyone on the way here?"

"No, we were coming from the south. He could have gone out north of the ranch and intersected I-25 and gone anywhere," Jake said.

"If he knows the area well enough. North of here there's not much traffic to slow him down," Barton groused.

The deputy was beginning to shoot pictures. I asked Barton, "Is Sam coming out tonight?"

"Yeah, I hated to call him out. Sam's no pleasure to work with right now. He's damn bitter about his own herd. But this cow's fresh. I want him to see her."

"Do you mind if I take a few shots?" I asked, slipping the small flip camera I carried everywhere from my jacket pocket.

"Naw, go ahead," Barton answered.

"How did she die?" I asked.

Barton pulled the big head back by the horns. A ragged slash dug deep across the throat. Blood soaked the dry grass. "Throat's cut like the one over at Foster's and look at her side.

Got the peace sign painted on it. She didn't have no testicles to cut, but look." He pulled up her hind leg. Blood oozed from the wound on her belly. "Maybe he took the ovaries. Sam will know."

Barton and Jake walked behind the cow. "He got the tail. That don't take much time. What the hell you think he does with the tail?" Barton asked.

Headlights pierced the darkness and a truck door slammed in the distance. "This happened at Foster's place?" Jake gestured at the peace sign on the carcass.

"Yeah, same sign," Barton said, looking up at Jake. "He got the testes on Foster's bull. Sam says he paints that peace sign with the tail from blood from the neck slash. We didn't tell the public any of these details."

"How about how close the cow is to the road? Any similarity there to the animal over at Foster's?" Jake asked.

"He makes it easy on himself," Barton said rising. "Neither kill was far from the road. He doesn't have to carry much but rope, sedative and a good knife."

"He's got to be delivering the sedative by dart gun. Only way a man can do this by himself," I said.

Sam followed Barton, rounding the perimeter. "The grass isn't stamped down this time," Barton said gruffly. "He was in a hurry."

"Cow didn't try to stand either. Look there." Sam pointed. "The dirt's smooth around her hooves. Bet he dosed her heavier than his first."

"Guy's moving up the learning curve," Barton said. "Get me the lab results on the drugs soon as you can."

"Yeah, sure. I got no real vet work to do," Sam grumbled. "Sorry you lost a cow, Jake. Sawyer, see you're working another one."

Barton kicked at the dry grass with the toe of his boot. "We walked Foster's pasture in a grid and we'll do the same on your ranch looking for anything to nail this bastard. Looks like this guy knows a little about your ranch and Foster's. The best way to keep your animals safe is for all of us to be looking out for anyone or anything in the wrong place. I know right now it don't sound like much."

"Were you able to find records of anyone buying Xylazine or turn up any more on the rope fibers from Foster's bull?" I asked.

Barton whirled around to me. "I'm doing my job. Told ya,

common rope sold everywhere. Don't know where he got the Xylazine *yet.*"

"And the Ketamine?" I asked.

"How the hell you know about that?" Barton shouted.

"Sheriff, I'm doing my job just like you are."

"Do your fuckin' job, but you share anything with me you find out. I got a cell about your size." Barton kicked up dirt walking off.

"My, you know how to piss off the local constable," Jake whispered.

I touched my finger to my lips. Sam was packing his gear back in the old truck. "I'll call you in the morning, Sam."

"Sure, get in line. I ought to have something later in the day."

I touched Sam's shoulder. "How are you doing with your own loss, Sam?"

"Managing," Sam mumbled, not making eye contact with me. He hoisted himself on the front seat and slammed the truck door.

"You ready?" Jake asked me.

"Yeah." We walked back to our vehicles and I popped the lock on mine. "Get in for a sec, Jake. Let's talk. I'll even run the heater for you."

"You interviewed me and now you want to pick my brain?" He sat in my passenger's seat and stretched.

"Oh, it won't be that bad or take long. How are you doing?"

Jake ran a hand through his hair that fell back on his forehead. "I'm angry. Worried for the rest of my stock. How about you? Second time you've seen a butchered animal."

"I'm okay. I've seen worse and had it happen right in front of me. Do you think Sheriff Barton can solve this?"

"Maybe. He's got experience. He's in his third term, but he doesn't have many resources. The county doesn't have many problems, and when they do, they've been routine. He's going to need some luck." He rolled his head on his shoulders. "What'd you do to piss him off?"

"We don't agree on what sharing is."

"Barton gets to pick what he shares with the media. Remember, I was an ADA. I watched the DA finesse what he told the media. You might have to cultivate Barton, not piss him off." He opened my car door. "It's late. I'll follow you up to your drive."

He poked his head back in the Jeep and added, "I'll call you tomorrow and we'll talk about getting together over at the ranch.

Chapter 12

Saturday dawned crisp and cool. I was lying in bed, thoughts ricocheting through my head, creating the monkey chatter that inhibited the Buddhist Zen I sought. I was going to have to forge a better working relationship with Barton.

Outside, the sky was the achingly clear, cold blue of early winter. Not a shimmer of the gold of fall left. There was already a touch of snow above the tree line in the high country. I pulled myself out of bed with the intent of driving the chattering monkeys from my mind with a pot of coffee. While the caffeine began to work its magic, I replayed the evening at the Drover. Jake had warned me off Hunter—something I was going to have to think about.

I had work to do this morning, but thinking about dancing with Jake was more pleasurable. The man certainly knew how to move. Plus, he was incredibly easy to look at and damned nice to be with. There was also that instant connection I felt when he touched me.

I went for a short run. I was getting acclimated to the altitude. A few short weeks ago, I gasped for oxygen the whole time I jogged. I unlocked my door and hit the shower, pleased with my distance and time.

Driving to the station I remembered Jake mentioning the Shoshone herd. I started my computer, searched 'Shoshone' and started reading. The Wind River Reservation website told the story. The herd's pasture abutted a cattle rancher's land who accused the Shoshone's buffalo of infecting his cattle with brucellosis. The rancher got his Senator to introduce SB432 in an effort to eradicate the Shoshone's entire herd and shut down their meat packing plant. The bill was still pending.

Benita peeked into the office. "Hey, I'm cutting out at noon today. You have time to tell me about the mutilation over at Jake's? Was it like the one over at Ray Foster's?"

"Similar, except it was a female. You want to see the video? I've got a couple of phone calls to make before I do the voice over." I passed her the camera.

"I can load the footage if you like. Does the sheriff have a lead?"

"Not when I talked to him last night. My story is going to be short, no more than forty-five seconds."

Benita left to load the video. I called Sam. He answered on the first ring. "Got those results. This animal had a much higher dosage of Xylazine than the first. Made his work a little easier this time, but he still doesn't know to add the Ketamine, the bastard. He took the ovaries all right. Damn good with a knife our boy is."

"You talked to Barton this morning?"

"Just gave him the results on the cow. I got patients, Sawyer. Gotta go."

I called Barton. "Good morning, Sheriff."

"You talk to Sam?"

"Yeah, he told me about the heavier sedation. Do you think the guy might be someone who works on a ranch out there north of town? He's making easy work of getting on and off the ranches."

"Could be," Barton said. "I got a list of all the hired hands. Ran them for priors, didn't get nothing." He stopped. "Sam's report on the drugs is off the record. Don't even think of using it, you hear?"

"Yeah. It's off the record."

* * * *

I drove up the wide circle drive and parked in front of Hunter's front porch. The house was a soaring two-story of wood and stone. He met me on his manicured front lawn. "It's a great afternoon for a ride. Feel winter coming on?" Hunter enthused. "Good thing you dressed in layers. Up on the ridge line the wind will be blowing. I hope you like this little mare I've picked out for you."

He was speaking too fast and too much, but his desire to please touched me. "I'm sure I'll love her. I can't wait to ride again."

He flushed. "Let me give you the tour of the house before we ride." He stepped aside to allow me to walk beside him.

"How's your work? Interviewed anyone interesting?"

"I talked with George Carlisle and Jake Spooner—"

"So you interviewed Spooner," he interrupted. "Bet Spooner had a whole different story." Hunter's body was suddenly rigid. His hands clenched in tight fists. "George Carlisle is the kind of man who made the cattle business in this state the success it is. Spooner and that conservation group of his have got some idea about saving the American bison."

Hunter had a full head of anger by the time we stepped on the broad front porch. "I don't have much use for Spooner. He rubs me the wrong way." He jerked open the front door giving me a dazzling smile. "I can't tell you how much I've looked forward to showing you my home."

My spine tingled. The man changed moods like a teenage girl changed clothes.

"I worked with my architect. He redrew the plans until I had just what I wanted." He ran his hands over the stone columns by the door. "The stonework is native granite from Colorado. Welcome to my home, Sawyer."

The entry was two stories high. A chandelier blazed in a cove ceiling that ran the length of the house. A large den opened off to the left. He took my hand and led the way into a dining room where a walnut table, surrounded by twelve chairs and a matching sideboard, filled every inch of space. The dining room was adjacent to a restaurant style kitchen with a large island facing a wall of windows. A set of copper pots above the work island glowed in the sunlight.

"You like to cook?"

"I can cook a mean steak on the barbecue, but I usually have caterers in."

The kitchen looked unused. Perfectly decorated and never used. Not a dish towel in sight, not a coffee mug in the sink nor even a coffee pot. A trophy kitchen—the man owned a trophy kitchen.

He beamed with pleasure, ushering me into his den. Two burnished leather sofas flanked an oriental rug. A bronze figure caught my eye. "Go ahead and touch if you like. It's a Remington. I couldn't resist buying it. The sculpture is called *The Working Cowboy*."

We walked up the grand staircase to the second floor. Even in Hunter's private spaces, there was no revelation of his interests. No candid photos, no plaques, no sign of hobbies or just the detritus of daily living. Fine art work, though. I could have sworn I passed a Russell and a Bierstadt painting. Hunter did well.

Back downstairs, I admired the bronze statue. "You have an excellent eye for western art."

"One of my many pleasures. I also love entertaining. I hope you'll enjoy my annual barbecue."

He slipped his arm around my waist, nestling me to him. "Let's get the horses saddled."

The warm smell of manure and horse wafted out of the barn. Hunter stroked the velvet nose of a brown mare. "There, there girl. I brought you someone special." His shoulders relaxed, his jaw became less rigid while he stroked the horse's neck, smoothing her long brown mane. I let her smell me before I touched her.

"You'll love this mare, Sawyer. She's got some spunk in her, but she'll give you a smooth ride. She knows her own head too." The mare nickered, bobbing her head up and down.

I rubbed the mare's neck. "Sweet girl," I crooned. "We're going to have a good ride today, aren't we?" She nuzzled my shoulder.

We led the saddled horses out of the barn. The trail wound through low hills gradually rising into the high country. The brown mare was a gentle ride with a good mouth, responsive to a soft pull on her reins. Hunter pulled his horse up on a low rise. "Look, there." He leaned across his saddle touching my arm and pointing. Pronghorn antelope covered the plain below. A large buck with curved horns above his black and white striped face sniffed the air for danger. "Look at that buck. Has his harem with him, five or six does. Their young will be born in the spring."

"Benita says people stalk them from pickup trucks."

"Yeah, I lease out to hunters every year." He eased back in his saddle. "People like them for their meat and the occasional trophy buck. Antelope's an acquired taste. Tastes a lot like the sage they're grazing on down there. Meat smells like sage when you cook it. Elk up in the high country are gathering their harems, too. We might catch a glance of one further on."

We turned the horses up the trail. He sat his large gelding well, guiding him almost imperceptibly around the sharp curves. I enjoyed watching Hunter's broad back and narrow hips sway with horse's step.

The trail had a steep drop off on the side away from the mountain and loose stones skittered and clattered down the cliff face to the valley floor below. "Not far now to the ridge line," Hunter called back. One more sharp turn and the trail opened up on a flat, grassy area bordered by lodge pole pines and a few aspen.

Hunter dismounted, tying his horse to a tree. He held the reins of my horse and helped me off the mare. My hands were on his shoulders, his hands spanning my waist. "Lunch is ready," he said.

I kissed him lightly on the cheek. "Great ride. Fantastic panoramic view up here." I broke the embrace. "I can see mountains to the west and all the way east out on to the plains."

"The view up close with you is pretty good, too." He grinned. "But yeah, I love this ridge line."

"How'd you find it?"

"I was out riding shortly after I bought the ranch. Followed an old trail up here." He untied the picnic basket from his horse. "Used to come up here to clear my head when times were tough. I'd been around ranching, but never done it. Lot of my high-wealth clients at the bank in Missoula were ranchers. I had a lot to learn and I needed to learn fast. I was leaking money." He spread a colorful old quilt on the ground, unpacking cold fried chicken, deviled eggs and potato salad. "I'm so happy you came up here to share this with me."

At my gasp of surprise at the bounty, Hunter threw back his head and laughed. "There's a great deli in town."

"And there I was thinking you cooked all this."

He laughed casually taking my hand up to his lips for a kiss. "Do you enjoy your work?"

I liked the feel of his work-hardened hand on mine. "I love my job. No day is ever like any other."

"Ranching's a lot like that," he said. "Banking was a day full of people with problems. What drew you to the news business?"

"I used to sit in Dad's study and read the newspapers with him. Grew up to be a newshound." I helped myself to a lemon tart. "Got a journalism degree from CU and worked my way back home."

"You still have friends here?" He refilled my wine glass.

My heart was beating a little faster—wine, altitude or Hunter? "Julia. She's a second grade teacher. We were roommates at CU." I flushed when he leaned in for a quick kiss before we tapped our glasses.

"I went to school out in Seattle." Hunter stretched out on his side. He crossed his booted legs. "Seattle was pretty liberal for a Montana boy. Got a very diverse population. I had friends who were real exotic people to a small town kid like me." He laughed. "Dated a girl who was half Chinese and half Samoan with Asian eyes and creamy coffee skin. Hell! Quite a deal for a kid from Missoula."

He held my hand, the warmth spreading to my whole body. "You still have family back in Missoula?"

He rolled over on his back, still holding my hand, and stared up at the cloudless blue sky. "Nobody left there. I have a brother, Joe, who's two years younger and graduated from West Point. Right now, he's over in Iraq serving his second tour. When he finishes his commitment, I don't know what his plans are. He's a trained engineer like most of them coming out of West Point. I don't know what Joe will do, but it'll have to be exciting." He said softly, "Lost my parents in a car crash two years ago."

"I'm so sorry." I squeezed his hand.

"It was bad. They died at the scene. Joe was over in Iraq at the time and he had to get compassionate leave to get home for the services."

He rolled the tension out of his back. "All I wanted was to see Missoula in my rearview mirror when I graduated from high school. I went to University of Washington and then I got into the U's medical school."

"Really? Did you finish?"

"No." He propped his head up on his hand. "My time in med school was mercifully short. I finished the first year, dissected that cadaver, and left. Just didn't suit me. I fit in real well over in the business school."

"Have any regrets about med school? Ever rethink it?"

"No regrets. I don't look back. Decide to decide, decide, and move on," he said emphatically. "Business fit me like a glove. Started at a bank in Seattle and then got the opportunity to go back to Missoula. Emily and I built a good life. Why don't you scoot a little closer? Or hell, just lie down by me and relax. You're way over there hugging the edge of the quilt."

I scooted closer to him, but remained sitting. "Were you married long?"

"Over four years." He traced his fingers down my calf. "We met at a party in the spring of my senior year. Married the following Christmas. I was so in love with her. Emily Alston, the most beautiful little blonde on campus. She had a hard time being away from her folks.

"First home you make away from your parents can be difficult."

He wiped one hand over his face. "That was just the beginning of the adjustments for us. We tried to have a baby. Emily couldn't get pregnant. We began the rounds to fertility specialists. Hormone treatments for Emily. Sperm counts for me. After a couple of years, Emily accepted we probably would never have children and she took it hard."

"A loss for both of you," I murmured, not sure about the personal turn of the conversation.

Hunter's hand continued to play up and down my calf. "She started to drink and her drinking was a problem for both of us. She couldn't or wouldn't control it. She tried to hide it at first, but soon, all our friends knew. She'd go to the club and be too drunk to play tennis. I was embarrassed. Anywhere drinks were served, I tensed up. I didn't know if Emily would drink herself into oblivion or do something stupid. Then she totaled her car. She was on her way home from the club and hit an embankment trying to exit the freeway. The judge gave her a DUI, took away her driver's license for a year. We were living in Missoula, for Christ's sake! You can't hide a scandal like that in a small country club environment."

"Sounds like a hard time for everyone."

He took my hand and kissed it. "I was worried Emily's drinking would keep me from making vice president. People want a squeaky-clean banker, no scandals in the family. We quit socializing. I began to make excuses. I couldn't risk taking Emily out anywhere alcohol was served. We spent more and more of our free time alone down in Colorado at the condo in Keystone."

"Did you get Emily any help?"

"Hell yes." He sounded indignant. "I got her the best, the Betty Ford Clinic in Arizona. Each time, I prayed it would take. Never did." His face tightened and his shoulders tensed. "The last time she went to the clinic, I didn't go for Family Day. Drinking was *her* problem. I stayed in Missoula."

"When you didn't go to Family Day, how did Emily react?"

"We never spoke of it." He gave a bitter laugh. "Speaks volumes about the depth of our marriage, doesn't it?"

Way too much disclosure. Trying to manipulate me? "Sounds lonely. How did Emily die?"

He gathered up his dishes into a neat stack. "I'll tell you how Emily died, Sawyer. I will, but I have to go to a dark place and a dark time in my life. I hope you understand. Emily died suddenly." He absently reached over to stroke the hair back from my face. "I know now to never leave someone without telling them I love them. You never know if it's the last time you'll see them."

He had to go to dark place? After all that personal revelation, he couldn't just say "Emily had a car wreck" or "her plane fell out of the sky" or "my wife was murdered." Why not? What really happened to Emily? A shiver of foreboding passed through me.

He eyed the sky. "We need to saddle our horses." He offered me his hand to help me get on the mare. "The high country gets thunderstorms in the afternoon. We don't want to get caught up here in a lightning storm." He lashed the picnic basket onto his saddle.

The clouds were building in the west. I zipped my Polartec jacket against the cold wind. The mare was snorting and stamping her feet. I reached over and soothed her neck. "You sense a storm coming in, don't you girl?"

"We'll get down to the main trail before it starts raining up here," Hunter said. We pushed the horses hard down the narrow path. Great gusts of wind blew leaves around us, making the mare toss her head.

Suddenly, Hunter pulled up his horse. "Look at these tracks—mountain lion. She must have crossed our trail while we had our picnic. Look at the size of that print. She's a big one. Probably interested in those antelope we saw."

"Is she up ahead?"

"No, she passed this way awhile ago." He reassured me. "If she were up ahead, she wouldn't bother two humans on horseback. A single hiker, now that could be problem."

Hell yes. Mountain lions were a problem. They stalked their prey, rushed in and killed them with a single bite to the neck. I rode on in uneasy silence. A hungry cat with a taste for antelope wasn't the only thing bothering me. A couple of puzzle pieces jockeyed for place.

The sound of Hunter's voice jolted me. "I'm going to Montana tomorrow morning for a couple of days to buy two new breeding bulls for my herd. I'll be giving my annual barbecue when I get back." He smiled. "You look like you were off on another planet there for a moment."

"I was. I was thinking about how saddle sore I'll be in the morning," I lied.

"Got to get you back in shape," he teased. "You'll love my barbecue. It's a lot of fun. I've had a terrific afternoon. You're just so easy to talk to. I usually don't run on at the mouth like that, telling Emily's story. I hope I didn't ruin the afternoon for you." He swung off his horse and helped me off mine.

"I had a great ride."

He swooped in and kissed me, lingering with his lips on mine. His kiss did nothing for me. "You're a hot woman and damned intelligent, too. We're going to have some good times together, I promise you."

* * * *

By the time I got home, I had an hour before meeting Julia for dinner at the Albany Grill. I scrolled through the viewer comments to the web version of my interview with George Carlisle. There was a lively discussion in the comments section between WyCowboy27 and ridgewalker52 about the dangers of ranching buffalo near cattle. Several other viewers echoed Carlisle's negative views of buffalo ranching.

I stripped and soaked in the tub, hoping to head off the saddle soreness I knew was coming. The hot water steamed around me and sweat ran down my hairline. Hunter was an interesting man, molded by the hard work of climbing the rungs at the bank and building a successful ranch. He had a lot to be proud of. He was almost anxious for me to accept him. I slipped down further in the warm water, just up to my nose.

Hunter had excised all traces of his wife from his home. A dead wife whose husband was so embarrassed by her that he had isolated her to protect his career. But he had revealed her life story on a picnic. Then, had ended the lunch by telling me that talking about her death drove him to "a dark place." Why? What had really happened to Emily?

Oh hell, Hunter was the classic approach-avoidance conflict. Attracted by his warm wit, his intelligence, his damn fine looks and his interest in me I was flattered. But his sterile house, dead wife and talk of going to a dark place made the hair stand up on the back of my neck.

More mental aerobics resulted in my decision that my unease trumped any pleasure I took from him. Avoidance rules. Conflict solved.

* * * *

Julia was waiting for me in a booth in the back of the Albany. She had a half-eaten basket of bread and butter in front of her. "I was early and starving. I see more of you on TV than I see of you in person. We gotta fix that. Sit down and catch me up."

I slid into the booth across from my old friend and relaxed. "I've been working some crazy hours."

"Looks like it from watching the news. The mutilations are bad for our town's family friendly image. Does Barton have any suspects?"

"Not that I know of. Hard to catch a guy who works alone at night in the middle of a pasture." I helped myself to the bread.

"He needs to catch him soon. How's your...?" She paused, staring at the doorway. I followed her gaze. Jake was following Morgan Hall to a table by the fireplace.

Julia buttered more bread. "I saw them at the deli last week having lunch. You know Morgan?"

"Not really. I met her once at the Little Bear. She and Jake were having dinner."

"Really," Julia mused. "When was that?"

"Maybe a week ago, I don't remember. Stop staring unless we're going over there to say hello," I whispered.

"Okay, but you gotta admit they look good together. Bother you?"

"No reason for it to bother me. Jake's free to do whatever."

"Your turn. Stop staring," Julia murmured. "Where were we? Oh yeah, how's your social life? Seen Hunter again?"

"I went riding with him today."

Julia smiled. "Really? Give."

"Have you been to his house? To a party there?"

"Yeah, once maybe. Why? I thought you went riding."

We did, but he showed me the house first. It's spectacular and weird. There're no photos, no personal items and not even a damp dish towel. It's sterile." I was tearing the bread into a small white mountain.

"What's with the bread? You nervous? About Hunter's house or Jake over there?"

"Neither," I snorted. "Doesn't it seem strange to you that a man who was married for nearly five years has no photos of his dead wife?" I swept the breadcrumbs off the table into a napkin.

"Maybe he hasn't gotten around to the personal touches." Julia shrugged. "Could be he just works and socializes with his guy friends. He could be waiting to meet the right woman to change his life."

"I don't think so." I tapped my knife on the table.

"Look, are sure you're not reading too much into this? Most guys are exactly what they say they are. You know the line, 'I'm just a simple guy.' And they are. Sometimes I look at Dave and think he was formed by two random cells careening across the universe and colliding. One screaming, 'Am I going to get laid?' and the other yelling, 'What's for dinner?'"

I erupted in a peal of laughter. "Seriously, old friend, I'm getting a visual I don't like."

"*Seriously*, Dave's a wonderful guy and a perfect husband. I love him with all my heart. But we overanalyze our men."

"Hunter's got a story. My news interest is just pinging about him."

"Find out. You're good at that."

I shrugged. "Maybe I'll do a little digging."

"Tell me what you find. Don't look now, but Jake has sneaked a peek or two at you. Have you seen him lately?"

"I danced with him at the Drover earlier this week," I said mischievously. Our server set down the grilled chicken salads. Julia peered around the young woman while she grated parmesan over her salad.

"Start talking," she demanded.

"I bought him a beer and interviewed him. Our dancing was interrupted." I let that hang there.

"What happened?" Julia's fork was in mid air.

I gave her the guts of Jake's story.

"How's Jake?"

"Frustrated. Angry. I think he felt used or that his ranch was violated."

"He's pretty passionate about that conservation program he works with to save the bison. Was it one of those conservation animals?" Julia asked.

"No, a hybrid animal for the meat market."

"What's he going to do?"

"His answer is the same as Foster's. Be vigilant. Not much else the ranchers can do."

"How about you? You have any ideas on who's doing it?"

"Not a list of names, but a list of skills the guy has and some personality traits."

"Be careful Sawyer." She laid her hand on arm.

"Thanks. I am."

"You gonna see Jake again?"

"He invited me over to his ranch."

"Perfect! Jake's a stand-up guy." She glanced at Morgan and arched a brow at me.

"Let's don't get ahead of ourselves here." I placed both

my palms on the table. "I've done some thinking about what you called my failure to trust. I think I like being the captain of my ship. I don't want to give up my captaincy, but I'm not sure I'm good with sharing the bridge."

"You'll work this out Sawyer," she said with that practical voice of hers. "In the meantime, think about this. You can share the bridge with the right person in the right relationship. So don't put your combat boots on and stomp on any opportunities," Julia advised.

"Deal," I agreed.

Julia and I walked out to the cars chatting easily. There was a square of white paper stuck under my windshield. Someone had left me a message cut from letters from a newspaper. *Quit stirring up trouble. Rodriguez died, didn't he?*

Julia peered over my shoulder. "Who, in hell, is Rodriguez? Oh, god. He's the dead gang banger from San Antonio? What trouble is he talking about? Oh, my god! It's your story, isn't it?"

I stared down at the patched message. "I got an anonymous email to my station account telling me to 'Leave it alone.' He knew we were here tonight and I don't like you being pulled into this."

"Did you call Sherriff Barton after the email to the station?" Julia demanded.

"No…"

"Why didn't you?"

"Because sometimes viewers email something they would never say to your face. This is different." I dug my cell phone out my purse. I had missed a call, ID blocked.

Barton found us waiting for him in the back of the Grill. He slipped into the booth, tipped his hat back, sighing like an overworked man with few ideas to share. "Two threats, two phone calls. He's warning you. He followed you two here," he said. "Look, I gotta call in the Cheyenne police. This is their jurisdiction. I'm a county sheriff. They'll send someone over to the station to look at your email account and they'll pull your cell phone records. Can't promise you it's gonna turn up much. I can assign someone to drive by your house out there in the country. You're going to have to be careful. You got somebody worked up. Don't stay out there at that house by yourself."

Julia grabbed my hand. "Come home and stay with Dave and me."

Barton jumped at the idea. "I'll follow you out to your

house to pack up your stuff and then follow you back over to her house. Do it."

"He's right. Don't over think it." She jumped up. "I'll go home and get the guest room ready."

I looked at Barton. "Let's get going. It won't take me long to pack."

* * * *

I woke up in Julia's guest room longing for the familiarity of my little house. I could smell coffee. Someone was running water in the other bathroom. *Better rise and shine, sunshine, you're meeting Detective Don Jacoby in an hour.* I rounded the corner into the kitchen to find Julia pouring coffee. "Did you get some sleep?"

"Yes. Thanks for putting me up. I can move to a hotel if you like."

"No!" She quickly crossed the little kitchen. "Dave says your place is here. We want you here. Safe."

I took the coffee mug she thrust in my hand. "Thanks, both of you."

"Good, it's settled then. Here's your key and here's Dave's cell number. You've got mine and the school's. There's some breakfast stuff on the bar. You meeting that detective today?"

"Yeah, I'm going to eat a bite and get going too." I poured my second cup of the day.

"Call one of us if you need anything, Sawyer."

* * * *

A heavyset, middle-aged man stood in the doorway of my office. "Ms. Cahill? I'm Detective Don Jacoby, Cheyenne PD."

"Have a seat Detective. Sheriff Barton said you would be coming by."

"Talked to Barton this morning." He perched on the small chair. "I agree with him that you should stay at your friend's house. Someone took the time to find out about that gang murder in San Antonio."

"That wasn't that hard to do. The story was in all the newspapers and we carried a video report on our station's web site. Just googling my name could have turned that up."

"Yeah, but someone took the time to research you. I talked to Detective Deaver this morning down in San Antonio. He says hello and told me to tell you to stay out of trouble here."

I smiled thinking of Deaver.

"Stay at your friends for a while. I don't think this trouble followed you up from San Antonio. I'll meet with your IT people and get a look at those emails. We have a man patrolling around the station." He handed me one of his cards. "Call me if you need anything. I'll be in touch."

The office seemed larger and empty without his presence. Am I afraid? Yeah, be an idiot not to be scared. I'm also damn curious.

My cell rang. "Hey, glad I caught you and not your voice mail. Hate talking to machines," Jake said. "How about touring the ranch this afternoon around three?"

The warm timbre of his voice chased back the chill. "Perfect. I'll be at your front door at three."

Chapter 13

Jake's home was a rambling 1930s ranch house with a long porch where two white wooden rockers flanked a gate leg table. Someone had been sitting in one of the white rockers. A bottle of bourbon, a glass with a thimble of liquor and a dog-eared copy of the *Wyoming Law Review* were on the table. Chet bounded around the side of the house. His toenails clicked on the boards and he skidded to a stop in front of me. He greeted me with a deep, rumbling bark. His tongue lolled out of his big head, slurping my leg.

The door banged open and Jake strode out. "Thought I heard you arrive." He scratched behind Chet's ears. "Good boy, Chet. I was having a drink and enjoying what could be the last of the season's sunshine. Can I get you something?" He held the door open for me. "Come in. Chet, mind your manners." He petted the big head.

When I brushed past Jake, I caught a hint of bergamot from his cologne. Chet casually bumped his head on my thigh, looking up at me expectantly. I scratched behind his ears. "What kind of dog is Chet?"

"A big ol' ranch dog who wants a lot of attention and love. I got him when I moved here. Nate Foster had his mom, a Great Pyrenees, and one ranch over had an Australian Shepherd with a roving eye. Chet was the pick of the litter. He's got the body and tail of a Pyrenees, but he got that black and tan coat from his dad. You're a good herding dog too, aren't you fella?" The big dog rolled over and presented his belly for a scratch from Jake.

The inside of Jake's home fulfilled the promise of the porch. Old photographs lined the walls of the pine-floored hallway. A couple of the sepia-tinted portraits of men and women vaguely resembled Jake.

"My great-great-grandfather and his wife." He tapped a stained and curling picture of an unsmiling couple, the woman holding a solemn-eyed baby. They homesteaded this land in 1890. It's been in the family since then." He pointed to another old print. "That shack there is the first building on the ranch, but not the first home. My great-great-grandmother raised her first two kids in a dugout with a dirt floor and no windows. My grandmother said her mom was proud when they moved into that shack." The photos changed from sepia to black and white and then to color, ending with prints of his parents, a young Jake and one of him and his granddad on horseback. "Come back here, I'll fix you something to drink." I reveled in the warmth of his hand on the small of my back.

The house was a classic old ranch style with a center hallway dividing the public rooms. The kitchen was located at the back. Someone had beautifully restored it, fashioning a modern wet bar in one end.

He held up a bottle of merlot, cocking his head.

"Red would be great. Comfortable home."

"Thanks. I've had quite a bit of work done. My granddad didn't do too much to modernize the old place. After my grandmother died, he lost his spirit. The kitchen and the bathrooms were pitiful and the porch had dry rot." He handed me the wine. "I wanted my home to still look like a working ranch house when the contractor walked out."

We took our wine into the den. A fire crackled in the huge stone fireplace flanked by floor to ceiling windows. "Who helped you with the remodel?" *Darn.* My cell phone vibrated in my pocket. "Excuse me." I looked at the number. "It's my mom."

"Go ahead and take it."

"No, I'll let it go to voice mail. I want to spend some time with her."

"Family's important." A boyish grin split his face. "I used the McMillan brothers for the contractors. I wanted to make sure the plumbing and wiring passed inspection. They did the restoration work on the old Cheyenne courthouse and train station so I knew that would keep the house's integrity in place."

"It turned out great." I drained my wine glass and crossed to the windows.

I felt his presence behind me. His hand rested gently on my shoulder and he pointed my chin to the left. "See those two over there? Don't often see twins. You know the difference between a bison and a buffalo?"

"No." The warmth pouring off his body behind me made it hard for me to concentrate on nomenclature. His square jaw filled my vision. The scent of his cologne mixed with the bourbon, and his bottom lip was so inviting.

"Same animal." He shifted his weight and the warm hand slipped from my shoulder. "Proper Latin name is *Bison bison.* French explorers got here first and called them 'les boeufs' meaning 'the beefs.' When the English got here a little later, they changed the pronunciation to 'la buff.' Pretty fancy name for an eighteen-hundred pound bull. 'La buff' went through a couple of variations and became buffalo, but the American Bison and the American Buffalo are the same animal." He put his empty glass down and turned me from the window to face him. "If you're ready, let's get a four-wheeler and get a look."

We stepped off Jake's porch. A huge yellowing cottonwood bowed its branches over the porch railing. "What's that on the trunk of the cottonwood?" I squinted. "Someone's carving?"

"Memories of my boyhood." His gray eyes twinkled with amusement. "Come." He grabbed my hand, pulling me toward the tree.

"JS and a brand? Is that your brand?" I fingered the gray-scarred bark.

"No it's Granddad's old brand. I carved my initials on this old cottonwood when I was about twelve years old and out here for the summer. I always knew someday I would live here."

"EH. Who is EH?"

My granddad Huddleston, Elliot Huddleston. He carved his initials in the tree when he bought the place." Jake whistled to Chet who gave up the scent he was following, woofed joyously, and fell into step with us.

We turned south toward the barn. "I passed some fields on the way in. Do you grow your own feed?"

"I grow alfalfa and hay. My herds graze the native grass except in winter when I put them on my own grass. I don't use herbicides on my crops or hormones in my animals. Makes for a much better beef animal."

"You use a lot of green farming techniques?"

"I try. I rotate my stock from one section of a pasture to the next. Their dung replenishes the soil. You keep moving the herd, the grass and the soil don't compact from overgrazing. The rains get down to the grass roots."

He pointed to small group of animals in the distance. "See the group in the north pasture? Next week, I'll be moving them across the fence line and let that land rest. Rains are coming toward the end of next week, too. Rain breaks down the dung, scattering grass seeds."

Except for the wind, the ranch was quiet. "So quiet here. Do you miss the noise and activity of the city?"

"I thought I would. The adrenalin rush of a new case, the flurry of activity. But I don't. Ranching is in my blood."

Jake's passion for ranching was contagious. "Does organic meat taste different?"

"You've never eaten organic beef? I need to cook you a steak! I do the final fattening on organic grains. Makes the meat sweet and tender." He cocked his head toward a dark corner of the barn. "The four wheelers are back here. Let's get loaded up."

There were three of them. A big bore Polaris model that seated two people and two smaller ATVs for single use.

"Driven much? If not, let's take the Polaris and I'll just drive. Chet, go home boy." Jake said, gathering two helmets.

I fastened the chin strap on mine. He swung his long leg over the wide seat, extended his right hand and hoisted me up behind him.

"Once we get going, it'll be too noisy to talk. Hang on. Put your arms around my waist. When we get past the barn, the trail is more of a washboard. Hang on and lean into the curves with me."

I reached around his waist and clasped my hands in front of him. I could feel his tight abs. I flushed like a schoolgirl. He wore a lightweight windbreaker and his muscles rippled when he turned the Polaris. I leaned when he leaned. When he reached around, touched my thigh and signaled with thumbs up, I let go long enough to return the signal.

He stopped the noisy Polaris well away from the fence line. "That's not much of a fence! That's all it takes to keep them in?"

I reached out to the fence wire to test the slack. Jake reached over and grabbed my forearm. "Don't touch the top wire—it's hot. All you need is four strands of barbed wire and sometimes an electrified fifth strand. Buffalo like to stay together once they get comfortable on a range. Even the old bulls stay with the herd."

A cow lifted her head and begin to lick her calf. "There's something beautiful about just watching them graze, isn't there?"

"Yeah. Those buffalo out there have ninety-nine point nine percent pure buffalo DNA. Without Goodnight's nagging wife, the American buffalo would've been lost. Out there is the American West."

I strained to get a better look at a calf. "They're branded. You've changed the brand from your Granddad's."

He nodded. "I use the Lazy E. Branding is the easiest way for law officials to identify stolen animals. There's been some talk of micro-chipping animals, but you'd have to get them in the chutes to get close enough to read the chip with the scanner. Lots easier to read a brand."

"Do you think there are enough left for the species to survive?"

"If they are left alone to breed, yes. Americans are interested in preserving this part of their cultural heritage. I think they're safe enough."

"What about competition between cattlemen and buffalo ranchers?"

"That's a war we don't have to have. There's room on the table for buffalo and beef to prosper."

"How?"

"I created a nonprofit organization, the Buffalo Breeders Association, whose mission is to expand the market for buffalo meat."

"Is it working?"

"Yeah. I just hired a lobbyist who represents us to Congress and we just launched our new web site. "

"Do you advertise?"

"You bet we do. We target all the major grocery chains in the nation. Denverites eat more buffalo meat than any other market in US. We're using the skyline of Denver in our new ads and we talk about how Denverites have the lowest obesity rate in the nation," he explained.

"I like your enthusiasm."

"You have it, too. You tear into stories. Life would be damned dull lived with a 'whatever approach.'"

"Are we headed to a range war like in the old black and white movies?"

"This is a twenty-first century version. Done with television interviews and proposed legislation. Galvanize your base and polarize them with lies. But some things never change. Like whipping up fear and threatening the opposition."

"I assume by legislation you're talking about SB432?"

"You know the story of the Shoshone tribe's herd?" Jake looked surprised.

"Don't look so shocked." I laughed. "I read the tribe has managed a brucellosis-free buffalo herd for decades, and has the vet records to prove it. Joe Long Knife and Dr. Henderson testified for the Shoshone. I doubt the bill gets out of committee."

"I know Joe. He's a fine lawyer. You know the back story of who introduced that bill?" Jake asked.

"Just that a senator from northwest Wyoming got the bill to the floor at the urging of one of his constituents."

"That senator is a cattle rancher. Like most of his constituents. The bill made the senator very popular."

"Bet it did."

"Market protection is a dirty fight. Brucellosis is a political disease," Jake said.

"One leg of the problem is tens of thousands of infected elk passing through ranches," I said.

"Right. Hunters caused the boom in the elk population by hunting wolves and mountain lions to near extinction. The elk population has increased nine times over since 2007 on my ranch." He rubbed my hands in his. "You're cold. Lets head back."

I pulled my windbreaker tightly around me. "Yeah, that wind cuts right through you." He angled his body to block the cold wind from me. "Maybe you could help me. I've been trying to set up an interview with Joe Long Knife. He hasn't called me back."

"I'll talk to him. We can go out there together if you like."

"Absolutely. Thanks for the introduction."

"Could I interest you in an Irish coffee by the fire back at the house?"

"Yes." I shivered. He started the four-wheeler. I tucked in close, snuggling into his broad back, safe from the icy wind.

* * * *

Jake's office had a scarred old partner's desk surrounded by brown leather chairs and bookcases. "Granddad's desk." He lighted the fire he had obviously laid before we went out. Nice touch. "Be back in a minute with the coffees. Stand by the fire. You're still shivering."

Chet joined me, pushing gently into my thigh. I rubbed his head and he settled on the rug with a doggy sigh of contentment.

My hands had feeling by the time Jake returned with the

two coffees. "Who's the couple in the little framed photograph on the bookcase?"

"That's Charlie and Mary Anne Goodnight."

I liked his respect for the past. "Nice touch."

"I'm glad you came. I wanted you to see what I was building out here."

He was earnest, and better, honest.

He broke the spell with a sip of coffee. "How long has it been since you've seen Yellowstone with fresh snow?"

"Long time since I've even seen snow. Not much snow around Alamo Square."

"If we go to the Wind River Reservation to see Joe, we could go to Yellowstone and see the thermals. How about a working vacation in fresh snow?"

A trip with Jake? In a nanosecond. "I would love to."

"I'll call Joe in the morning."

I ricocheted between raging lust and relaxed conversation. "I'm going to talk to Javier Contreras about diseased elk and deer."

"He's a good man. Contreras has guided for hunters on my ranch over in the foothills."

"I hope to talk to him this week. You want to come along? He might be more talkative with you there."

"Give me a call. I'm beginning to enjoy this news business. You still working with Hunter?"

Immediately, I was alert. "I've never been working *with* Hunter. I've interviewed him, toured his ranch, but he's not my colleague."

"You visited the Bar-A?" Jake asked quickly.

"Yes. Have you been there?"

"I've been to some big parties at Hunter's. The Bar-A borders the east side of my ranch, but I doubt he would show me his operation."

"What did you think of his house?"

"Large." He shrugged. "What are you getting at?"

"See any personal touches?"

Jake looked puzzled. "No, but I wasn't really looking at his dresser top or in his bathroom."

"I wasn't snooping. But I did notice there isn't a single photo of his wife, no family photos, no mementos, nothing personal in any of the rooms I saw."

Jake's posture hardened. "There could be a good reason

there's no photos. I know a little about Hunter."

"Personally? From here in Cheyenne?"

"Both. I knew of him professionally in Denver. You remember I told you once there was more to Hunter than you might know. To be careful around him?" Jake persisted.

"You were a DA in Denver, right? That kind of professionally? From the DA's office? I'm assuming Hunter wasn't your gardener."

"Correct. Hunter wasn't my gardener."

"You're not going to tell me anymore, are you?"

"Nope. Just that he's opportunistic. Whatever else you're thinking or feeling about him, remember that."

"Let's clarify this. I think about Hunter in the context of my work." I walked to within an inch of Jake. He stood still, watching me. I reached up, draped my hands over those great shoulders, looked into his sexy gray eyes and kissed him.

Both his arms swept down and he pulled me to him. His mouth melded to mine. An explosion of lust coursed through me. Still holding me in his arms, he pulled back and rested his forehead on mine. "That's useful information, Ms. Cahill."

Chapter 14

Clay looked around a mountain of paperwork. "Come in, whatcha got going, kid—er, Sawyer? Sorry, it's going to take some time."

"Thanks. I've got a couple of new leads, Javier Contreras, the game guide from here in town and a Shoshone lawyer who testified before the Senate against SB432. I'm going out to Wind River to talk to the lawyer, Long Knife."

"You still looking for a tie in with brucellosis and the buffalo mutilations?"

"Yep, I don't believe in coincidences."

"Chew on it awhile longer." Clay nodded to me. "Keep thinkin' about the lawyers."

I was chewing on it when I ran into Benita in the hallway. "Hey. Will you need me if you get an interview with Contreras? I've got a ton of work to do for Clay today."

"No problem. I'll take a flip cam and shoot it myself."

"Thanks, Clay's got me nearly double booked today."

No message from Contreras. I checked his web site and read his blog before calling him, "Mr. Contreras? Sawyer Cahill with CBS3 News. "I'm working on a story about brucellosis and the elk herds. When would be a good time for us to meet?"

"What did you want to talk about exactly?" Contreras asked.

"I talked with George Carlisle and he said there was brucellosis infection in the elk and big horn sheep herds—"

He cut me off before I could finish. "You bet there is," he barked. "I'm going to Laramie tomorrow afternoon to scout some hunting land for a party of California hunters coming in later this month. They're expecting a fine hunt. It's getting damn hard to find them a trophy animal to shoot."

"Mind if I join you on that scouting expedition?"

"Why the hell would I take you? None of your business." He hung up.

I dialed him again and on the third ring he answered, "Contreras Game and Guide Service."

"It's the community's business when a local businessman's cash flow is at risk due to brucellosis. Those hunters you bring in stay in hotels, drink in the bars and eat in the restaurants. Probably rent a car to get around town in, too. There's a ripple effect in the local economy if the hunting business falls off."

"Why the hell would I care about hotels and restaurants? I got my own business to make work," he said.

"I can help you with that. My news report will include a shot of your business. I'll use your face on camera with your name and your business name under it. You'd like the free advertising?"

"Noon tomorrow," he growled. "Dress warm and keep your spike heels at the office. You know where I am?"

"Yeah, I'd like to bring Jake Spooner along with my boots."

"Getting real crowded. Slow me down and I'll leave you out there." He hung up.

"Jake?" I talked to his answering machine. "I'm meeting Contreras tomorrow at noon to scout some hunting land over by Laramie. Let me know if this works for you. Oh, and leave your spike heels at home."

Detective Jacoby was waiting in the hallway. "Ms. Cahill? I left a message, but didn't hear from you. You have a minute?"

"Sure." I gestured to the one empty spot in my office for him to perch on. "Were you able to find out anything?"

"Not yet, but we're not closing this case." He reassured me.

"Can you get anything from the paper, anything at all?" I eagerly wanted something on this guy.

"No." He shook his head. "He probably wore gloves and the letters were cut from common newsprint. Could have come from any paper."

"And the email and phone records? Anything there?" I tried not to sound plaintive.

"The IP on the email leads to a public computer. We

talked to the librarians and they say those computers stay busy. The caller ID on the phone messages is untraceable. Probably a throwaway phone. It's very easy to be anonymous in the digital world. We like to think we know who we interact with on the web, but frequently we have no idea."

I shuddered. I wouldn't be going home soon.

"I took a drive out where you live. I could have a guy from our home security division come out, talk about home safety and outdoor lighting. It's a free service the department offers to the citizens. Be happy to set it up for you."

"Yes, I'd like that." He passed me a card.

"Give them a call. You might think about getting a dog. They're the best. If you get an email, a note, even a hang up call you're worried about, call me. Don't hesitate."

* * * *

Everyone leaves tracks. All you have to do is find the database. Start out broad and general. Then, drill down deep. The Missoula newspaper archives featured the write-up of Hunter and Emily's wedding. Their black and white wedding picture filled the screen. Damn! Emily and I looked enough alike to be sisters. I couldn't tell if her eyes were blue, but the resemblance in our faces was eerie. Emily and I were about the same size and height. And there were the names of Hunter's parents.

I pulled the station's account number for using paid databases and entered it into Searchsystems.net, which would link me to five thousand databases. Hunter's parents were both alive and living at separate addresses in Missoula. They divorced when Hunter was five. Joe had barely been three. The boys went to separate foster homes. I found the foster care records at Knowx.com, sanitized but still bleak. Hunter had three foster home placements. Each caseworker commented on what a bright, personable little boy he was. Suspected sexual abuse by his second foster father led to his placement in his third home. Joe had fared better—staying with the same foster family until the boys reunited with their father when they were eight and ten. The court denied maternal visitation rights. She had a long history of legal problems including two stints in the state's prison for women.

Their father held a string of jobs working for construction and landscaping firms. When Hunter was fifteen, he ran away from home. Juvenile officers returned him to his father. Hunter told police his father beat him. Social workers investigated, finding no evidence. Hunter ran away again at seventeen, never returning home. He and another boy solicited sex from an undercover policewoman, landing him in a juvenile facility until he was eighteen.

I found Joe's high school graduation notice. After that, Joe disappeared from any database. His last known address was in Missoula. No record of a Joe Kane at West Point. No service records for a Joe Kane.

I searched student records from University of Washington. Hunter Kane graduated with a BS. He dropped out of the School of Medicine in the summer of his first year, going on to earn an MBA. Five facts of Hunter's story were true, including he had a brother and a wife.

Much of what Hunter glibly told me was a lie. Charming, flirtatious Hunter lied, and lied easily. Why would Hunter leave Seattle and go back to Missoula? To gloat and preen with a successful career and a beautiful wife on his arm? No one would pity him then.

Chapter 15

I worked all morning to cover another reporter's beat and had no time to research Emily's death. Before noon, I headed over to Javier Contreras' guide business.

Javier was loading an extended cab four-wheel-drive pickup. Jake and I squeezed in with a thermos of coffee to ward off the chill. Contreras pulled off the highway onto a dirt road that corkscrewed up the mountain pass. He expertly parked in a flat plateau with a breathtaking view of snow-topped peaks.

"I was up here two days ago scouting a site for a client from Salt Lake. I saw two stumbling sick elk trailing the herd. Wasted with disease." He looked up from the game trail and I focused my camera on him. "My clients expect a good hunt. That means a trophy animal. Big part of my livelihood is made off the fall elk hunts."

He was scanning the ground and kicking through the grass. "Look over here. A couple of animals laid up here. Grass is all matted down." He pointed to a barely discernible trail littered with scat. We followed him into a small clearing. Two dead elk were lying in the brush. The bodies were drying in the sun and flies sipped from their open eyes. Their swollen tongues protruded from cracked mouths.

I held up the little camera and began to shoot. Jake said, "These are young elk, look at the size of those antlers." He rolled the dead elk on its back and pulled up one small leg. "His joints are enlarged. If he wasn't lame when he died, he would be, and then the predators would take him."

Javier joined Jake by the carcass. "Once the elk get infected with brucellosis, they don't have any resistance to other diseases. Look at the eye inflammation." Javier pointed to swollen, sightless eyes.

"Will you bring hunters up here?" I asked.

He stood up. "Hell no. I can guarantee you the herd these two came from are all infected." Javier shot a glance at me. "You know part of the problem is eradicating their natural predators, wolves and lions? Cattlemen saw to that. Now, we have huge herds, fewer trophy animals and a lot of disease."

"I know. Meddle in the natural order and you have to pay the price."

"That's a good one. Put that in your story." He dared me. "Let 'em know we hunters hold the ranchers responsible. Did you know brucellosis can spread to humans? It's called undulant fever in us."

I focused the camera on his face. "Is it fatal in humans?"

"No, antibiotics will kill it. But who wants to get injections of several different antibiotics for months because he went hunting? Guy wants a trophy animal, not the chills and shakes." Javier replied.

"Is the meat infected?"

"Yeah, it is. You know about that, Jake. You can get infected when you field dress an animal. Even inhaling the bacteria will get you."

"Does cooking kill the bacteria?" I asked.

"Yeah, but butchers have gotten the fever." He shook his head in disgust.

Jake said quietly, "We all depend on the wildlife. We're their stewards."

"Put that in your story, too." Javier shot back at me.

We rode most of the way to Cheyenne in silence. I shook Contreras hand. "Thanks, Mr. Contreras. Good interview. I appreciate your time."

"Show them those dead elk," he pleaded.

* * * *

"Got a minute to sit in the truck?" I asked Jake.

"Sure." He climbed in.

"Hunter Kane is a liar." Jake made no move to interrupt me. "Hunter spun some fantasy version of his childhood for me. He was an abused kid in foster care and served time in juvie. There was no loving and supportive mom and dad for those two boys like Hunter described."

"You accusing Hunter of something? Because if you are, I haven't heard any proof," the lawyer in Jake answered.

"Hunter can be fun, flirting and charming the pants off you—that's figurative by the way. Then something trips his trigger and he's someone else."

"And?"

"He has the skills, access to tools and drugs. He knows the area. And he's angry!"

"So you suspect him," Jake said. "Tread lightly until you have some proof. He may just have that hair trigger you describe and the mindset to react. He might sue the station. Or worse." Jake grimaced.

"I know, I know." I dragged a hand through my hair. "Sam has all the same traits. Hell, half the ranchers in the county have the tools and drugs and all the cattle ranchers have motive."

"You'll figure it out. Until this is over I don't think you should be staying in that house of yours alone." Jake said.

"I'm not. I moved into Julia and Dave's for a while. I've gotten a couple of messages warning me off."

"What kind of warnings?" Jake asked sharply.

"Email and a note under the windshield."

"You've called in the police? Tell me you've called in the police." Jake shook his head impatiently.

"Of course," I soothed.

"Good. So what did the messages say?" Jake demanded.

"The first just warned me off. The latter referred to an old story I worked."

"What happened in that story? I'm going to pull it out of you."

"I was interviewing a gang member in a San Antonio bar when he was shot to death in front of me." I held up my hand when he started to interrupt. "But a simple Google search would turn that up. No relation to what's going on here. No south side San Antonio gangs in Cheyenne."

"True," the lawyer in him said cautiously. "It doesn't, however, make Cheyenne a safe place for you either, Ms. Cahill. It's a good time to get the hell out of dodge and go see Joe Long Knife. I talked with him this morning. He could meet us Friday morning. Can you get away that soon? Say yes, and give the police some time to do their job."

I'd already told Clay I was going. Why not this week? "I'll be ready."

"We'll have a chance to enjoy the park over the weekend. I checked and there are cabins available at the Old Faithful lodge. Okay by you?"

"Absolutely. And thanks for helping me score an interview with Joe."

He grinned. "I'll take care of the reservations for both us. I know a great little bar and grill. You'll love it."

"Sounds great. Thanks for coming along today. I had some preconceived notions about Contreras but I was wrong. He's concerned for the health of wildlife, not just providing trophy bucks for wealthy men's den walls."

"He's lived his whole life here," Jake agreed. "The police have any suspects for the notes?"

I blew out a breath, exasperated. "No news. Do you think it's odd there were two mutilations close together and now nothing for a couple of days?"

"No, I don't. A lot of physical work for one guy. If he's doing it because he has pent up rage and needs the release, he may be feeling good now. But the rage will be build again."

"Yeah, it's a waiting game. I want to go out to your ranch and Ray's. There has to be a dirt track between the ranches so you don't have to get on the county road each time you go on a ranch. Could be where that truck was heading to from the windmill."

"You have off-road tires?"

I shook my head no.

"Didn't think so," he said. "We'll take my truck. Better, you're not out by yourself. How about tomorrow?" His hand was on the door handle.

"Works for me. I can be at your place after three o'clock."

* * * *

I was turning out the light for an early night when the phone rang. "I hope I'm not too late," Hunter said. "I had dinner with a friend of mine out on his ranch and I stayed a little longer than I planned. You would have loved the sunset out there."

I hoped I sounded neutral. "Did you have a successful trip?"

"Always," he answered. "Bought two fine bulls. I'm arranging their transport in the morning. I think I'll wind it up tomorrow and be back late Tuesday, maybe Wednesday by noon. I'd like to see you."

"Clay is keeping me hopping. I've had to cover for another reporter who has been sick. I've got interviews to book and stories to file." Crap. I sounded like a chattering fifteen year old.

"Not even a quick dinner?"

"I can't Hunter."

"Then I'll see you at the barbecue. Put it on your calendar. It's going to be the big event around town. Oh, I need your friend Julia's address. I want to make sure to send them an invitation and anyone else you would like to add from the station."

A cold shiver surprised me. I sure as hell wasn't giving him Julia and Dave's address or anyone's address from work. "Drop me an email at my station account and I'll send you their email addresses tomorrow. An e-vite will be fine."

Chapter 16

Jake reached down and handed me a thermos without taking his eyes off the road. "Pour me a cup, will you? There's a second thermos for you at your feet."

I managed to keep most of the coffee in the thermos' shallow cup when I passed it to him. I grabbed a wad of Kleenex and blotted up the coffee in the console. "The gate into Ray Foster's pasture is just up past the forty-seven mile marker." I stowed his thermos and reached for mine. The coffee smelled wonderful.

"How'd Foster take it when you asked to get back on his ranch?" Jake asked.

"He was curious. Mostly he whined about Barton not arresting anyone yet."

Jake slowed the heavy truck, put his blinker on and shifted into four-wheel drive. When we pulled through the old gate and rocked on the washboard road, I grabbed the chicken hold.

"Someone thinks I'm getting close enough to make it worth his while to try to scare me off." I gasped when the truck scraped bottom. "I gotta figure this out. I can't sleep and hate it when my phone rings or my email buzzes. I want to live in my own house!"

"Don't let him surprise you when you get close to him. Better yet, don't get close to him without me," Jake said, jerking the truck out of muddy spot.

"Fat chance we'll just happen to be together." I braced myself between the dashboard and chicken hold. "After Contreras' interview ran, a couple of regulars on the website demanded all buffalo be slaughtered to keep cattle and humans healthy."

Jake rolled his shoulders and tapped his thumbs on the steering wheel to a drumbeat of frustration. He tore his eyes from the rutted road, locked eyes with me and demanded, "Tell me about the guy shot to death in San Antonio."

"Rodriguez was a teenage Latin Kings member who was a source of mine."

A look of shock passed over his face. "Jesus! How'd you handle his death?"

"Badly. One minute, seventeen year old Joey Rodriguez was talking, and the next he was dead. The barrio is full of young men like Joey," I said tiredly. "I reported on all those initiatives to help kids, The Gang Intervention Program, the Anti-Gang Initiative and a half dozen more. The gang wars kept raging. Boys kept dying. Our cities are full of lost boys."

Jake reached over and took my hand. He stroked my palm with his thumb sending little quivers of excitement up my arm. "I spent time prosecuting gang crime in Denver. A lot of painful time watching young men who thought they were tough guys all the way to the prison door. The success rate for Denver's gang programs was abysmal."

"I couldn't stand it anymore, the dead kids, the living kids with no future. We don't rehabilitate them. We warehouse them and turn them back on the streets. No one wants to hire a felon who dropped out of school."

"Not much opportunity for felons," he echoed.

"I mentored a kid. I tried so hard. Got him a job in a warehouse making ten bucks an hour while his friends were living the high life selling drugs and robbing 7-11s. He quit the warehouse and went back to the gang. He asked me, 'Why would I hump my ass in a warehouse for ten bucks?'"

"I'm proud of you for trying." He squeezed my hand, taking his eyes off the road for a second to make eye contact with me. "We slam the kid who's selling, and too often wink-wink-nudge-nudge at the recreational use buyer."

"I'm not a quitter. I liked working one-on-one with that kid. I'll find some program like that here."

He brought my hand to his lips, nibbling and kissing my hand. "We have to keep you safe enough to do that. You're putting pressure on a guy who's unstable and violent."

I started to speak, but he held up one hand. "Hear me out. I have ranch hands around my place all the time. You'll be safe there. There's plenty of room and all the privacy you need to work. Plus," he said, grinning like a deal closer. "You're near your house in case you need anything." He quickly placed one finger on my bottom lip. "Take some time and think before you say no. I know you're stubborn and independent. I'm not asking you to back away from your story. Give it some thought."

"Stubborn and independent? That's what you think?"

"That's not all I think. Not by a long shot," he swiftly retorted.

"I'm happy to hear that," I said before getting serious. "I'm settled in over at Julia's. I'll just stay with them."

I could tell he wasn't satisfied with my answer. He parked the truck and wrenched the door open. "I doubt he's finished," he said grimly. "Offer's on the table for you."

We easily found the spot where Jake's cow had died. Recent rains had raised the trampled grass, but the ground still showed the ruts churned by vehicles.

"According to the county road map there're only two exits, one on the north end and one on the south end. Both take you to the interstate. Remember the nights we went to the ranches? The killer would have passed us if he headed south back toward Cheyenne, but we never saw another vehicle. Logical explanation is there is a dirt road connecting your ranch and Ray's. Each time he took the road going north. Then he exited onto the county and hooked into I-25. Once on the interstate, he blended into the traffic."

"Possible... Brad interrupted him that night on my ranch. He had to know he'd be seen heading south by the Sheriff coming up north." He idled the motor for a moment before shoving the truck in park.

"Gotta be local," I said opening the truck door. "He knows these ranches like the back of his hand. I checked who owns the ranches north of Ray's place. No local owners." I stepped off the running board and finished the conversation over the Ford's hood. "The gossip at the courthouse says the land isn't leased. Nice and deserted up north of Foster's ranch."

We walked in circles parting the dry grass, looking for any sign of a trail.

"Here!" I yelled for Jake. I stood in damp brush up to my knees pointing to barely visible tracks in the dirt. Before he could answer I said, "We're going to see how tough that truck is."

We left the kill site on Jake's ranch, bouncing on head-banging ruts. "There." Jake swung the truck left and over into the faint rut animals had worn into the packed dirt. He idled, marking the point on his GPS. He looked at his headings. "We're heading due north. Foster's ranch is straight ahead."

Five minutes more of clinging to the hold and I could see a sagging gate. Jake threw the truck in park. "We're no more than ten minutes from where my cow was killed. I bet the trip is a lot faster trip when the trail's dry."

I opened the truck door. "I'll get the gate. Let's see how long it takes to get to where that bull was killed."

The dirt track passed the kill site and meandered to the far north side of Foster's ranch. Twelve minutes from the gate between Jake and Ray's ranches to the county road. Someone had picked familiar ground.

We headed south toward town passing hills dotted with early snow. "No traffic," I said. "Good place for someone trying to exorcise his personal demons. He didn't have time to finish his ritual of tramping down the grass and piling up a rock cairn on your place. I bet he's obsessive compulsive enough that he's furious about that."

"Good guess. You hungry? How about dinner at the Albany?" he asked.

"Deal." I leaned the seat back, stretching my legs. "How's your association doing?"

"We just got a new marketing study." He slowed for a tight curve. "The northeast coast consumes the least buffalo meat of any metropolitan area. We have a new campaign up and running in all the target markets in New England. Our lawyer is proposing that we hire an additional lobbyist to pressure the USDA to pass some friendlier regulations."

"I don't know how you have the time—"

"What the hell?" Jake cursed. He grabbed the wheel with both hands and squinted into the rear view mirror. He stamped down on the accelerator urging his truck up the hill. A dark truck filled the rear window. The roaring of the big engine deafened me to what Jake was saying. My head bounced off the dashboard at the same time I heard crunching metal. I was dizzy with the pain and my vision blurred. I moaned, scrambling to find the chicken hold in the bouncing truck.

Jake's truck lurched to the right. He yanked the wheel to the left, centering it.

In the side mirror I saw the dark truck coming up fast behind us. "Can you go any faster?" I yelled. When Jake's truck careened into the guardrail, I cracked my head on the side window. Pain roiled through my head. I screamed and then the high whining of metal scraping metal filled the cab. Sparks shot off Jake's truck as it screeched along the rail.

"Pull left! We're going to go over!" I could see the treetops in the ravine below us.

The dark truck veered into the left lane zooming past us. "Damn it!" Jake fought his shuddering vehicle to the shoulder of the road. He slammed the truck in park and pulled me to him. "You hurt?"

I shakily answered, "No...yes, a little. My head's banged up."

Jake was punching numbers into his phone. "Yes, this is Jake Spooner," he shouted. "Someone tried to run us off county road 2218. A dark pickup truck running with no lights, heading into Cheyenne. Tell me where we can meet the Sheriff... We'll be there." Jake tossed the phone in the console. "Let me see your head."

He gently felt the bump on my forehead and another in my hairline. "You're getting the mother of all bruises on your face. How bad are you hurting?"

"I'm okay. It doesn't hurt much."

"We can go by the walk-in clinic on the way into town."

"Don't need it. Are you hurt?"

He put the truck in gear and turned out on the road. "No." His face was set in a grim mask of anger. "Can you identify the truck?"

"Extended cab pickup, I think. Mud was all over the rear plate. I don't even know the brand."

"I didn't get much either," he said grimly. "His headlights were off and the pickup was so dirty. It could have been black or any dark color. He was hiding inside a damn hoodie."

Jake stopped at the first traffic light. He leaned over and kissed me lightly on the cheek. "He scared the hell out of me." He cupped my chin, turning my head from side to side. "You sure you don't want to stop at the clinic?"

"I'm sure."

We slipped into a booth opposite Sheriff Barton. He clattered his coffee cup into his saucer when he half rose to shake our hands. "Heard a bit from the dispatcher. Why don't you tell me about it?" He dipped his chin to his deputy. "He'll take some pictures of your vehicle before you go."

Jake waved yes to the waitress who was hovering with a coffee pot. "We'd just left Ray Foster's ranch and were heading south on 2218." Barton looked quizzical at the news we had been on Ray's property.

"There's a dirt road leading from the kill site on Jake's ranch to a gate onto Foster's and on to the county road," I said. "Not much risk of being seen on the way to the interstate."

Barton sipped his coffee and patted his shirt pocket like a man craving a cigarette.

Jake picked up the story. "The pickup rammed us twice. The second time he nearly pushed us over the ravine."

"You get a partial on the plate?" Barton asked.

"No," we both said.

"Don't make our job any easier. We'll get some pictures of your truck and the guardrails. Deputy will take some scrapings of your paint around to body shops in case someone needs a little bodywork fixed. Guy might be too sharp to get the work done local. Enough hills out there he could have been following at a distance for awhile and you'd never know it." His big-knuckled hands set his coffee cup down. He threw a few bills on the table. "I'll be in touch. You call me anytime."

He maneuvered his big frame between the tightly packed tables at the Albany. "Y'all want this table? I can have it bused for you in just a sec," the waitress said to Jake who cocked his head at me before answering yes to her.

Jake reached across the table and took my hand. "I don't know what Barton or the city's cops can do, but I know what I can and will do. So far, they've turned up jack shit. This isn't about just trying to scare you off a story anymore. That guy could have killed us. You need to come to the ranch." I started to interrupt and he finished, "I have a comfortable guest room for you. I can see someone coming out on my ranch."

I looked down in my lap. I had shredded my napkin into little bits of brightly colored confetti. "I'm scared. The land dropped away on the other side of the guardrail."

"Hell, I'm still scared spitless. Be an idiot not to be. So what's your answer?" Jake asked.

"The ranch. It's unfair to put Julia and Dave in danger."

Jake winked at me across the table. "We'll pick your things up after dinner."

"Jake, I can't gather up everything I'm going to need tonight." It sounded so trite to be obsessing about files and clothes when we could be dead at the bottom of the ravine.

He arched an eyebrow. "I'll take you over to get whatever you need whenever you need it. Don't go alone. Now—" He leaned back in his chair and smiled at me over his menu. "Consider it settled. Let's order. We're going to need our strength if this guy keeps trying to kill us."

I picked the avocado out of my salad, shoving the wilted lettuce to the sides of the taco shell. I jumped when the door to the Albany banged open. Hunter hung his coat and hat on the rack by the door. The wait staff seated him immediately and Hunter busied himself with the menu.

"Don't stare," Jake whispered.

Hunter's drink arrived. I watched him idly worry the swizzle stick. He put the stick carefully on the table, nudging it into alignment with the napkin. He locked eyes with me and got up.

He strode over to our table, bending over to gape at my face. "Sawyer, my god what happened to you? Your face is bruised and swelling." Hunter didn't acknowledge Jake's presence.

"Someone tried to run us over the guardrail into a ravine. Could have been a long drop off 2218," I said.

"My god are you hurt bad?" He ran his hand through his hair making it stick up in blonde tufts. "Do you need me to take you to the hospital?" Hunter leaned in and stroked his index finger down the bruise.

I recoiled from both his touch and the fact that it hurt like hell.

"Had she needed healthcare Hunter, I would have seen that she received the best." Jake's body was very still.

Hunter jerked back. "Did you call the police? Report this?"

"The jurisdiction is county, Hunter. We've filed a report with the Sheriff," I said.

"You get the license plate?" Hunter's eyes bored into mine.

"Barton will find him," I said.

He straightened to his full height, both hands linked behind his back. He raised himself on his toes. "I'll be checking on you, Sawyer."

"I'm fine. Just a little bruising," I said.

"You're too important to me to take this lightly. I'll be in touch." He pivoted on his heel and gathered his hat and coat.

"Where the hell you suppose that solicitous bastard was this evening?" I hissed in Jake's ear.

Chapter 17

I stood in the doorway of the bedroom feeling a warm tug at the sight of Jake's lean body dwarfing his sofa. He had dozed off while we watched TV. I didn't have the heart to awaken him. He had scrunched a throw pillow under his head. I took a thick wool blanket from my room and tucked it around his body. His shirt was unbuttoned, hanging loose from his jeans. What would it feel like to trail my hand across his muscular chest to the shock of dark hair on his flat belly? I felt desire rising, warm and fluid. I realized that somewhere in the past forty-eight hours Jake had ceased to be just a source for me. *If it's going to be a complication, I hope it's a pleasurable one.*

I went to bed doubting he was as comfortable on his sofa as I was in his guest room. I took my laptop to bed with me. I reread my file on the Shoshone's herd and meat packing business and the Senate bill. Joe Long Knife would make one hell of an interview.

At first light, I awoke thinking of Jake's taut body and the frisson of delight from his hand on me. Another woman might slip quietly beside him on the sofa, but I, according to Julia, suffered from failure to trust enough to let someone get close. So instead, I tiptoed past him and started breakfast.

"Good morning," he mumbled in a sleepy voice behind me when I was I plating the eggs.

"Good timing. Breakfast is ready. I hope you slept better than I think you did." I picked up two napkins and nearly bumped into him. "I slept a lot better knowing you were here last night."

"That's my job." He leaned in and kissed my forehead. "Now let's see what kind of cook you are."

Within a half hour, we were hauling our suitcases to the front door. My phone vibrated in my purse. Julia. "Sawyer, we got a delivery to the front door sometime during the night."

"What do you mean a delivery? You two okay?"

"Yeah, we're fine." Her voice sounded high, breathy. "Someone taped an envelope on the front door. There wasn't a name on it so Dave opened it. There're two pictures of you and Jake in it. I guess he doesn't know you aren't staying here anymore."

I looked up at Jake. I was unsure how much he heard. "We're about to leave the ranch. We can come now, if you can wait."

"I'll wait," Julia said. I could hear Dave in the background telling Julia he was staying with her.

"They're still at risk." I dropped my small overnight bag into the truck. "I feel guilty! The guy still thinks I'm staying with them. I can't just take an ad out in the newspaper saying I'm out at your place."

"You won't have to. All my hands and the people at the station know where you are. The Sheriff's office and Cheyenne PD know. No place has more leaks than a cop shop. Stop feeling guilty," he said, parking at Julia's.

"I don't want to put anymore finger prints on the envelope," Jake said when Dave thrust it out to him. "You have any gloves?" Julia handed him her yellow kitchen gloves. His hands stretched the bright rubber across his big fingers.

The metal butterfly clasp on the brown mailing envelope was barely hanging closed and two photos slipped out onto the floor. I toed the photos further apart on the floor lining them up with the edge of my boot. The four of us bent over to stare at them. One picture was of us sitting in Jake's truck in front of Contreras' business. The second was a more distant shot of us on the front porch of the Drover.

"I'm sorry. I never meant to bring trouble to your door. Until he figures out I'm not here, we need to get the city to patrol around your house."

Jake was already dialing his phone. "Barton? Jake Spooner. Sawyer received an anonymous envelope with two pictures of us taped to the Graham's front door. We'll be bringing it in on our way out of town."

"Dave!" I fished Detective Jacoby's card out of my bag, "Call this guy. He's good. Talk to him about the patrols. Maybe get an alarm system. Jacoby's working with Sheriff Barton."

Dave took the card from my outstretched hand. "Will do. Julia won't be here alone either. Good time for you two to leave."

Once I was in the truck with Jake, I exploded. "Damn it! I won't ever forgive myself if something happens to them. I can't stand feeling helpless about their safety." I slammed my balled fists on my thighs.

He parked in front of the Sheriff's office. "Good time to get away and dump this on the cops. Dave'll take care of Julia."

Barton took the envelope from Jake with a pair of big tweezers. He dumped the two pictures out on his desk and examined the empty envelope. With a pencil, he lined the photos up in front of him. "Guy's pretty organized. We might get a print off one of these." He flipped one with a pencil. "These photos are out of someone's home printer. See, no commercial stamp. You can tell they were hand cut out of the photo paper. It's a home printing job all right, didn't even use a paper cutter."

* * * *

Jake drove west on I-80 holding fast to my hand.

I broke the silence. "They're too many suspects and no hard evidence. I could make an argument for each of them being guilty. Sam, Hunter, Carlisle.

"I figured you'd get around to telling me what you were thinking about over there. "They're lots of greedy and vengeful people milling around this story." He glanced in my direction. "Don't underestimate any of them."

Jake steadied the wheel when a gust of wind blew red dirt across the interstate. "Barton's told me privately he has a person of interest—and it's not Hunter Kane. That's off the record."

"Who? How long have you known?"

"I'll answer the 'who' first." Jake grimaced. "He's a cowhand who works for Nate. Nate says he knows his way around a cow camp and has no problem with him," Jake emphasized. "Guy's name is Tom Walker."

"Walker? I met a guy named Walker when I interviewed Hunter over at the auction house."

"Yeah, Barton said he worked over there for awhile shoveling shit out of stalls. Nate gave him a raise to work cattle for him."

"I remember him. He was Hunter's pet humanitarian project. A foster care kid that Hunter said he 'lived his life to set an example for him.'"

"So, he ties back to Hunter. Interesting. And they were

both foster kids."

"Is Walker a local?"

"Barton says Walker turned up in Cheyenne in the foster care system."

"Why did he change foster homes?"

"He set his other foster mother's cat on fire."

"What? That's animal mutilation!"

"Yeah, he's no angel. Firing up the cat screwed his home life, but his juvie record is sealed so I don't know anything else. Barton's getting pressured. Hunter and a couple other cattlemen are putting the screws to Barton, clamoring for the governor to appoint a special investigator. Newspapers out of state are carrying the story of the mutilations. That puts even more pressure on the cops."

"How long have you known about Walker?" I demanded.

"Barton told me late yesterday. He may have a couple of leads he's not sharing. He was coy when he talked about Walker, called him a drifter. This is a good time for a road trip for you and me. Let Barton follow those leads while I have you in a safer place. When was the last time you saw Old Faithful in a snow storm?"

"First, before you have successfully changed the subject, I want to know anything you find out from Barton about Walker. Who the hell calls anyone a drifter? Sounds like a term from a 1930s movie"

"Agreed. Now can we change the subject?"

"Not quite. A new cowhand and a kid from foster care? Barton's looking at a shit-shoveler turned cowhand who burned a cat?" I warmed up. "Maybe Walker is a scapegoat—got paid for the dirty work by someone who wants his hands clean."

"You have no evidence at this point that Walker's guilty. You have to draw the line between the dots. Until then, you're speculating. Now, can we change the subject?"

"For the moment, I guess." I rolled the tension out of my shoulders.

Jake talked happily about Yellowstone. "I reserved rooms with views of Old Faithful. The buffalo gather around the thermals for the graze. The lodge has great food and a nice hot tub. And I booked us two snowmobiles for tomorrow morning. Ever been?"

"In Colorado—" My phone rang. Logan Matthews. "Excuse me. Hi Logan."

"Hello, my dear. I'm curious about your mutilator. Any

more incidents?"

I filled him in.

"So he has acted out again," Logan said. "I thought he might. You may be triggering him to act out. Watch your back, my dear."

I listened for a few minutes, thanked Logan, and dropped my phone in the console.

"Let me guess," Jake said. "Logan said be careful."

"Yeah, he did."

Jake pulled the truck into a turnout and faced me. "The cops can chase cyber leads and scrape paint off my bumper and try to match it, but the truth is they don't have dick all. I don't want you hurt. Until this is over, you're the houseguest of Jake Spooner, so get used to it. And that, Ms. Cahill, is the end of the discussion."

I put one hand on his chest, tilting my eyes up to his. "We haven't begun to discuss it. I can be grouchy in the morning. I work odd hours and come and go at all hours. And sometimes I roam the house in the middle night while I work on a story. I'm not a good houseguest—"

He swooped in for a quick kiss. "Nice try. You'll have to scare me more than that. You can be grouchy all you want."

A savage jolt of lust bolted through me. His taste was intoxicating. I felt the punch to my libido as I trailed my fingers down his magnificent jaw. "Your call, but you may rue the day."

He pulled the big truck out into the streaming traffic on I-80. "I won't." Jake held tightly to my left hand. "Blow off some of that tension. We'll do some hiking, snowmobiling and eat some good meals. Have long hot soaks in the hot tub." He gave me that quirky little grin. "Which could lead to more interesting developments."

"You could be a dangerous man, Jake Spooner." I stiffened my back. "Jake, I have to know what's between you and Morgan Hall. I don't share."

Quiet reigned in the truck. "I'm not seeing Morgan Hall. Morgan Hall handles the PR account for the association. She's a paid consultant and I'm the President." He glanced at me. "I don't share either, Ms. Cahill."

"That's not going to be a problem."

"All right then, that's taken care of." Jake grinned.

"Look over to the left," Jake said, pointing out the driver's window. A small herd of deer grazed on the edge of the forest. They lifted their heads, watching us speed by. I looked in the side view mirror and saw them leaping into the darkness of the sheltering trees.

I rolled down my window to smell the tangy crisp scent of pines and the dampness of the loam. "Do you smell it? I've always loved it here."

"Enjoy yourself. I'll take care of you."

"I've never let myself get used to someone looking out for me."

He lifted my hand to his lips, lingering with the kiss. "Get used to it. It's your new normal."

"You could be a good co-captain Jake."

"Pleasure to serve. Trust me enough to shift that to 'You are a good co-captain.'"

"I can probably do that. "How about you fill me in on Joe?"

His fingers nimbly tapped out a rhythm on the steering wheel. "I bought a bull from him couple of years ago. He's an activist for Native American causes, plus he's legal counsel to the Shoshone."

"Is he a member of the breeders association?"

"Yeah, the Shoshone have a big herd." He turned into the lodge's drive.

Jake schlepped our bags up to our interconnecting third floor rooms rather than wait for a bellman. I was delighted with my tiny gable window that looked out on Old Faithful and dark pines silhouetted against a sky caught between last light and moonlight. I hummed in anticipation going downstairs to meet Jake for dinner.

I caught my breath when I saw him seated at a cozy table set for two by the fireplace. He was wearing a white button down shirt with no tie and a fabulous sable brown leather jacket. The firelight flickered shadows across his rugged, tanned face. He looked up, caught me staring and winked.

I blushed when he pulled out my chair and he whispered in my ear, "You look beautiful."

My hand grazed the stubble on his chin. "You look incredible in that sexy jacket."

The waiter was hovering for our orders and made a small harrumphing sound.

"What do you suggest?" Jake asked him.

"Our filet for the lady and perhaps a rib eye for yourself." He scribbled our orders and complimented Jake on his choice of wine to pair with our steaks.

When the waiter slipped out of earshot I asked Jake, "Do you think the waiter ever tells some diner he made a lousy wine choice?"

"I sincerely doubt it." He laughed.

We talked quietly enjoying our meal. His eyes were expressive and reflected the firelight. He was hard, smooth and cut in all the right places, and I was mesmerized by his voice and flushed with lust.

He picked up my hand and caressed it. "I had a wonderful time with you today."

I wanted this man! I'd sat two feet from him in the car for hours looking at his thigh muscles, the way he threw back his head before his rumbling laughter tumbled over me. I swallowed hard. "Me too. I think I'll pass on dessert."

He grinned as he scooted his chair back. "Maybe you won't have to completely do without. Why don't we take a dip in the hot tub?"

He extended his hand to me and pulled me gently to my feet, guiding me to the open elevator. When the door slid shut, we were alone and I kissed him softly on the lips. We rode in silence wrapped in each other's arms.

After I had changed into my skimpy black bikini, I met him outside where he'd already settled into the hot tub. He stood to help me step in, then turned to pour us a drink.

I sank into the bubbles, the cold air on my shoulders in opposite sensation to the steam rising up from the hot tub. He licked a drop of brandy from my bottom lip. "Delicious." His tongue softly teasing my bottom lip. I sighed, releasing my tense muscles and folding into his embrace. His lips captivated my mouth, sending an unbridled hunger through me when he deepened the kiss.

The wind kicked up, blowing the first stinging drops of rain into our faces.

He nibbled my neck. My lust rose again and I ran my hand down the flat plane of his belly. My voice was low and husky. "Oh god, you have a marvelous body."

"Our lovemaking will be beautiful like you," Jake whispered.

The stinging rain turned to ice. Jake grabbed his towel, offering it to me. "Let's take our brandy upstairs. It's going to be miserable out here in a minute." We wrapped up in the hotel robes, rubbing our icy hair with the towels.

Outside his room, he said, "Yours or mine? I laid a fire in

my fireplace before I left."

"Yours it is. I'll be there shortly."

When I knocked a few minutes later, a barefoot Jake clad in jeans and a t-shirt opened the door. I enjoyed the view of his ass while following him to the crackling fire.

"Sit down," he said softly.

I sank into the soft cushions. Jake held me close while his hand gently caressed my throat. His mouth nibbled mine softly, then with the urgency of a lover. He stretched out on his side, pulling me down beside him. My skin burned when he cupped by breasts. His thumb stroked my nipples and they hardened under the exquisite attention. "Don't stop, please don't stop."

His intense gray eyes mesmerized me. Fire spread through me when he reached under my shirt. "Oh my god, you feel so good."

Jake's hand slid down my belly to the top of my jeans. His mouth never left mine. "You're beautiful Sawyer," he murmured "I want to make love to you," he whispered above my swollen lips.

He unbuttoned the top of my jeans, jerking them to the floor. His long fingers pushed aside my silk thong. He stroked the essence of my pleasure, pushing me from lust to aching need. I arched my hips to his waiting fingers, begging for more. He slipped his fingers into me. I was wet and ready.

I parted my legs for him. His tongue stroked a ceaseless rhythm, stoking my desire to fire. "Now! I want you inside me, *now*."

I wrestled his shirt over his head, exposing his hard chest and smooth abs. I had only one thought, getting him inside me. I jerked his jeans down his slim hips, grabbed his hips and pulled him to me.

"Look at me," he said softly. "I want to remember when we join our bodies together." He thrust into me and I cried out with relief. His strokes were deep and fast. I rode him over the top, crying out his name. Ripples of release swept through me. He shuddered to a climax, rolled us on our sides and we lay intertwined and spent.

His hand traced down my side resting on my waist. Kissing me tenderly he whispered, "You are a beautiful woman." He cupped one buttock in his hand, massaged it. His gray eyes were level with mine. He lingered over my mouth. "I hope you were able to concentrate on me like you wanted to."

With a snort of laughter, I pecked him a quick kiss. "I did

a damn fine job of concentrating." I tucked into the curve of his body and we lay quietly wrapped together in our shared warmth. Jake's breathing was even and rhythmic, but sleep wouldn't come to me. I eased myself out from under his arm. I left Jake's room door open, slipped into my room and retrieved my laptop. Something about Emily buzzed in my head.

Chapter 18

I typed *Emily Alston Kane* into the search engine. A dozen hits popped up on the screen. Newspaper articles from *The Denver Post*, the *Colorado Springs Gazette*, and the *Summit County Daily*. Then the hits came from the papers on the west coast, the *Seattle Times* and the *Seattle Post Intelligencer*. The *Missoula Independent* screamed headlines, "Mystery Death: Wife's Fatal Plunge" and "Socialite Dives to her Death." Story after story from the center of the country to the west coast scrolled across my screen. I read with morbid fascination.

A picture of Hunter and Emily took most of the column, inches above the fold of the front page of the Summit County paper. Emily with her upswept hair and sequined black evening gown smiled into the camera. Behind her stood a younger Hunter in his tuxedo, his hands resting lightly on her shoulders. The headline read, "Husband's Version of Death Arouses Suspicion." My stomach roiled. Her face, my face, stared eerily at me. *Was that why you asked me to go riding and to picnic with you? Because I look enough like Emily to pass for her?*

I couldn't stop reading the reporter's story. My god, he'd interviewed friends, colleagues, business members of the community. They had gone to their Beaver Lodge condo in Colorado where they hiked the trail to Eccles Pass. The couple who ran the deli reported that Emily and Hunter talked about seeing the lupines blooming in the meadows on the way to the summit. Three days later, the couple asked them to make their favorite sandwiches for their hike back to the top of the pass. Hunter excitedly told them Emily wanted to take pictures.

The trail up Eccles Pass is a series of switchbacks that

widens to a flat top at the false summit at eleven thousand feet. They had planned their romantic picnic to celebrate their reconciliation. Come morning, rescue workers found Emily's partially clad body, broken and battered, twenty stories from the summit, perched on a narrow granite ledge.

In April, before the fatal August vacation, Emily had returned from the Betty Ford Clinic in Palm Springs to their Missoula home. Once home, her friends recalled that Hunter had persuaded her to go rest at their condo. While she was in Colorado, Hunter filed a petition for divorce in Montana, claiming that Emily had abandoned him. Hunter complained to his friends at the club that after all he had offered Emily, she had left him. Emily's friends called her, telling her of Hunter's divorce petition. Emily surprised Hunter, returning unannounced to their Missoula home. He stood in the doorway denying her entrance to their home. Emily sought refuge with Leticia Dominguez, her neighbor who claimed Hunter yelled, "Drink and be a bag lady for all I care."

The next morning Emily saw a divorce attorney and filed her petition with the court. Hunter withdrew his petition for divorce, sent her flowers and begged her to come home. Emily told friends when she moved back. "Hunter wants us together."

What was Emily thinking? She had an unsupportive husband who had said, "Your drinking is your problem. Deal with it."

Hunter wanted her home all the time, wanted to dictate who she could see. Once she started to drink, he smirked and joked about her. "It was embarrassing to listen to," one Missoula country club member told *The Independent*.

Hunter told the Summit county sheriff that Emily had started drinking merlot early the day of their picnic. According to Hunter, when they reached the Eccles Pass summit she switched to a sparkling wine and drank steadily while she ate her chicken salad sandwich. She wanted to shoot the view from the top of the world. Hunter told the sheriff, he didn't know how she would be able to operate her camera she was so drunk.

Hunter told the police Emily wandered behind some rocks and removed all her clothes except her blue windbreaker, gray wool socks and hiking boots. She smiled, twirled the sparkling wine bottle and laughingly curled her finger in invitation for Hunter to join her. Hunter told authorities he took her arms from around his neck, encouraging her to dress and sit down, telling her she was she was drinking too much. Instead, she began a slow seductive dance on the cliff's edge. Emily tossed the empty bottle into the brush and continued dancing. "And then she stumbled and fell, plunging to her death. I tried to get her away from the edge. I begged her over and over." Hunter explained to authorities.

During the endless interviews, Hunter's story changed. He told the forest ranger that he fractured his lower left leg trying to grab and hang on to Emily to keep her from falling. To the search and rescue team at the mountaintop, he claimed he didn't see her fall and that he hurt his leg stumbling down the trail searching for help. To the Sheriff, he said he turned in time to see her plunge from the cliff.

Sheriff McAfee and his deputy searched the summit top and found only the remnants of a picnic lunch, the cork from a bottle of sparkling wine and the foil top from a bottle of merlot. No wine bottles or bottle glass or wine glasses or cups. Police found Emily's camera at the condo on the top closet shelf where she kept her bags.

Phones started to ring. Friends from her social circle and from the civic boards she served on called the Summit county authorities. With one voice, they painted a horrific picture of Hunter—controlling, manipulative, obsessively domineering and caring very little about the well being of his wife. Before she had left Missoula for the August vacation in Colorado with Hunter, Emily had asked Leticia, "If something happens to me, look into it, will you?"

Emily's body was difficult to find in the thick brush. A rescue pilot finally located her, radioing the mountain top rescue unit. "I've found her body. You couldn't die in a lonelier place." Another fifteen hours passed before daylight came again and rescuers could descend the cliff with rappelling and climbing gear.

Emily's metal litter banged gently on the side of the ledge. The team at the top reached over and unhooked the harness, pulling her litter to safety. Hunter, his left leg bandaged, stood by Sheriff McAfee and told him, "I would never have dreamed this place was dangerous. I never knew the drop off was there."

The coroner's report ruled the death an accident. Emily suffered a broken neck and pelvis, a punctured lung, broken legs and fractured ribs. Her blood alcohol was 0.22, nearly twice the legal point of intoxication in Colorado and far more debilitating in the thin air at eleven thousand feet. When her body was released, Hunter asked that Emily's remains be immediately cremated and placed in the least expensive urn. Her ashes sit in a small plastic urn in a back storage room of the funeral home. Unclaimed.

A year after her death, Hunter sold out in Missoula and bought his ranch in Wyoming, leaving Emily's ashes in the small back room of the funeral home.

Sherriff McAfee closed his case comments with, "There are only two people who know what happened up on Eccles Pass that bright August morning and one of them is dead."

Emily had lived my greatest fear. Trust someone, commit to him and lose yourself—lose your individuality and the right to control your own destiny. Slowly all that is you, the very essence of you, burns away under the demands of another until you become a brittle husk.

Where was the coroner's report? What did he say? There was a high blood alcohol level, a punctured lung, broken legs, broken neck and pelvis. What was missing? A tox screen. Why was there no tox screen mentioned?

From the bedroom doorway, Jake said softly, "Are you still working? It's late. Come to bed."

"It's Emily."

"What about Emily?"

"She died. Hunter was a suspect. I was rattling through the facts, trying to comprehend her death.

"From Seattle, a socialite and civic fundraiser in Missoula who plunged twenty stories to her death under suspicious circumstances off the peak at Eccles Pass," Jake finished softly.

I stared up at his grim face. "How do you know? How do you know about Emily?"

Jake put his hands gently on my arms. "I was an assistant district attorney in Denver, remember? We were called in on the case. We were the largest city adjacent to Keystone. The feds joined in because she died in a wilderness area. Together, we spent a year investigating Emily's death. We were Emily's only advocates. Her parents were dead and she was an only child. There were too many discrepancies in Hunter's story. Most damning for me was Hunter's statement to the Sheriff that he didn't know the cliff was there when he and Emily had hiked that same spot two days before."

I turned toward the early sunrise barely tinting the sky with golden hues. Jake stepped behind me, his hands loosely resting on my shoulders. I shrugged them off, then turned and faced him. "You should have told me what you knew. Better for me to know with whom I'm dealing with early in the game.

Instead, you just alluded to something in Hunter's past." I accused. "You deliberately withheld from me."

Jake sighed and responded, "The death was ruled an accident. He was never indicted."

I pointed to my laptop. "Look at the picture of Emily. Who does she look like, Jake?"

"You, Sawyer. I saw the resemblance the day I found you lost on my front porch." Jake rubbed his hand over his face.

"I look like Hunter's dead wife and you didn't tell me his story?" I shouted. "He killed her, Jake. He had an opportunity to clean up his life, tidy up his reputation in the community and cash in on the insurance. He grabbed it and Emily paid for it with her life! You weren't going to tell me about Hunter's past, were you?" I thumped my finger on his chest. "You hinted you knew of him when you were in Denver. Why not just tell me you investigated him? It's a public record!"

"Tell tales to you about a man who might be your lover?" He shot back. "Hell no. Because I knew if you wanted to, or you needed to, you'd find out about Emily. You do damn fine work," Jake said tightly.

"He was never my lover! You've known that for a while now. You didn't trust me enough to tell me." I hissed.

"Never was about trust." Jake defended himself. "At first, I did think you and Hunter had something more going on than his being just a news source for you."

"He was a fun date for a ride and a picnic, but then I was through. Not only through, but creeped out!"

Jake's long fingers drummed the desk. "I know that now. I didn't earlier. I didn't!" He flung up his hands. "But babe, I sure like hearing you say it. I didn't want you to come to me because I told you tales about Hunter."

I was still angry, but my heart melted at the site of Jake's concerned eyes and contrite face.

"I'm sorry," he murmured.

My shoulders sagged and the exhaustion overwhelmed me. "I need your help."

"I'm yours. Ask away."

"Emily deserves justice. He had the most to gain from her death."

"I know, but there's no evidence to prosecute him."

I interrupted. "Why did Hunter keep calling and asking if the cremation was done? Why was he in such a hurry? Was a substance missed in the autopsy? There's no tox screen mentioned." I whirled around and looked at Jake. "You did know Hunter did a year of medical school at the University of Washington? He quit after one year saying 'those people were the most uptight anal group of assholes I ever met.'"

I could see Jake's logical mind was racing. "Yeah, I knew he went to medical school and that there was no tox screen. Hunter had the remains cremated the same day the coroner released her body. The coroner shrugged off not doing a tox screen saying, 'When I have a body that fell two hundred feet and an eye witness saying she was drinking, no tox screen is needed.' He was a semi-retired, part time coroner. He didn't have the best facilities either."

"Did he keep working as the coroner after her death?"

"No, he resigned within three months. We got a look at his bank records and there were no unexplained cash deposits. He told the sheriff that he was retiring to Durango where he had family. I checked on him once and awhile, and he was living quietly out there. No evidence of a payoff."

"What else do you know about Emily?" I asked.

"I did a prescription history for Emily in Summit County and back in Missoula. She had a prescription for Oxycodone, a powerful narcotic. Prescribed for Emily by her orthopedist for back pain."

"When had she last filled it?" I asked

"Two days before she died…"

"Alcohol and a narcotic, a powerful double punch. You know the side effects?"

"Yeah, it can impair your motor skills," Jake answered. "When the drug is mixed with alcohol, the effects are exaggerated."

"She was drunk with eleven thousand feet of air between her and the bottom. Drunk, maybe on pain pills, and alone with a husband who gained if she died. How convenient for Hunter," I scoffed.

"We couldn't find any proof the coroner was bought. No one could ever prove how she got the wine and we'll never know if she had a dose of Oxycodone that morning." Jake recited all the problems with the case he tried to build. "Sit down. I made coffee in the tiny hotel pot. Not much, but it'll give us each a cup." He handed me the coffee "What is it?"

"I'm a damn good reporter, but he suckered me. Not for long," I corrected. "All that glibness and superficial charm. He built an elaborate social facade, carefully held in place to hide who he really was. His boasting about his house, his ranch, his art." I shook my head, chagrinned at my gullibility. "I was disarmed by his charm and flattery until he started talking weird shit about going into the darkness."

"Don't," Jake interrupted. "Don't beat up on yourself. Men like Hunter sucker punch even the smartest people."

"Emily deserves more than a plastic urn in a mortuary closet. I want the truth told. For her." Tears stung my eyes. "Emily's story is what I'm so afraid of."

"Why are you crying? What do you mean Emily's story scares you?"

"I'm not crying." I blew my nose. "Not now anyway."

"What are you afraid of? Of marrying a sociopath? Of your husband killing you for money?" The linear thinker responded.

"No. Emily lost herself. Hunter erased all her dreams and hopes until she no longer existed. He remolded her by the force of his will to meet his needs." I wiped my face on my sleeve.

"Sawyer, listen to me," Jake commanded. "Emily's story is of a woman who was too weak or too afraid to kick Hunter in the nuts and establish her boundaries. That's not you. Look at who *you* are. Look at what *you've* accomplished. Look at how strong you are when you interact with other people. You're fearless. Sometimes the way you go after things scares the hell out of me. You *look* like Emily. You're *not* Emily." Jake gave me a little shake. "And I sure am no Hunter Kane."

"I know. But the fear still creeps up my back," I whispered.

"We'll conquer your fear together. You can do this. Find your strength." He raked his hand through his hair.

"You think that's possible?"

"Yeah. We're smart enough to solve it together."

"What if the fear never goes away?" I shivered.

"Your fear is our enemy. We'll defeat it." Jake promised. "And together we'll get justice for Emily."

Chapter 19

The night was dry and crystalline cold when we stepped out on the on hot tub deck.

"Drop your towel and get in quickly." Jake slipped into the steaming water and held out his hand to me.

"Oh." I sighed with relief. "God, this heat feels great on my poor shoulders." I positioned my back over a jet. "I can still see you parked at the top of the mountain yelling, 'Tighten up your curve. Tighten up. You're going to go over!'"

"I wasn't sure you could hear me over the motor and the blowers. But you were *damn* close to driving over that cliff."

"I could hear you all right. I was just too busy to answer." I plunged in the hot water all the way up to my neck. "I was trying to pull left while I was staring down a long, long drop."

"You think the ride was worth it?"

"Sure, the view was spectacular. The whole back side of the mountain was getting pounded by snow." I arched my brow at him. "And I took that curve like an expert on the way down."

He leaned in for a quick kiss, whispering in my ear, "You took that curve like a grandma on the way down."

"Grandma my ass, I had it all under control. If we had another day here I'd race you to the top," I retorted.

"Have to be another trip, babe. Tomorrow we're headed up to Gardiner so you can work for living."

"It's been good to get away."

"You bet it has." He hugged me. "You about done here? Let's have dinner and a little wine in the room. Yours or mine?" Jake asked, toweling off in the cold.

"Depends. I had the maid leave two fresh hotel robes in

my room. You have two?"

"Your room it is. Lead and I'll follow."

I unlocked my door and disappeared into the bathroom to claim a robe. "Here is yours." I tossed him the other robe. "Get decent before dinner arrives."

* * * *

My buffalo burger was cooked to medium-well perfection. Jake's was dripping pinkish red blood into a stream by his French fries. I motioned with my free hand at his bloody plate. "I could build you a dam around those fries, if you want."

"Woman, your burger is charred and probably tasteless. Could be porcupine and you wouldn't know." He tore off a piece of his and handed it to me. "Now this is how buffalo should be seared and served."

The dubious piece of meat and pink stained bun landed on my plate. I nudged it away from my fries. "I prefer my food to be dead, not just wounded."

The fire warmed our wet hair and added great yellow light to the room. "What are your favorite things to do in Cheyenne?" I asked.

"Coming up is the Cheyenne Rodeo and Frontier Days. You ever been?"

"A couple of times to the rodeo when I was a kid. I remember there were Indian dances." I conjured up memories of colorful moccasins and thumping drums.

"They still dance. In fact, they do a reenactment. Set up tepees and cook over open fire pits. The Frontier Day's committee snares some great music, too. George Strait headed up the last one I saw. The city fathers put on a pretty good week." Jake took a long draught of his wine. "Brad Paisley is in concert. Let's go and we can catch the finals of the rodeo."

"Sounds good. I'll get Clay to let me work the earlier performances. I used to cover the rodeo down in San Antonio before moving to the crime beat. I interviewed a nineteen-year-old bull rider who had won nearly two million since he turned pro. His purse was down the past year because he was nursing a bad injury."

"He get on the wrong end of a bull?"

"Yeah, the bull broke his jaw and crushed his nose and orbital bones. He got his rhythm off and his head went forward just when the bull threw his head back. He talked about it so casually. Just another day in his office."

"How'd he look?" Jake asked.

"He looked damn good, but he put on the vest and helmet for his winning ride."

"The adrenaline attracts you, babe." He rolled his head from to each side, his neck making little popping sounds. "Want to go?"

"Sure." I kissed him.

* * * *

We slept late, then munched on granola bars and drank take-out coffee in the truck. I brushed the oat bits onto the truck mat. "Owe you one vacuuming." I spread the park map over my lap. "Pull over here for the geyser basin."

Jake hooked his arm around my waist, holding me close while strolled the boardwalk around the geysers. "Feels like a steam room when you get close, doesn't it?" We watched a bubbling geyser rumble and erupt. Three buffalo were dark hulks covered by steam. "Sometimes you can see dozens of them here. They've gathered here for centuries to survive the winter."

At dusk, we passed under the stone Roosevelt Arch leaving the north entrance of Yellowstone. Gardiner looked like a movie set with quaint log buildings and wooden sidewalks.

He parked in front of the lodge office. One side of his mouth quirked, revealing one perfect dimple. "Before I register, am I getting one room or two tonight?"

"One. You just got lucky. Don't morph into a snorer or a bed sprawler."

* * * *

The hot water drove down onto my shoulders. Jake pulled the curtain back and stepped into the shower. He turned my body to the tile wall.

"Your sighs of pleasure sounded so good I had to join you." His hands soaped my shoulders and then eased their way down my back. He lathered up again, slipping his hands down my buttocks and between my thighs.

I groaned with pleasure. I reached back, trying to get my hands on his gorgeous body.

He stepped in closer to me. "No yet," he whispered in my ear. "I'm just beginning."

I rested my head on the cool tile wall, feeling his warmth behind me. His fingers slipped in and out of me. My need rose. I reached behind to stroke him. He wrapped his free hand around my waist and pulled me back further to him. I came in an explosion of wetness. I turned to face him grabbing his hips, pulling him into me. He plunged into me, needy, hot and hard.

My pleasure built again. He arched his back and thrust so deeply we came together in a shuddering embrace. Warm water cascaded down our shuddering bodies.

Close in a lover's tight embrace of legs and arms, he whispered in my ear, "Ready for bed now?"

"Not just yet." I stepped out of the shower, flipping a thick towel off the heated rack, wrapped him in it, pinning his hands to his sides. I smiled. I kneeled and licked his thigh. "I like this game." My tongue worked up under the towel eliciting groans of pleasure.

"Stop you're killing me," he begged hoarsely.

He whirled me around bending me over the counter. He rammed into me, thrusting hard. The mirror reflected him, head thrown back, mouth stretched in a rictus of arousal. He was driving me to the top of lust and need. I came in a noisy rush. He climaxed, slumped over me, sweating rivulets. "You better be ready for bed, I got nothing for you."

I was panting for breath. "I give. Bedtime."

* * * *

A tall, graying man of about fifty with a single braid hanging to his waist welcomed us to his home. Jake was right. Joe Long Knife's study had a spectacular view of the Rockies

"My law degree is from the University of Montana and I really am that old." He gestured to the diplomas I was studying. He poured coffee into incredibly fragile looking china cups, setting out the cream and sugar, and sat in an armchair across from the sofa.

I set my digital recorder on the coffee table and punched record. "Would you mind if I record our interview, Mr. Long Knife?"

"Joe, please." He voiced his approval to be interviewed and recorded.

"Tell me about the Buffalo Field Campaign."

"It's a nonprofit organization whose mission is to stop the slaughter of wild buffalo in the Yellowstone area. We monitor any legislative initiatives that would affect the herds. Right now we're trying to stop SB432 from making it out of committee."

"How would the passage of the senate bill affect the Shoshone tribe?"

Joe sipped his coffee. "We run two herds on the Rez. One for our meat packing plant and one to breed the American bison. The American bison is a unique part of our native heritage. Passage of the Senate bill would put us out of the meatpacking business, causing widespread unemployment among the tribe, and deny us our native heritage."

"But the land belongs to the Shoshone nation. How can the federal government pass legislation that would slaughter the herd and put the meatpackers out of business?"

"The federal government claims jurisdiction on the basis that brucellosis is a trans-border problem. There is no precedent case. The Shoshone may have to litigate to see if the federal government has the right to destroy native property fenced on our own reservation."

"Do you think the feds can win?"

"I think it will be a difficult challenge for our people. The FBI has more authority than our tribal policemen. So the feds already have a precedent for making decisions about Native people. There are only about fifteen thousand animals left with the DNA of the original American buffalo. He is sacred to us, linking us to our past and our ancestors in the Yellowstone Basin," he emphasized.

"Is that why you testified against SB432?"

He laughed and looked at Jake. "You told me she was good. I represent my people. We need the jobs at the plant and we need to breed our heritage animals."

Jake leaned forward and joined the conversation. "Breeding these animals is their only hope for a future and it's not rocket science. We buy stock from each other so none of our small herds becomes inbred."

Joe agreed. "We've all benefitted from working together. Keeping the parts of the herd in several states also safeguards them from a single catastrophe wiping them all out."

"I read your testimony before the senate that the elk were infecting cattle."

Joe poured more coffee in my tiny cup. "No one has ever documented a case of a buffalo infecting cattle with brucellosis."

"Why doesn't that happen?"

"Buffalo calve in the early spring when the weather is still below freezing. Brucellosis can't survive in the birth fluids in subfreezing temperatures."

"And elk?" I asked.

"Elk calve much later in the spring when the temperatures are warmer and the bacteria can stay alive longer in the birth fluids."

"Elk spread the disease," Jake said firmly. "They calve in cattle pastures."

"He's right." Joe nodded at Jake. "The elk population has exploded since we got rid of the natural predators. The current elk population is unsustainable. The State Wildlife department needs to manage the elk population to help eradicate brucellosis."

"What kind of management are you talking about?" I asked Joe.

"A two prong attack." Joe stood and paced in front of the fire. "Wolf packs need to be reintroduced. Wildlife experts can chip them and monitor their range. Same with the mountain lion. The state needs to issue more permits for hunters to take elk."

"What about the cattlemen?"

Joe gave a succinct and lawyerly response. "Vaccinate cattle when they are about four months old. The legislators ought to drop SB432 and mandate the vaccination of cattle."

"Will you introduce a bill to require that all calves be vaccinated?"

"The Shoshone already have. We'll protect our cultural heritage," Joe said.

* * * *

I listened to Joe's interview in the car. Jake looked over. "Did you get what you wanted?"

"Yes, he corroborated your story. I still need a sound bite from the research expert, Dr. Henderson down at A&M."

"So I'm just another news source now?" He shook his head in mock sadness.

"Yeah, right. You can reassume the role if you like."

He picked up my hand, kissed the palm and answered quietly, "Thanks for the offer I can easily refuse. What would you like to do this weekend?"

"Hunter's barbecue is Saturday night. I assume you're invited since Hunter said it would be the event of the season."

Jake burst into a fit of laughter. "I didn't know Cheyenne had a season. I'm invited. Want to go?"

"I wouldn't miss a chance to be back in Hunter's house, but we'll have to meet there. I won't know when I can leave the six o'clock news until the second I get to walk out the door."

Jake's cell phone buzzed in his pocket. "Spooner here." His gray eyes darkened. Hard anger contorted his face. "Is Barton still there with you?" He barked to someone. He snapped the phone down in the console. "Nate. There's a mutilated buffalo over on the north range at his Wildcat Ranch."

"Jake!" I grabbed his forearm. "Is it like the others?"

"Yeah. Slashed throat, tail taken. More importantly, Tom Walker was found standing over the carcass." He looked at me grimly.

"Tom Walker! I can't believe he'd screw up where he's working!"

"Unless Walker never intended to be caught next to the carcass. Unless he's one sick fuck," Jake responded roughly.

"Is anyone hurt?"

"No," Jake replied. "Nate sent a couple of men to the north pasture to round up strays. They saw Walker standing over the downed buffalo, wiping his knife in the grass. They held him until Barton got there."

"What's Walker's say?"

"Walker claims he found her suffering, slit her throat and put her down." He grabbed his cell.

"Barton, Spooner here. Nate called me. Right. You got enough to hold Walker? How long? I'll swing by on my way to Nate's."

"Fill in what I couldn't figure out," I demanded.

"Her front and back legs were both trussed. Sam's on his way over, but it'll be a day or so before he's got the drug scan. Barton searched the area for the tail." He shrugged. "Couldn't find it. Wasn't in Walker's Jeep or anywhere in the area."

"Does he have enough to hold Walker?"

"On animal cruelty charges," Jake said grimly.

"How does Walker explain being caught over the carcass?"

"Walker says he was coming to see a hand on my ranch and he 'just came up on her suffering.' Says he likes the back roads so he can four-wheel in his Jeep."

"Did Barton verify there was a man expecting him?"

"Yeah, the man owed him money from a craps game. What's bothering you about this? You're fidgeting like a cat over there."

"It's just too neat. Man who has a stain on his past just happens to be wiping his knife over the dead body. I don't see Walker sending me emails and taking photos of us. Where'd Walker get a big pickup to run us off the road?"

"We've been linking your stalker with the mutilations. Could be Walker did the mutilations, but not the stalking," Jake answered.

"Yeah, right," I snorted. Suddenly there're two crazies in Cheyenne, both connected to me. I'm going out to Nate's with you."

"I figured that was going to happen."

Barton's tiny office had two holding cells and only one was in use. Walker shifted his weight a little and his arms hung loosely from his rounded shoulders. He wiped his hands on his dirty jeans and cleared his throat. He had an air of resignation.

Barton rose to meet us and said, "He's told the same story at least three times. Step out with me."

"What's his story?" I asked Barton.

"He claims he didn't mutilate her. That she was down when he came up on her."

"What about slitting her throat?"

"Claims she was down and suffering. Says he woulda shot her if he'd had a rifle with him. What he did have with him was a sharp knife."

"You believe him?" I asked Barton.

"Can't say that I don't," he replied laconically. "He didn't have a rifle. He's got an old beat up vehicle with a roll bar and off road tires so the four wheelin' part's plausible. That old Jeep is a dark color, could have been the vehicle that ran you off the road."

Jake ran his hand through his hair and looked at Barton. "That last part is a stretch. You think he's the one sending emails and shooting pictures?"

"Library has public computers." Barton pushed himself off the doorframe. "Could have. We'll be working to see if we can tie him to the other killings. I can tell you that bail will probably be set low enough someone can make it for him. I doubt Walker's in here tomorrow afternoon."

"Thanks, Sheriff. We'll be in touch." Jake said.

Jake held the truck door for me. "You sure you want to go on over to Nate's? That carcass isn't going anywhere."

"Yeah, I do. We're going to drive right by my place. Stop, so I can pick up some of things. I'll be quick."

Chapter 20

I was out of Jake's truck hurrying to the front door while he was still sliding it into park. I ran through the kitchen, stumbling to a stop when I saw blood dripping off the wall. My breath hitched in my throat. I grabbed a knife from the rack and backed up to the counter, peering into mid afternoon gloom in the hallway. Over the pounding of my heart, I listened for any sound.

The front door slammed shut and I heard footsteps. "Jake," I croaked.

"Sawyer?"

"The kitchen!" I screamed.

"Sawyer," he yelled. He careened around the corner.

"There! On the wall." I pointed to the bloody lopsided peace sign. "Oh my god, I didn't see it." One hand covered my mouth. Draped across the kitchen counter like a belt in a spatter of blood coiled a severed buffalo tail.

Jake yelled, "Take your cell and go outside on the porch. I'm going to look through the house. Call Barton *now*."

I raced for the door dialing Barton's number.

"It's Sawyer Cahill. Someone broke into my house. There's blood on the wall. Yes, I'm okay. I'm waiting on the porch."

Jake swung the front door open. "No one in there. You better? You were really pale in there."

"Okay, I'm okay." I shivered. "Barton's on his way."

"You think you can drop that knife now?"

I set the knife on my porch chair. "How'd he get in?"

"Broke the window by your back door." He rubbed his hands up and down my arms. "I'd go crazy if you were staying here." He clung to me, kissing the top of my head, murmuring and stroking my hair.

"I want to see if anything is missing."

"Just don't touch anything," Jake said. "Not that I think the bastard left prints on the tail. But maybe around the window."

We stood in the kitchen staring at the wall. "That's not blood." I pointed. "See how the color is spread evenly on the peace sign? It's red paint. You couldn't get enough blood from the severed end of a tail to do that. The sick fuck broke into *my* home and tagged my wall like a damn gang banger!"

Barton's voice interrupted my anger. "Sawyer, you in there?"

"Back here." I called.

Barton stood in my kitchen with his feet splayed and his hands on his hips. "Could be the tail of the dead animal from Nate's ranch. Sam can give us an idea." He strode over and scratched at the peace sign. "Looks like red paint." He produced a small plastic bag and scraped some of the paint into it. He took a larger evidence bag out of his vest pocket and stuffed the tail into it. "Where you stayin'?" he asked me.

"Over at Jake's. When can I board up the back window?" I motioned to the other room.

"Not just yet." Barton looked at the broken glass. "Looks pretty straightforward. Deputy'll have to dust for fingerprints. Then you can get her boarded up."

He cocked his head at Jake. "You gonna be watching out after her?"

Jake's arm circled my shoulders. "Yeah, she's not going to be alone."

"Good." Barton nodded.

Damn! He was a man who had irritatingly few words and none for solving the case. His worn clamshell phone rang and he unsnapped it. "Barton here. Yeah. Uh-huh. You got all you need? Right. Got some new evidence I'll drop by your clinic." He snapped the old cell shut and looked at me. "Sam's just left Nate's."

"Let me know about the tail." I moved toward my bedroom. Jake was already calling a hand and telling him what he would need to board up my broken window.

I climbed into the seat of Jake's truck, clutching file

folders and another small bag. "One person didn't do all this. Walker would have had to leave the kill site, break into my house, paint the wall and drive back to Nate's to be found standing over the carcass by the other ranch hands. No way, it happened that way. A second person took the tail to my house." I was thinking aloud. "Or there could be three people involved. Maybe Walker and the other man did this and someone else planned and paid."

"It's a plausible theory," Jake answered slowly.

"Yeah could be. Or my other theory is Walker's telling the truth. He walked up on that animal and he put her out of her misery. The mutilator botched the job or got scared off, then broke into my house, leaving the tail."

"It's late." He swung into his drive. "I'll drop you at the ranch house."

"No way. I'm going with you."

"You don't have to do this tonight. You can go in the morning. She'll still be there," Jake said.

"I'm going. It's not just a story anymore."

"You sure you're up to it?" He asked. I nodded. "Okay, we'll stop by the barn and get some battery operated lights. Everyone else is probably gone by now."

She had died near a rock ledge like the first one, probably to provide a little cover for the killer. The windmill creaked, trickling dirty water into the tank. Under her trussed hooves, the mud bore deep gouges. We walked around the carcass. Jake bent down and probed the throat wounds with his knife. "Look, in places it's so superficial it didn't even cut through the fascia. First wound's not deep enough to kill her. But look here."

In the harsh light, the second wound was an ugly slash. Its path followed the first until it veered off in the center of the neck. There, the second wound cut was distinctly parallel to the first, cutting deeply into her neck and severing the jugular.

"That's the cut that killed her," Jake said, picking at the edge of the deep wound with his knife. White fascia stretched tightly over the neck muscle until the point where the knife slashed through the jugular. A pool of blood congealed around the massive head and mouth. Blood spatter peppered the dirt around her.

"Either it took Walker two tries to kill her or he's telling the truth," I said. "Question is, why didn't the mutilator finish the job? Nate's boys scare him off?"

Jake pointed north of the animal. "Don't know. There's

where Barton said Walker parked the Jeep. Look at all those tire tracks in that dirt."

"There were no tire prints around the other kills. If Walker did this, why would he drive his Jeep right into the kill zone?" Jake repositioned the lights. It was nearly midnight and the wind cut through my light windbreaker. "I'm finished. How about you?"

"Me too. You can't just intellectualize your way through the attacks on you and the break in at your house. You need to deal with your emotions. Or it'll come back to bite you in your sweet ass. It's normal to be mad and scared, but you got to own it and deal with it." He hugged me tightly, soothing my frazzled nerves. "I want to see that beautiful smile of yours again."

I put my arms around him and kissed him softly on his neck. "Anyone tell you lately that at times you can be perfect? No? Well, don't let it go to your head." I patted his sweet ass.

* * * *

I was so achingly tired I fell into a deep and thankfully dreamless sleep. I awoke before dawn, slipping quietly out of bed. I set up my laptop on the desk in the guest room. The story flowed from my fingertips. I pushed the chair back and stared at the screen. *Looks good,* I thought, dragging my hand through my messy hair.

"You in the mood for coffee or you going to keep working?" Jake asked from the doorway.

"Coffee, now." I said shutting down the laptop. "You been up long?"

"Long enough to watch you pound that thing for awhile. He handed me a steaming cup of coffee from the pot he kept in his bedroom. How civilized. Coffee in your own bedroom.

"You don't have a bagel up here somewhere do you?" I asked over the rim of the cup.

"No," he laughed drily. "You have to go downstairs for food in this house."

"No time," I said.

* * * *

An hour later, I was sitting in Clay's office while he read the script of my story on the Senate bill. "Fine piece of journalism, Sawyer." Clay set the script down on his desk, peering over his cheaters. "News desk caught the business out at your house on the police scanner. Guy on the desk last night tried to call you. You need anything?"

"No, I'm okay. I guess. I'm staying over at the neighbor's.

My house is a mess." I didn't want to talk about how I didn't feel safe enough in my own home to stay there, even with the window boarded up.

"You need anything? You have friends here at the station," Clay said. "We got your back." He picked up the script, flipping through the pages. "We'll lead with your story tonight on the six and the ten. Really good. Substantive. I like the bite you have from the researcher. You got his verbal release, right?"

"All the releases are on the digital recorder. I'll pull them off and amend them to the story file."

"You know kid—er, Sawyer. This is going to bring out the knives." He was shaking his head. "The senate bill is controversial. Gonna divide this community right down the middle. That bit about bringing back the wolf packs? Locals aren't going to like that."

"I'll deal with it. No investigative story is worth the airtime if it doesn't make people think."

I stuck my head in Benita's office and interrupted her visit with Tobin. "Ohh, good to see you. How are you?" She got up and hugged me. "I just heard about the break-in at your place. You need a place to stay?"

Her warmth thawed the knot of cold fear in my belly. "No, thanks though. I'm staying over at a neighbor's."

"Offer stands. I don't think you should go back into your place for a long time." Benita shivered.

"Clay's running my senate bill story tonight on both the six and ten." I was excited.

"He must really like it." She sat on the corner of her desk. "We're both here for you." She included Tobin who gave me a thumbs up.

"Thanks." I walked to my office. In daylight and surrounded by friends the gnawing anxiety retreated.

I had missed a call from Julia earlier. By now, I was sure she had heard about the break in at my house. "Julia?"

"Sawyer," she said breathlessly, "I heard what happened at your house. Are you okay?"

"I'm okay. I'm glad Jake was with me."

"Me too. Dave and I will do anything you need, you know that, right?" Julia said.

"Yeah, thanks. You and Dave having any problems over your house?" I was still dragging a load of guilt for getting them involved.

"No, we're fine. It's you we're worried about," Julia

answered. "How's it going with Jake?"

I smiled for the first time since finding the tail. "Good enough that I don't want my trust thing to screw it up."

"We need to have lunch. Oops, art's over for kids and I hear them coming down the hall. Talk to ya later."

"Hey, one more thing. You get the invitation to Hunter's barbecue?"

"Yeah, we plan on going."

"Good. I'll see you both there."

I had one more missed call. Hunter. Probably checking on my health. He could wait, the bastard.

* * * *

I forced myself to run my two-mile loop in the morning hoping to slap the stress level back to high-normal before driving to work. After my first cup of coffee I logged in the station's server. The web version of the story had garnered twenty comments so far. *Good number of responses.* I began to scroll through them. I recognized three of the regulars. Wycowboy27 called the story a "flat-out lie." Barkeep272 wanted to know "why we care what a Texan ivory tower shit thinks about our cattle business." Only ridgewalker51 agreed, "the elk population should be managed by culling the herd." Barkeep272 started a petition in support of SB432 at change.org asking people to log in and sign it. No one favored reintroducing wolf packs or mountain lions.

I closed the file and reached for the phone. "Sam, Sawyer here. Did the buffalo at Nate's have traces of Xylazine?"

"She did. I talked with Barton late yesterday. The best I can tell from the cut marks, the tail in your kitchen came from the same animal. How are you holding up?"

"Better than yesterday."

He grunted a reply and hung up.

"Sheriff Barton, Sawyer. Is Walker still there?"

"Nope. Made bail and he's gone. Didn't get any prints from out at your place. He wiped that windowsill or wore gloves," Barton was loquacious today.

"Who made the bail?"

"George Carlisle."

"George Carlisle! What's the connection between him and Walker?" I asked.

"Don't know. Walker's one phone call was to Carlisle. He came in and made bail," Barton replied.

"Do you know where Walker is?"

"Back at Nate's," Barton spat out.

"Why would Nate take him back?"

"Ask Nate."

* * * *

I parked in front of a deserted looking ranch house. "Nate, Sawyer Cahill," I said into my cell. "I'm here on your porch. How about a few minutes of your time?"

"Sure. Look over toward the barn. You'll see me headed your way. When he stepped onto the porch he asked, "What can I do for you?"

"Nate, why did you take Walker back to work?"

Nate's head shot back in surprise. "I don't believe he mutilated that animal. I think he's telling the truth about finding her."

"Why?"

"Who the hell are you interrogating me!"

I chose to ignore that jab. "Why didn't you make his bail?"

"Carlisle beat me to it. Not that it's any of your business."

"How well does Carlisle know Walker?"

Nate threw up his hands. "How would I know? We're through here." He strode off.

I called to his back. "I'd like to talk to Walker for a minute."

"That's his choice. He's branding over in the north pasture where we found the cow."

* * * *

A cluster of pickup trucks marked the spot in the north pasture where Walker was working.

"Mr. Walker."

He cocked his head, screwed up his face trying to figure how he knew me. "Yeah?" He took off his hat and wiped his face with the filthy rag knotted around his neck.

"Sawyer Cahill." I moved forward extending my hand. "From CBS3. We met the other night."

"Yeah, I remember now. What do you want?" He restlessly shifted his weight from one well-worn boot to the other.

"A few minutes of your time." I maneuvered him away from the rest of the men. "Tell me what the scene looked like when you found that cow."

"What?" He snapped in surprise. "I didn't cut her up none..."

"Mr. Walker, I didn't accuse you of mutilating the cow." I took a step toward him closing the distance between us to inches. "I just want you to relax, close your eyes. Tell me what you saw out there."

He scrunched his eyes shut. "I was drivin' when I saw her down by the windmill tank." He was silent for a moment. His face creased with the effort of thinking. "She was kickin' a bit. When I walked up, she rolled her eyes up in panic. Blood bubbles was comin' out her nose and mouth. She was struggling like she thought she'd be able to get away from me." He was running the rim of his dirty hat through his fingers.

"That's good Tom, real good." He kept his eyes tightly closed. "What do you see around her, Tom? Anything out of the ordinary?"

"I see blood everywhere. She's making gurgling sounds. Blood bubbles pop on my hand when I get my knife to her throat. She's hurting bad."

"Then what happens?" I asked softly.

He opened his eyes. "I pulled her head back by her horns. I didn't know where to start cutting or how deep. I tried to stay in the first cut, but I couldn't do it. The knife slipped outta the first cut and I just bore down hard. She bled out bad, real bad, but she weren't suffering no more."

"You're doing great Tom. Now think about the dirt around her. You see anything, any tracks, anything in the mud?"

"Well." He paused.

I was close enough to smell his nervous sweat. "You found something, didn't you, Mr. Walker?" He stumbled back a step. "What did you find?"

"I didn't find nothing..."

"What did you see?"

His red-rimmed eyes opened. "I seen a trail of dust way off down the pasture, truck of some kind. Lit out when I pulled up."

"Which way was he going?"

"North. That's the only way out from the windmill tank unless you go cross-country. Real rough country 'round that tank. Couldn't do it without a real high chassis," he said.

"Do you know what kind of vehicle it was?"

"Dark truck. I don't know nothing else. The boys came up and found me standing over that cow and everything went to hell in a hand basket. Look, I gotta get back to work," he said, eyeing the work crew.

"Thank you Mr. Walker."

* * * *

I found Jake on his back porch talking on his cell. I waggled two beers his way and waited until he pocketed his phone.

"Beer?" I said handing him one.

"Sure. I just talked with Nate."

"So did I. Walker, too."

"I heard from Nate," he said dryly. "What did you get out of Walker?"

"When I took him back through it, he remembered seeing a dust trail heading north. Says he saw a dark truck."

"He know the brand of truck, plate number?"

"No such luck." I swigged my beer. "Could have been the guy who rammed us."

"Circumstantial. There're a lot of dark trucks," Jake said. "If Barton doesn't have any evidence that Walker mutilated her, the case will be too weak for the DA to want to prosecute."

Chapter 21

I headed out to work and Jake called after me, "Ms. Cahill, what we need is another little diversion. How about dinner and dancing at the Drover this evening?"

"Good idea, cowboy." I waved to him.

I drove past the station and parked in front of Cattleman's Auction. The metallic clang of chute gates and bawling cattle pierced the morning.

"I'd like to see Mr. Carlisle, please," I said to his secretary.

"Do you have an appointment? I believe Mr. Carlisle is busy with arrangements for the morning sale." She tidied the papers on her desk.

"I don't. Please tell him Sawyer Cahill is here to ask why he made Tom Walker's bail."

She sat still with a shocked look on her face before she recovered to say primly, "I'll see if Mr. Carlisle will see you." She disappeared behind the heavy wooden door to Carlisle's office.

She reappeared and settled herself behind her desk. "He'll give you a few minutes."

George Carlisle sat at his desk surrounded by a pile of papers. "Good morning, Mr. Carlisle. Why did you post Tom Walker's bail?"

"Sit down, sit down, Sawyer. Ah yes, poor unfortunate Tom Walker."

I remained standing. "Not really unfortunate. He had a savior swoop in and make his bail," I said. "How do you know him?"

"Why do you ask? Are you interviewing me for a story? I might refuse to answer." Carlisle sat back in his chair and folded his hands over his stomach.

"That's your choice," I said. "If you refuse to answer, I'll report your refusal to comment, Mr. Carlisle. How do you think that will sound to our viewers?"

"No big secret," Carlisle deferred. "Hunter hired him to work around here. Some foster kid Hunter was trying to save. I heard about his arrest and went down to help him out. I thought he was down and out, running a bad stretch of luck. Just helped a man." He shrugged.

"Just helping a kid down on his luck charged with animal cruelty? You're a stockman, Mr. Carlisle. Don't you think that sounds odd?"

"I have no idea what you read into it, Ms. Cahill," he huffed. "But if you slander me in one of your news stories, you'll find yourself sued." He rose. "I'm out of time this morning."

I stepped up to the edge of his desk placing my palms flat on the top, jutting my face into his. "Did you pay Walker to mutilate that animal?"

"That's preposterous," he roared. "You're clutching at straws to make a story for yourself. I'm warning you. You slander me and you'll hear from my lawyer—you and the station both."

"Good day, Mr. Carlisle," I said, moving out of his office.

That should stir the pot.

* * * *

Music drifted out from the Drover. Jake slipped his arm around my waist. "No shop talk or you have to do the dishes for your dinner," Jake warned with a grin and a wag of his finger.

We wove through the throng of dancers and diners to a secluded table in the back. Before I could sit, Jake pulled me out to the dance floor. "You're going to work up an appetite before dinner." His held me close to him. We moved in step with the group of dancers. Jake bent down and whispered in my ear, "You know dancing is foreplay, don't you?"

"Ah, the guy promises dinner and hopes to get lucky," I teased.

His amusement turned serious. "With you, I am lucky."

After a bottle of wine and dinner, we slow danced to Reba's "I Miss Him" ballad. "Let's go home," Jake said softly.

"Good idea."

At the bottom of Jake's stairs, I kicked off my shoes and

unbuttoned my shirt, enjoying him watching me. He reached out for me. I nimbly took two steps up the staircase. "You're going to have to be faster than that," I said, tossing my shirt on the stairs. He took the stairs two at a time, racing me for the landing. Desire softened his face, making his eyes luminous. Slowly, I unzipped my skirt, wiggling so it pooled at my feet. I was clad only in two wisps of black silk.

"I hate it when you get ahead of me," he rumbled. He bolted to the landing. I walked into his embrace, dragging my hand through his hair, down his jaw, tracing his full bottom lip with my finger. He kissed me with a ferocious hunger. I put one leg around his waist, his body holding my weight. Heat sizzled in my belly. "I can shorten this trip," he growled, picking me up. He booted the bedroom door open and laid me on the bed. He stood before me shirtless, unbuckling his jeans. I pulled them down over his fine ass. When he straddled me, I gripped his shoulders pulling him closer.

"This, Ms. Cahill, is the result of dancing," he smiled skimming his hands down my shoulders and breasts.

"I love dancing," I murmured.

He reached behind me and removed my bra. I arched my back to receive him.

"Not yet...shush, too soon," he murmured.

His hand made tantalizingly slow circles across my belly. He kissed his way to my thighs, pulled the silk past my feet and cupped my buttocks, kneading and spreading.

The heat sizzled between my legs, filling me with an aching hunger. His fingers slid urgently in and out of me driving me almost to the edge of climax.

"Now, now!" I gasped. "I want you in me, *now*."

He pushed himself up on his elbows. Sweat slicked between our bodies. He plunged hard and fast. I encircled his waist with my legs tumbling us over. I threw back my head, riding him until pleasure thundered through me. I shouted his name when he took his own release.

We lay entwined. "God, I love pleasing you," he breathed huskily.

I stirred, aroused from my sated warmth. I ran one hand down the V-line of dark hair and gently laid my hand on him.

"Don't do that unless you want to go again," he whispered in my ear.

"But I do." I rolled on top. I lazily nibbled his neck, teasing him with kisses down his belly. He was rock hard. I took him in me, slowly, inch by inch, delighted to hear his groans of pleasure.

"You're killing me," he said roughly.

I rose up and slid slowly down on him watching his eyes widen. He thrusted into me, bringing us together in a shattering release.

I lay in his warmth beside him. He kissed me gently and rested his forehead on mine. "I've fallen in love with you." He stroked my hair back from my face.

I was jolted from my satisfied state by clanging internal alarm bells. I pushed up on my elbows and could hear myself backpedaling, "Are we feeling this intense closeness because we are being threatened? Is that what this is?"

Jake smiled his quiet smile and answered, "No it's not, and you know it. Yeah, we're experiencing something no one else is, but a guy ramming my truck and a break in at your house are not the reason I love you. Have I upset you?" He smiled and tucked my hair behind one ear.

"No, I think I'm in love with you. You startled me by getting there first," I said, pulling one hand through my messy hair.

"Why, Ms. Cahill, would loving me alarm you?"

I groaned and flopped down on the bed. "Ask Julia. She has it all figured out. She thinks I have a failure to trust a guy in a relationship."

"A failure to trust? Well, I think I just demonstrated I can rise to any challenge," he said with a wry grin.

"It's not funny." *God, I refuse to sound whiny.* "Here I am baring my soul to you and you're grinning like an idiot. I don't know if Julia's right. I don't *want* Julia to be right. Sometimes in a relationship, I've felt like a bird whose wings have been cut. And all I can do is hop morosely on the bottom of the cage."

He held me gently. "Then you've been with the wrong men, babe. Not me. There are not any cages in this relationship. You're not going to lose yourself with me. Why would I love you and want to change you?" He kissed my forehead. "Besides, loving me can be a helluva lot of fun."

"Don't get puckish with me. I just declared my love to you."

"We could be puckish together in the shower," he said, peeling back the covers.

"We could shower in the shower and you could show me your cute ass. Come on."

Chapter 22

I tapped my pen on my desk, rolled the worry out of shoulders and stared at the evening runsheet with no interest. Jake's telling me he was in love with me sent me into a tailspin. *Oh hell, have I botched that?* A man doesn't want his declaration of love to be an alarming proposition. How did loving Jake fit in with me being the captain of my ship? What if I can't share the bridge with a mate? In a perfect world, two people would stand together on the bridge of their ship mutually respecting each other. Decisions would be the result of input from each, and each would find the relationship satisfyingly supportive while they sailed through calm seas or rip tides. *Yeah, right*, I snorted to myself.

By four o'clock, when the evening anchors rolled in, I had a working run sheet of the show ready for master control. The evening news producer was still writing segues, but the stories were nailed down and the video logged. Time for me to go to Hunter's barbecue.

After a quick shower, I stood in the closet trying to decide what to wear, thumbing through a wardrobe that didn't offer many choices. Casual would do. It's a western barbecue and going to be outside. *Casual and warm, I corrected*. I pulled out jeans with a white wrap shirt and wool blazer. My silver jewelry would look great.

The parking around Hunter's house looked to be at a premium. Then I saw the valet—*go figure, a valet for a barbecue!* Crowds surged through the house. "Sawyer!" Julia called. Snagging a glass of white wine from a server, I worked my way over to her and Dave, hugging her warmly.

"Have you seen Jake?" I asked.

"Last time I saw him, he was in the backyard where the caterer's tents are." She motioned through the throng of people in the living room. "Go on and find him and we'll meet up with you later. Let's eat together," Julia said.

"Good idea." I gave Dave a quick hug, "I haven't seen you in awhile. It'll be good to catch up."

I worked my way through the crowd to the kitchen door and out into the backyard. Big propane heaters were blasting heat into the tents. Caterers were filling the buffet tables with huge slabs of fragrant barbecued beef and pulled pork. All that blasting heat was wilting the cold salads. An arm went round my waist. I smelled the Jim Beam before Hunter was close enough to whisper in my ear, "I'm so happy you're here." He reached out, trailing a finger across my cheekbone. "Your face looks much better. I can barely see the bruise under your makeup. You'll be so proud to be with me tonight. Best party in town every year." He quivered with excitement.

"Hunter we're not—"

The band blared from the speaker above my head. He leaned down and yelled in my ear, "Come meet some of our guests who are pretty special to me." He took my arm, leading me to a small knot of couples. "This is Wayne Johnston and his wife Abby." I nodded at Wayne and smiled greetings to Abby. "And," Hunter continued, "Mike Wiley. He owns the Iron Horse ranch. His wife, Sarah." Hunter snatched another drink from a passing server.

I chatted with Wayne Johnston about the loss of his herd, and he offered he had to bring his boy back from the university because the government destroyed his livelihood. His wife looked stricken with embarrassment so I turned to Mike Wiley and asked how long he had ranched in the area. Abby and Sarah began to chat with each other.

"Hunter, why don't you show me that new bronze you told me about?" I asked.

"Now? Well, maybe we have time before we need to welcome the rest of our guests. See the microphone up by the band? Be thinking about what you're going to say."

I took another glass of wine from the server. "You're the host of this party! I think you should be the only one to welcome everybody." He straightened his back and lifted his chin.

"I've been dying to see that bronze. You have such an eye for western art," I wheedled.

His vanity helped him decide. "Of course," he said. He looped his arm back around my waist. Inwardly, I shrank from his touch. To him I warbled, "I feel so lucky to have the opportunity to see such art."

"I have a new gallery in Jackson Hole that represents my interests. You know, to build a true collection one has to have a gallery scouring the auctions for just the right pieces." He ushered me through the door with his hand in the small of my back. "They found me a Remington. Just an exquisite piece, cost me a fortune. Wait 'til you see it."

On a marble table in the upstairs hallway, we admired a bronze of a buffalo and a mounted Indian entitled *Buffalo Hunt*. Instinctively, I ran my hands down the smooth flanks of the horse.

"Careful. Your fingers aren't greasy are they? That'll leave smudges."

He puffed out his chest and linked his hands behind his back. I ran a finger down the Indian's thigh just to make him uncomfortable. "Nice addition to the collection." I could see him twitching when my finger lingered on the cool metal.

"I'm so proud to own this piece." He pulled a Kleenex from his pocket, deftly wiping away any errant greasy prints. He widened his stance, bouncing on the balls of his feet. "I've had them hunting for a piece like this for about a year now." He gestured down the hall. "I had the upstairs painted the neutral white color museums use to set off the tones of the bronze. Come down here and look at it under that spotlight."

"Nice, Hunter." We were standing in the hallway near what I assumed was his master bedroom. "Your master bedroom?"

"Yes, you may take a look."

I followed him into his bedroom, spying a framed photograph on a small chest. I picked it up. "Who's the man with you?"

"That's my brother right before he shipped out." He took the photo and lined it up carefully with the right angle of the edge of the chest.

"Do you have any pictures of you and Emily?"

"No. Absolutely not. If I put out pictures of Emily, the memories would drag me back to that awful place. I've worked so hard to leave that darkness. You understand, don't you? I can't live in there. I can't." His warm bourbon breath wafted over me.

"Yes, of course," I said softly. "If you'll excuse me, I'm going to use your restroom. I'll meet you downstairs."

"Certainly, Emily—oh, I'm so sorry, Sawyer." Confusion marred his handsome face. I watched him gather his old bravado. "It's back to your right in my dressing room. I'll be downstairs. Don't go too far. I want you by my side when I open the food line and we welcome our guests." *Does he think he's talking to Emily?*

Hunter's bedroom was immense; a king size mahogany-framed bed anchored two huge windows, giving a magnificent view of the ranch. The bureau and dresser tops were bare. Both bedside tables were empty except for a single lamp and the one photograph of his brother. I turned a full circle. Nothing on his walls.

In the bathroom, one perfectly folded hand towel hung from a pewter ring. Two closets with substantial wood doors covered one wall of the dressing area. One was slightly ajar. I tiptoed to the bedroom doorway and listened. Silence.

I hurried back to the bathroom and opened the closet door. Double rods of expensive men's clothes hung organized by type. Racks of shoes and boots, each with their own shoetrees, lined the floor. I closed the door, leaving it ajar. I pulled the other closet door and it didn't budge. It looked like a simple spring lock. *Who locks their clothes closet?*

I silently slipped open the drawers under the countertop looking for something long and very slender to slip into the lock. Damn. Just toiletries and razors. He had pinch pleat drapes in the bedroom. Of course he'd have formal drapes. I cracked the door to the hall—no sound, nobody drifting upstairs. Balancing on a small overstuffed chair, that Hunter would look ridiculous perched on, I worked a drapery pin out of the curtains and straightened it.

I slipped the pin into the lock and pushed, expecting the spring pin to release and the door to pop open. Nothing happened. I inserted it harder and turned the knob. Nothing. I was running out of time. Crap. I reshaped the pin and attached the drapery to the rod. Looking around the bedroom, everything was in place. Even the chair was resting in the dents the legs left in the carpet. *Another time.*

* * * *

Jake and Nate warmed their hands over a fire pit in the backyard. "Sawyer, you look good." Jake swooped in for a kiss.

"Hello, Nate." I was wary about what his response to me would be.

"Sawyer." He nodded in my direction. "Walker told me you found him. Hope you got something useful."

Jake and I started to speak at the same time, but I said with a shrug. "I asked Mr. Walker some questions, Nate. Just part of the job."

"Just so you both know. I don't see Walker cutting up an animal or breaking into your house. When a man's got some shade in his past and he's trying to turn himself around, somebody oughta give the guy a chance," Nate said.

George Carlisle sidled up by Nate. "Ah, you're talking about Walker. I made his bail, you know. You must think a lot of him too." George continued smoothly. "Took him back on your place, didn't you Nate?"

"Gave the man a second chance. See what he does with it." Nate nodded brusquely at Carlisle.

"Fair enough. If Walker's innocent, he deserves a chance," Jake said. "If he's not, then the rule of law will decide what his fate is. Come on, Sawyer. I'm getting hungry and the line is getting longer." We left Carlisle and Nate standing by the fire pit. I turned around to see Carlisle lift his glass in mock salute and snark a smile at me.

At the head table, Hunter was toasting his guests with another shot of Jim Beam. Hunter's eyes tracked us to the end of the food line.

He finished his toast and joined us at the end of one of the long tables.

"Hunter, these are my friends Julia and her husband Dave."

"Happy you could come. I hope you're having a wonderful time. Sawyer, I'm sorry you weren't free to join me in welcoming our guests." Hunter surprised me by offering his hand to Jake. When Jake took his hand, Hunter grabbed Jake's forearm and pulled him in. "Evening, Spooner." His lips curled in a snarl and he dropped Jake's hand.

"Hunter!" I stepped in front of him. "These people are your guests. *You* are the host. Stop acting like we're a couple."

"You're with Jake? That's it?" Wet spittle flew on my cheek.

Jake inched closer. "Yes, she's with me, Hunter."

"The master of all trades, Jake Spooner." Hunter snaked his arm around my neck cinching me close. He gulped from his bourbon. "You think you know Jake Spooner? Do you?" His breath was hot on my face. "You don't. You know what? Huh? He was a dickhead little Assistant DA who did just what Daddy said." He slurred. I pulled out from his grasp. "That's what he was. Now he thinks he's a big successful rancher," Hunter mocked. "A real leap in expertise from the law you tried to practice in Denver."

I put one hand on Hunter's chest, leaned in closer and said in his ear, "That's more than enough Hunter. You're rude and drunk on your ass."

Jake's voice was low and hard. "You damn well know I quit my law practice to ranch my family land. If you'd like, we can discuss my law career further. Your call, Hunter." Jake raised his beer to his lips and sipped casually.

"You're making a big mistake, Spooner." He jabbed his finger in Jake's chest. "You're in my world now, not some fancy DA's office." He shook his head in mock sorrow at me. "I'm so disappointed in you, Sawyer."

Jake glanced at Julia and Dave. "If you'll excuse us, I think we're finished here." He held out his hand to me.

"Julia, I'll talk to you later." I grabbed our plates. "I'll drop these by the kitchen and meet you out front, Jake. Here's my key. Will you ask for my car?"

"Sure. I'll have it ready for you."

I cut through the kitchen and found Hunter pouring diet Pepsi into Jim Beam. He spilled the Pepsi on the counter, clumsily wiping it up. He missed the sink when he tried to score one with the dirty towel.

"Ah," he said, taking a halting step forward. "Sawyer. I see you're finally alone," he mumbled. "My time now." He toasted me. "Drink with me. I could always count on Emily to have a nip with me. Not time for you to go yet." He slurred his words. He over extended his reach crashing his glass down on the edge of the counter. "Time for you and me, Emily." He picked up his Beam and Pepsi and took a big gulp.

"Hunter, I don't want to have a drink with you."

"You know what I want? I want to talk about our lives together. You and me, babe. You won't have to work. You can devote yourself to me and our children." He finished his drink and clattered the glass down on the granite top.

He swayed off balance. "Together, we can go to Paris. We'll have a good life. Travel. Money. You'd have all this." He gestured out the back of the house to the ranch. "And my heart." He stumbled, catching his balance on the counter top.

"Hunter, get this in your head. There's never going to be an *us*." I kicked a bar stool out from under the counter and pushed him on it. "Sit Hunter, and don't get up."

"No, you're wrong, Emily," he called softly to my back.

I found a waiter in the living room. "Mr. Kane needs some coffee, a lot of coffee. He's waiting for you in the kitchen."

* * * *

Lights blazed out Jake's front windows, lighting the parking area. Jake held the door for me. Chet waited expectantly in the hall reaching me first and bumping his big head on my leg. I obliged him with a head rub, receiving his delighted doggy grin. "Well, Ms. Cahill, you certainly know how to liven up a party." Jake tossed his keys onto the lamp table.

I dumped my purse and keys and opened my arms. Jake stepped in close, holding me fiercely.

When he let me go, I joined Chet on the sofa. "Hunter called me Emily twice tonight. Weirded me out. He's like a Svengali, so commanding, but nuanced in his controlling behavior. Like saying, 'our guests'. Behind that mask is something evil."

Jake sat down by Chet. "Hunter's a sociopath. All the classic symptoms—liar, glib, manipulative, no empathy," Jake said.

I shivered. "Even when he was showing warmth and compassion when he was telling me he would give me—or Emily—everything, it was more an act than a display of real feelings. And the lying, oh my god, Jake he was so charming and believable. What a narcissistic asshole."

Jake put his arm around my shoulder. "Sociopaths fool everyone with their charisma." He squeezed my shoulder. "I called an old FBI contact and told him about what was going on here. He put me in touch with his buddy, an FBI profiler who said the actions fit the profile of a sociopath.

I sat up. "Did you do that research before or after you told me to be careful of Hunter? Answer me Jake Spooner! How long have you thought he was a sociopath?"

"After. That's why I moved you in with me and took you to Yellowstone after we were run off the road," he said. "I'm your co-captain, *remember*?"

Swamped with regret, I apologized. "That was a knee jerk response. You've been more than a good captain, Jake. You've placed your life in danger to protect me. I'm so sorry." Crap, I felt awful about accusing him. "You didn't deserve that."

"Apology accepted. See how easy this trust thing is? I think you're getting the hang of it, Ms. Cahill."

"I'm afraid."

"Tell me about it."

"Tonight I asked Hunter why he didn't keep pictures of Emily in the house. He gave me his old line about having to go to a dark place. Remember he kept telling me that someday he would tell me how she died? But now, he's calling *me* Emily."

"What do you think he means by a dark place?"

"I don't know—it's just eerie. Foreboding. I feel something malevolent when I'm around him and I'm not a woo-woo woman! You know what else?"

"What?" He smoothed my hair behind my ear.

"Hunter has a locked closet in his bathroom."

"What you were doing in his bathroom looking at his closets?" Jake shot back.

"He took me upstairs to see his new bronze and I asked to use the bathroom." I blurted out, "But I couldn't get the lock open."

"You what? You tried to pick the lock on his closet? I don't know how much more you want to tell me without counsel."

"Yeah, well, I couldn't find anything to pick it with."

"There better not be another time. Breaking and entering is a crime. Some homeowners get a little upset about strangers in their closets. Some of them keep guns too, and know how to use them."

"Be interesting to know what Hunter needs to lock up in his closet."

"Leave it Sherlock. You wouldn't want to run into Hunter in his own house while you're picking his lock," Jake warned, getting up to close the curtains.

He yawned. "You ready for bed? I am."

"I'm too wound up. I'm going to work a bit."

Chapter 23

Morning came much too soon. I slept fitfully with Emily crowded into all my dreams. Her socialite picture morphed into my face. *What happened on Eccles Pass?* Clay buzzed my cell before the Laredo had cleared Jake's cow guard. "Yeah, I'm on my way in now. What's happening?"

"A couple of cattle on a ranch just west of town tested positive for brucellosis. The herd's going to slaughter today. Thought you might go out there and get some footage and a couple of interview bites."

"Sure. Give me directions," I answered. "His name's Wiley? Mike Wiley out at the Iron Horse? Yeah, I've met him. What mile marker off the highway? Okay. Got it." I scribbled the number on a post-a-note. "No, I have a camera and a microphone with me. Save me time in the first news block for the six o'clock."

By the time the Laredo rocked over the cattle guard onto the Iron Horse, a cattle truck was backing up to the pasture gate aligning with the narrow chute. The cattle were already in temporary pens, the bawling calves separated from their mothers. I hung my ID around my neck, checked the camera and headed toward Wiley.

"It's Sawyer Cahill with CBS3, Mr. Wiley. We met at Hunter's barbecue. Can you give me a minute?"

"Hell no, not now! That's my whole life they're hauling off out here." Mike rammed his fist down on the metal gate.

"Later then, Mike. When they're loaded. Tell my why they're taking the whole herd."

Two men rattled guide sticks on the sides of the narrow

chute forcing cattle up into the truck.

"You gonna tell your viewers what's happening out here?" He shouted over the din.

"When you *tell me* what's happening out here." Two cows bawling for their calves tried to turn and run back down the narrow chute. Two men stood on the railings and beat the ground, turning the cows back.

The final three cows bolted into the truck. "That's the last of them," Mike said, wiping the perspiration off his face with a dirty bandana. His sweat mixed with the thick dust making mud rivulets run down his neck. I used a lens cloth to wipe the brown dust from the camera several times before I framed Mike's face.

"Get that thing outta my face. I haven't said I'd talk to you," Mike bellowed.

"What happened out here, Mike?" I lowered the camera.

"What does it look like?" The wrinkles of anguish feathered through the sweat-streaked dust on his face. "I lost my herd, the whole lot of them. I woulda fed those calves out and sold them next year for a good profit. The government boys took 'em all, even though just a couple tested positive." Mike buried his face in his hands.

"I'm so sorry for you loss, Mike. How did you know you had a problem?" I asked.

"Had Sam Jordan out here to help with a cow in breach. He noticed two heifers lost their calves. He took some blood tests on the two who aborted. Called me the next day and said the mamas lost their calves because they had brucellosis. Sam said he'd have to report the outbreak. Next thing I know, I got trucks coming to my yard hauling away my herd." He ran his hand over his face.

"Do you get paid for your animals?"

"Next to nothing." He grimaced. "You're looking at fine breeding heifers and their calves hauled off to a slaughter. Robbed, I was robbed by my own government," Mike yelled, thrusting his fist into the sky.

"Mike." I refocused the camera. "Why does the whole herd have to be slaughtered?"

He dropped his fist. "The fuckin' USDA requires 'em all to be slaughtered!" He turned and glared at a man with a clipboard.

The man with the clipboard started moving our way.

"You get 'em all? Make sure you take my whole livelihood, you bastard," Mike said to clipboard man.

"I'm the Wyoming state veterinarian, Doug Gibbs," he said, shifting the clipboard to his left hand and extending his right to me.

"Sawyer Cahill. CBS3 News."

"Mr. Wiley, this is always a very difficult decision for the USDA and for me. I'm a vet. Nobody's happy about your loss."

"Why did they all have to be put down if they weren't all infected?" I asked Gibbs.

"Once any animal in a herd is found to be infected, the USDA requires all to be slaughtered to preserve the state's brucellosis-free status."

"Why can't you wait to see if any of the animals that tested negative get the disease?" I asked.

"Efficiency, I'm tellin' ya," Mike sniped. "These cattle were out in a pasture together. Hell, I don't know which ones of them came in contact with the after birth. So our government slaughters them all. Keeps the government boys from having to come back out and retest the herd."

"Not exactly, Mr. Wiley. We need to protect the other cattle and the livelihood of these other ranchers," Gibbs said. "We can't have a long, slow rolling of contagion through the herds."

"Wyoming is just brucellosis-free on paper." Mike's mouth turned down in a sour grimace. "The vet here is the Dutch kid putting his finger in the dike."

"The USDA studies Wyoming very carefully. If one more animal tests positive, Wyoming will lose its Brucellosis-Free state certification," Gibbs explained.

"Well, it doesn't look brucellosis-free to us cattlemen," Mike snorted. "Better come up with a better plan or dicker with your paperwork."

"What happens if Wyoming loses its designation of brucellosis-free?" I asked.

"No cow or buffalo will be allowed to cross the Wyoming state border. Not for grazing rights, or breeding and not for sale. No out-of-state rancher is going to send his animal here for stud either," Gibbs answered.

"When could the state reapply for a change of status?"

"The soonest the state can apply to regain class free status is a year from the date the last positive animal was killed."

"Do you have any recommendations, Mr. Gibbs?"

"Yeah, vaccinate your herd," Gibbs responded, checking boxes on his clipboard.

"Yeah, you're a state boy all right," Wiley said. "Add more costs to the rancher. Squeeze his profit down to nothing. But keep the state boys and the vets working."

* * * *

When I got to Clay's office, he was viewing a story off a camera. He looked up at me expectantly. "How much time did you give me on the six o'clock for the Iron Horse ranch story?" I asked.

"Look at this video clip," he said, turning the viewfinder toward me. George Carlisle was talking from behind his desk, but the volume was too soft for me to make out his words. "Carlisle called and said he'd make a statement to make to the press. I sent Benita over to cover it. Listen to it," Clay said.

I hit rewind. Carlisle walked into the frame and sat at his desk. Gazing directly into the lens, he said, "Today, I contacted all of our state senators asking for their support of the bill that our friend, Senator Mack McCormick, introduced. That bill demands the domestic buffalo herds be moved to state park land and put under state proprietorship until the brucellosis epidemic is under control. Our duty is to protect the primary business in Wyoming, cattle ranching."

I handed the camera back to Clay. "You know how many of the state senators are cattle ranchers?"

"I don't know." He scratched his head. "At least a couple," Clay ventured. "Why?"

"More than that I bet. Hold me some time in the six and ten," I said to Clay.

Out of the sixty state senators in the 61st Wyoming legislature, the top two occupations were rancher or oil-gas businessman. I called Senator Joe Phillips in his Cheyenne office. He was in his second term, representing southeastern Wyoming. "Good morning, Senator Phillips. Sawyer Cahill from CBS3 here in Cheyenne."

"Good morning to you too," his voice boomed in my ear. "Always happy to give you press people a few minutes. What can I do for you this morning?"

"This morning George Carlisle made a statement calling for all the state senators to support Senator McCormick's bill. Will you support the bill?" I asked.

"Well, my study of Senator McCormick's bill is in the very early stages. My aide called George's office not more than thirty minutes ago asking that he send us information he might have that is relevant to his bill."

"Is that a yes or a no, Senator?"

"Now, I've known George Carlisle for many years. My staff and I will give this my complete attention—consider everyone's interests. At the very least, there is the question of efficiency in implementing this bill. The state may not have the resources to impound and move the herds."

"Shall I tell your viewers you have no response?"

"I didn't say that, Ms. Cahill."

"What response would you like me to report?"

"That my staff and I are giving our utmost attention to this bill."

"Do you think the senate will be able to act on this issue without the perception of bias? Thirty-nine senators list their occupation as rancher."

I could hear the note of anger in his tight voice. "The senate debates legislation that affects ranchers during every session. Ranching is the primary business in this state." He lectured me. "The media can whip up their audience by alluding to perceived bias, but I can assure you that the senate is independent and unbiased."

I thanked Senator Phillips for his time and cradled my office phone. Clay had promised me the lead on the six and ten. Carlisle's demand and the senator's sound bite finished my story.

Dwayne stormed into my office. "I have to have the lead on the six o'clock. The university just hired their new football coach. We've been waiting for weeks for this announcement." He tucked his clenched fists into his crossed arms. "Your story will have to follow mine."

"Dwayne," I said, tapping my pencil on my note pad. "Clay's the news director. You'll have to convince him to change his decision of the run sheet order. Excuse yourself on the way out. I have to finish my story."

"I'm going to talk to Clay about this."

"I think you'll find that Clay is perfectly capable of doing his job," I called to his back.

So Dwayne was going to challenge Clay, and hopefully Clay would find a sports anchor that wasn't such a pain in the butt.

Chapter 24

Emily had wormed her way deep in my mind, churning my thoughts. I grabbed my cell phone. "Jake, do you remember the name of the coroner in Summit County?"

"Offhand I don't. Been awhile, but Sherriff McAfee is still around and he'll remember. I might have his number at home."

"Thanks, I'll get it online. I'm having Julia over for an early happy hour this evening."

"'Kay. Call me when you leave for the ranch. You've pissed off a bunch of the locals."

Sherriff McAfee's receptionist said he was out on a call and she didn't know when he would be back. I left my cell number, telling her I was reporter looking into an old case of his. I googled the white pages of Missoula, Montana and there was one L. Dominguez. "Hello," the female voice said.

"Ms. Leticia Dominguez?"

"Who is this please?" She asked with a bit of wariness.

"I'm Sawyer Cahill with CBS3 in Cheyenne. Here is the number of the station if you would like to call me back, 307-627-3741." Maybe that would put her at ease.

"What do you want?" she asked.

"I am looking into the death of Emily Kane. From the newspaper reports, you were a close friend of hers. Her husband has moved to Cheyenne—"

Leticia exclaimed bitterly, "He's in trouble I hope. Bad trouble."

"None that I know of." I answered smoothly. "Would you tell me what happened?"

"Poor Emily. She was afraid of him. Wanted me to call the

police if anything ever happened to her. That night he turned her out with no money, she came down to my house. She was so distraught. He'd called her a sniveling drunk and slammed the door in her face."

"How long did she stay with you?"

"Not long, maybe a week. When he found out what a divorce was going to cost him he called her saying it was all a mistake and they could start again. Emily wanted to believe him so badly. The fucking liar."

"Why didn't you believe Hunter?"

"I never believed anything the son-of-a-bitch said," she said angrily." I saw him one morning at the tennis club when Emily was staying with me. He said to me, 'I'm sure Emily can develop the mental maturity to accept my viewpoints.' How demeaning is that? The pompous ass. Moving back in with him wasn't gonna be any better for Emily."

"Why couldn't they make it be different?"

"The son of bitch wasn't capable of loving anyone but himself! He was so goddamn vindictive when Emily's drinking got out of control. Hell, she drank because he was destroying her. Here's this husband telling her he loves her and wants her back, but he's the same guy who threw her out in the street with a bag of clothes and wouldn't go down to Arizona to support her in rehab."

"Did you see Hunter after Emily died?"

"No, never saw the fucker. What would I have to say to him?" Her voice broke.

"Keep my number Leticia, and call me if you think of anything else."

"I will. I want to hear when they nail that asshole for something…anything."

* * * *

I was putting a few snacks together for happy hour when I heard Julia's car in the drive.

"Hello," Julia called. "I'm hungry." She snatched a chip. "Dave's busy going over accounts so he'll be late. I haven't seen much of you lately. So what's up?"

"What makes you think something's up?"

"I've rarely seen you handle food. Here you are, cutting up fresh fruit and heating something in the microwave. Something is up. What gives?"

I erupted into laughter. "Have some food." I handed her a plate.

We sat with a view of the short winter sunset. "I found out how Emily died."

Julia held her fork in mid air. "Bad? It's bad. I can tell by looking at you."

"Yeah. It's also off the record."

"How did she die?"

I told her the short version watching horror, disgust and anger converge on her face.

"Did they do an autopsy?" Julia asked.

"Barely. The coroner believed Hunter's story that she was drinking and lost her balance. 'A tragic accident,' the coroner said. Tragic accident my ass." I poured myself more wine.

"Is anyone still investigating?"

"Emily's death is a closed case. No one is asking any questions."

"But you are, aren't you? Asking for her sake?"

"I am. She deserves justice and a decent burial."

"How are you going to act like you don't know about Emily when you're around Hunter?"

"I can't act like I don't think he killed Emily. I'm no actress."

I listened to Julia vent about Emily's story and marital injustice. We gathered up the dishes in amicable silence and loaded the dishwasher.

"Change of subject," Julia said. "How long have you and Jake been lovers?"

"What?" I burst out, dropping a plate in the dishwasher. Damn, how did she know?

"You're smiling to yourself, humming too. Never mind saying 'yes' because it's so *obvious*." She hugged me. "I'm so happy for you Sawyer. You look so damn happy."

"I am."

* * * *

Jake had come home hours ago slipping into his office to give us girl time. One small lamp threw a circle of yellow light over him asleep on the sofa, a half-drunk beer in his hand. I almost had the can on the coaster when his hand reached out and circled my wrist. "My beer, woman. Don't take my beer."

"There's half of a warm beer in there sleeping beauty. It's all yours."

He brought the can to his mouth, thought better of it, and set it on the table. "You and Julia have some good time together?"

"We did. I told her about Emily."

"Figured you would," he said, putting his arm around my shoulders.

"She understands it's off the record." I relaxed into his warm chest

"How you doing with all this?" he asked.

"Better. Hunter's façade is so well crafted that I wonder if he has any discernment about who he is."

"Doubt it," Jake said. "That normal demeanor he so carefully projects hides all kinds of unpleasant traits from him too."

"God you feel good." I cuddled to him.

He pulled me into his lap and kissed me. "You know my shower is vacant."

"I have plans for it," I said, rising, taking his hand and pulling him into the bathroom.

"Let me see what we have here." Jake tugged my sweater over my head and tossed it on the bathroom floor. His hands moved across my shoulders gently unhooking my bra.

I jerked his tee shirt out of his jeans, running my hands down his hard chest. "I can't wait to see you standing here deliciously naked," he said, kissing one nipple.

My pants pooled at my feet. I kicked them to my sweater. "Much, much better," he said, bending to kiss and caress my breast.

Heat rippled through me. "My turn." I unbuttoned his jeans.

"You are so beautiful. You take my breath away," he breathed into my ear. I pressed myself against his hard cock. His fingers circled between my legs.

"I want you now." His lust wrapped around me, exciting me, emboldening me.

I jumped up on the counter and wrapped my legs tightly around his waist. My desire stoked his. His bent his head and that gorgeous mouth was even with mine. I nipped his swollen bottom lip, sucking it rhythmically before I ravaged his mouth. He turned to stone between my legs.

Jake licked and tasted down to my belly. Desire lashed through me. His tongue dipped below my navel, finding the wetness between my legs. I held my breath, pleasure racing through me when his tongue entered me. "Be in me *now*." I cried out.

Jake braced one arm on the counter. I begged him. "Now, now." His biceps wrapped around me, then he rose on his toes and thrust into me. I clung to his hips. The wild ride pushed me to the brink of my climax. Faster and deeper. I came wet, thrusting with him when he took his sweet release.

His head rested on my shoulder and my hands felt the muscles of his back ripple.

His breathing slowed to a gentle rhythm. He kissed my ear. "I believe we came in here to shower, did we not?"

"Can't remember. But we are in a bathroom and you do have a big shower."

Within thirty minutes, I was in a deep and dreamless slumber.

Chapter 25

Jake watched the six o'clock morning newscast, frowning and shaking his head no. "Babe, I don't think Carlisle has any possibility of enticing the legislature to take over buffalo ranching. There is no precedent in state law for nationalizing a private business, even if there were an epidemic."

"I don't either. How's the association reacting?" I asked.

"We're out ahead of this crisis, not reacting to. We're getting in the face of every legislator, lobbying them to support a vaccination program. The state's wildlife agency paired with us and they're demanding the reentry of the wolf and mountain lion. Morgan has a dual press conference scheduled tomorrow afternoon."

"Good work." I felt proud of his resourcefulness. "Pairing with a state agency should rock Carlisle back on his heels. His move was a brilliant media ploy, especially honing in on Wyoming being one diseased cow away from losing its brucellosis-free status."

"The press sets the agenda and the public forces the legislators to react."

"How are you justifying the costs of vaccinating?" I asked.

"We had a third party do a cost comparison of vaccinating and reintroducing predators to cull the wildlife versus doing nothing and risking losing our brucellosis-free status. Guess which provides profitability and stability to all the interested parties?" Jake asked.

"There's a lot of animosity to reintroducing predators..."

"I agree. But other states have successfully done it. I have a judge who will issue an injunction if the legislators pass the senator's bill. There won't be any implementation until a court of law looks at the issue of the state's commandeering private businesses."

"Do you think the state will lose its USDA status?" I asked.

"Definitely. There's a cow out there somewhere that's infected. It's not the end of the world for ranchers. Cattle ranching will still be a huge business in the state. When we lose our brucellosis-free designation, the legislators will have to address mandating vaccinations and reintroducing predators. They'll want a USDA free status for Wyoming to cover their own asses."

* * * *

I had barely sat down in my office when the phone rang. "Ms. Cahill, Sheriff McAfee from Summit County. You wanted to talk to me about a case?"

"Yes, thanks for the call back. I've talked with Jake Spooner—"

"Spooner, he was with the DA's office in Denver," he interrupted. "Then you want to talk about Emily Kane."

"Yes, Hunter Kane is a rancher here in Cheyenne…"

"He causing any trouble there?"

"Not that I know of."

"Then what stirred your interest in Emily's death, Ms. Cahill?" McAfee got to the point.

"Mr. Kane told me about her untimely death. He dodged my questions. Piqued my reporter's curiosity." I hoped that would convince him to talk to me.

"Damn straight, Emily's case would pique anyone's curiosity. The case may be closed, but I think about it every time I'm out near Eccles Pass."

"Jake told me the coroner who did the autopsy retired and left the area shortly after she died. Do you have contact information for him?"

"Last I heard he was in Durango. I wouldn't call what he did an autopsy. He'd made his mind up before he pulled back the sheet," McAfee said. "Her body was broken and battered. Had an eyewitness that said she was drunk when she fell. Didn't take long for him to rule it an accident."

"Do you think the coroner was paid off to rule it an accident?"

"Couldn't prove it," he said. "But maybe he was either careless with the autopsy or someone got to him."

"Do you remember his name?"

"His name is Barstow. Dr. Dave Barstow. Don't have a phone number." I heard him rustling paper. "No, don't have a number."

"Do you think Hunter killed his wife?"

"I think he was capable of it. I tried hard to prove it. Spooner did too."

"Will you call me if you think of anything else?"

"Yeah, and I want to know if Hunter screws up in Cheyenne," McAfee said.

* * * *

Benita caught me in the hallway outside my office. "Good stories the last couple of days," she said. "I checked the website. Plenty of viewers posted comments."

I grabbed my third coffee of the day and logged into the website. Scrolling through the comments, WyCowboy27 was drawing support for his idea of "having a special election and recalling any legislators who didn't support the senator's legislative request." Angus42 called George Carlisle a savior for cattlemen. Only Ridgewalker51 tempered the brewing stew by suggesting, "The legislators study the senate bill carefully to be fair to all involved." Plenty of viewers voiced their concern over "government bureaucrats who had never been out of the corner office killing our cattle."

I found Dave Barstow's number on one of the websites that sells private addresses, phone numbers, birthdays and anything else they can data mine. I called his house in Durango. All I got was the ex-coroner's voice mail. I identified myself and left a number. Best not to tell him I wanted to talk about Emily Kane.

* * * *

Mid afternoon, the station's receptionist brought a small box wrapped in brown paper to me. "This must have been hand delivered," Margery said puzzled. "I found it on my desk after my coffee break."

I took the box from her outstretched hand. "Delivered, not mailed." She tapped the top of the box. "See, it has no return address. Are you gonna open it?"

My focus narrowed to my name and the station's address cut out of letters and pasted haphazardly on the box. I speed-dialed Detective Jacoby.

"Detective Jacoby here," he answered distractedly.

"Sawyer Cahill. A package was hand delivered to me at

the station. Left on the front desk. I'm not expecting anything."

"Get everyone out of the station," he said urgently. "Put the box down gently and get everyone out of there. We're on our way. Get one hundred and fifty feet from the building. Go *now*."

Margery bolted down the long hall of offices toward the front door screaming, "Evacuate. The police say to evacuate. Get out *now*."

I sped down the other end of hallway toward Clay's office, located inside the soundproofed studio. Plus his hearing was crappy. "What the hell is Margery screaming about?"

"Suspicious package. The police are on their way. Come on, Clay. Get a move on. Move now!"

Clay and I joined the others huddled in the far corner of our parking lot. We couldn't get any further from the building without climbing over the fence into the supermarket's lot next door. Two squad cars roared up, followed by a windowless van.

A man dressed in an army green bomb suit sidestepped down the narrow metal stairs of the van. His suit was so bulky he had to turn his shoulders and head to look at Jacoby. Jacoby beckoned me to him. "Where's the package?" I gave directions to my office. The bomb-suited technician slapped down the visor on his helmet. He swiveled his hips more than bent his knees in the heavy suit, making slow work of carrying the container into the station. The crew and I stood quietly staring at the front door.

"Portable X-ray," Clay said. I bet he's got it in that van. He may even have some kind of high performance sensors in there. Thermal, infrared. Who knows what they got these days?"

Minutes later the technician emerged, carrying the container into the bomb squad's van. People swiveled their heads to stare at the closed metal door on the back of the van.

The technician popped his head out, flung up his visor and waved Jacoby over to the van. They talked a minute and Jacoby joined me, huddled on the fringe of the parking lot.

"It's not a bomb," he said. Nothing inorganic registered. No metals. Nothing. There is an object in the box though and the box is leaking," he said. "It's your property."

He turned to the small crowd that had gathered. "Show's over folks. Everything is fine. False alarm. You can go on back to work." He lowered his voice and said to me, "Come with me please." I followed him to the van. "You have to wear gloves and I suggest you open it inside the police van. Not because I think it's going to blow, but because I want whatever is in there kept quiet until we see what it is. Shall we?"

The technician had the box sitting on a metal fold down table. A damp spot covered the bottom of the box and one corner of the brown paper was wet. Jacoby handed me some gloves. I pulled off more of the sodden paper and opened the lid.

I gasped and rolled the metal chair back clanging into the van wall behind me. I wasn't sure what lay in the quart sized freezer bag, but I was sure it had once been alive. The rounded white ball was about five inches in circumference and came to an oval tip on one end. I poked it through the bag and it seemed to be semi frozen. The tip was soft, but the center was frozen hard.

"Wh-What is it?" I asked Jacoby. "Part of an animal?"

"My guess is you're looking at a slightly thawed bull testicle. If we're lucky, someone saw the dumb bastard delivering it or he left prints on the box." He pulled a plastic evidence bag from his coat and snapped on a pair of gloves. He tightened the lid on the box and slipped it into the evidence bag.

"Why send it to me?" I stammered before I thought.

"How the hell would I know?" Jacoby asked, irritably sealing and tagging the bag. "I'm a detective, not a shrink. Reconfirms my belief he's a sick bastard. Don't go anywhere without

texting a friend your plans. Don't go anywhere alone."

"What can I say when I go back into the station?"

"Tell 'em what you want to. Thing like this is going to leak." He enjoyed the pun.

"So you think the mutilator sent it?"

"How many guys with sharp knives do you know who are currently pissed off at you? Yeah, I think it's him." Jacoby said. He softened. "You want a man to stay here at the station for awhile? Follow you home? I got the man power for that, but I can't give you a permanent body guard."

"Yeah, thanks," I said. A uniformed policeman followed me back into the station and took up his position in the reception area. I waved a thanks to him heading toward the newsroom. I felt safer with him sitting up front by Margery. Poor him, she would chat his ears off.

Everyone was amped. We report the news; we rarely make it. I could hear Margery's high-pitched shrill telling her story to anyone who came near the reception desk.

"What was in the box, Sawyer? Did you get to see it?" Tobin shouted over the din in the newsroom. I explained the contents of the box, but refused to give a sound bite on camera. I didn't want to give my harasser the pleasure of seeing me upset on television.

"You wanna call it day, sounds fine by me," Clay said. "You call me if you need anything." He patted my shoulder.

"Thanks, Clay. I'm leaving."

I punched in Jake's number hoping he was already at the ranch. "Jake? You at the house? I'm on my way."

"What's wrong? You sound different."

"I got a package delivered here at the station. Shook me up. I'll tell you about it when I get there."

"Do you want me to come pick you up?" He offered quickly. "We can go back and pick your car up anytime."

"No, I have an officer who is following me home. Be there shortly," I answered. All I could think about was getting away from the station and to the warmth of Jake's home.

The house never looked better. Porch light on. Smoke pouring out of the chimney into the cold evening. The officer behind me flashed his lights and turned out of the drive.

I grabbed Jake and clung to him. "God, I'm glad to be here." The relief poured out of me and I relaxed into his embrace, appreciating his calm strength.

"Sit down, babe." He steered to me the sofa. "What's happened? Tell me."

I told him. A look of repugnance passed over his face.

"I can live with this crazy bastard in my life until he's caught. I can do this." The repetition was to convince me, not Jake.

"You don't have to do it alone. I'm not going anyplace."

"I want my life back. The one where I don't have to watch my back."

"Can't right now, babe." He kissed me gently on the cheek. "But you're safe here. I have a lot of ranch hands who are watching your back. You'll have a shadow every day."

My breathing quieted, my hands stilled. I was suddenly very tired.

His mouth quirked up on one side. "Plus, I have a great shower."

"Ah yes." He had made me smile like he meant to. "The shower."

"I bet you're hungry. I'll make us some sandwiches." Jake said, moving into the kitchen. I watched him slice the meat, joining him at the counter. I helped him prep the food and pretended everything was normal.

I stacked my plate in the dishwasher. "I talked to Leticia Dominguez today."

"You have been busy today. I remember her. McAfee and I both talked to her during the investigation." He poked the fire and added a log.

"Was she bitter and resentful about Hunter when you talked to her?" I asked.

"No, she was just grieving the loss of Emily."

"Well, she's bitter now." I told Jake about my call to Leticia.

"I'm going to call Dave Barstow again. Maybe I can catch him at home."

"Barstow...Barstow," Jake murmured.

"The coroner who performed the autopsy on Emily." I filled in. "I talked to McAfee today too." Barstow's phone rang five times and went to voice mail. I left my message again. "Wonder if Barstow is screening his calls." I tossed the phone on the coffee table.

"What did you learn from McAfee?"

"Nothing new. He's hoping I catch Hunter doing something. Guess what? Leticia said the same thing."

Jake leaned back into the sofa and crossed his long legs. "We need something to look forward to. Another diversion. I swear I never had to think of so many diversions for one woman," he teased. "I got tickets to the Dierks Bentley concert next Saturday night at Cheyenne Frontier Days. You on?"

"I wouldn't miss it. Let's go to the rodeo on Saturday, too."

He reached into his front pocket and held up two box seat tickets for Saturday night. "Got them. Wear tight jeans."

Chapter 26

I've always had the ability to stand back from myself and dispassionately analyze my feelings. I think I learned by copying my Dad who trained himself to stow his emotions and rely on logic. I'm not perfect, but I can freeze frame the facts long enough to keep the emotions at bay and make a good decision. I was on a quest for facts.

There were fewer pink phone messages impaled on the spike on my desk. Flipping through them, I found one from Barton. No fingerprints but Margery's and mine on the box holding the testes. Another dead end.

I glanced at my watch. Logan Matthews was probably in his office by now.

"Logan, Sawyer here. How are you?"

"Good to hear your voice, my dear. I guess you have something you think I can help you with." I could hear him rapping his stained pipe on that chipped ashtray of his.

"I do." I laughed. "Have a minute?"

"I've got a few minutes before my patient walks in."

"Thanks, Logan. Here's the short version." I told him about the testes and the tail left in my kitchen.

"Sending you a totem is interesting behavior. I could argue he is sharing his power with you or that he's threatening you. I don't have enough information to make a decision." His chair creaked under his weight. "Breaking into your home and defiling it is a personal act of primitive rage fueled by unmet needs."

"Does he know what he needs?"

"Probably not. He's created a social facade, walling his anger off from his conscious mind."

I heard a buzzer in the background. "Well, my dear, my patient just came in the waiting room. Stay in touch."

I was scribbling notes on Logan's opinion when my mom called. "Hi Mom."

"Sawyer, you haven't called me in days. Do you know how that makes me feel?"

"I'm sorry, Mom." *How many times have I said that?* "Really, Mom, don't be upset."

"If you ever have children, you will understand. A mother doesn't want to be cut out of her daughter's life."

"Mom! You are an important part of my life."

"I don't know about that Sawyer. I don't know at all about that." She changed her tactics. "You still working on those disgusting stories? Can't you find some other...some other, er,—beat—isn't that what you people call it?"

"Mom, I'm a news reporter. I investigate. I tell the stories of the world people live in. For them. For their lives."

"You make it sound like a higher calling, a duty."

"A free press *is* the bedrock of democracy."

She retreated from talking about my job. "How's that young man up here?"

Maybe this ground would be easier to cover. "He's wonderful, Mom."

"Is he good to you?"

Well of course, he's keeping me safe from an attacker.

"Yes, he's very good to me. I love you. I'll be in touch. I promise."

Dwayne was standing in the threshold of my office. "Finished with the personal call? Good. Clay has assigned me as field producer for the rodeo and all our news coverage from Frontier Days. He knew I had the ability to cross over from the sports angle to the soft news we'll cover from out there. I've got your assignments for Frontier Days." A smug smile inched across his face. He made a show of flipping through several sheets of his reporter's notebook. He reminded me of preening peacock at a zoo. "Here we are. Benita will be photographer for both you and Tobin's remotes."

"Tobin's doing the weather as a remote from the site? Our truck will handle his graphics?"

"The truck will handle the challenge. Tobin? That remains to be seen." He turned back one page, his finger running down the paper. "Friday, I want you to do a series of feature stories. Cover the Art Show early Friday morning. Then, go to the Indian encampment and get some video. Dancing, get them dancing. You're covering the shopping in Wild Horse Gulch, too."

"Look Dwayne, I'm not a features reporter. My strength is hard news reporting."

He interrupted me. "It's an opportunity. You can broaden your scope of experience. Use it on your resume. Several people here need to work on their resumes." He cocked one eyebrow. He was looking better and better for the peacock. *Insufferable little man.*

Dwayne droned on about the assignments. "By the time you finish covering the Balloon Glow, we'll have to get Tobin's evening weather update." He stood in the doorway of my office. "You've heard him lately, haven't you? He's been working with a voice coach to help him with his southern boy accent. I could get the voice coach to work with you too. You picked up a trace of an accent working in Texas. Not good for your career." He angled out of my office.

"I'm declining your sweet offer of voice lessons," I shouted to his back.

My cell was tap dancing on my desk. "Sawyer, Hunter here. I think I owe you an apology for my behavior Saturday night. I wet my beak a little more than usual. I apologize."

"You're right. You put on quite a drunken show."

"I'm so glad you understand." His breath whooshed out in relief. "I want you to join me at Cheyenne Frontier Days. We need some fun together. We'll be in my box seat for the final rodeo performance and you'll be on my arm on the floor of the arena when I award the grand prizes. I promise you a special time. You can join me for the other events, too. I'm awarding the trophies for the balloon races. I'll be involved in just about every event of the Frontier Days. Be out there most of the weekend. We'll have a great time! Say yes, Sawyer."

Is this the way you planned everything and announced it fait accompli to Emily? I don't dance to your tune. "No, you misunderstand. We aren't a couple."

"Well then." His voice stiffened, becoming more formal. "I assume I'll see you there. We can have a drink together. Until then, Sawyer." He hung up.

Chapter 27

Dave Barstow's phone rang for the fourth time as I rocked over the cattle guard. I knew I needed to come in fast and hard with him. He wouldn't talk to me if he knew I was a journalist. Especially if he had taken a bribe. He had a new life, and after this much time, he probably thought he was safe from discovery—and he damn well might be. I figured the only way to approach him was to ask questions first before I had to reveal my identity.

I thought I would once again get his voice mail when a women's voice answered, "Hello?"

I pulled to a stop, cutting the engine. I didn't give my name, just asked to speak to Dave Barstow.

"Dave's not in. Would you like to leave a message?" She asked.

"No, thank you." Before I could say anything else, the line was dead.

Barstow, Hunter, Carlisle, Walker, Sam. The list was too long, frustrating me. Carlisle was an old man. Calling the senators was probably all the strength he had. But Carlisle had money to hire anyone to do his bidding. Maybe Walker had the brains to plan and do the dirty work. I just didn't have much information about Walker—it was like he materialized out of foster care to employment at the auction house. Sam had the brains, motive and skill. Vets don't mutilate animals, right? Hunter? Hunter had brains, skills, money, motive and a locked closet. It was what I missed that always came back to bite me in the ass.

* * * *

I found Jake in the kitchen, adding greens to a huge salad. Wafts of grilled chicken made me ravenous. "Will you do this every night?" I asked.

He bent down and kissed me softly. "Expect it and you shall have it." The kiss lingered until Jake broke the spell. "Hope your day was more interesting than mine. I've spent the day calculating how much auxiliary feed I'll need this winter and then bidding on it." He moved efficiently around the island to the refrigerator. "Oh, and I also talked with Barton today."

"What did Barton say?"

"No new leads. He's trying to hang it on Walker," Jake said, stirring his salad dressing.

"Does the district attorney think he has enough evidence to put Walker on trial?" I snagged a tomato out of the salad. "Would you try him?"

"Unlike the district attorney, I can't see all the evidence. From what I know, I wouldn't put Walker on trial. He was at the kill site carrying a knife. I'd have to know his knife was the weapon used. Remember, Sam said the mutilator used a small, very sharp knife. Walker had an ordinary, large-bladed knife like a lot of guys."

"I can't see Walker as a planner. But I can see him being bought," I mused.

"Don't talk to Walker." He looked up from the salad he was tossing. "Saying that to you is like waving a red flag at a bull."

We sat at the kitchen bar in companionable silence enjoying dinner. "I talked with Logan Matthews today. Without more information he doesn't know what leaving the tail means." I popped a sweet pepper in my mouth.

"Oh, and let me guess, he told you to be careful." Jake wasn't smiling and his fingers were tapping his leg.

"Yes, he did." My voice softened and I trailed a finger down Jake's cheek. "He can't forecast what's going to happen, Jake."

"I can. If this doesn't get resolved soon, you're taking a leave of absence and we are going on a nice long trip involving beaches, hot tubs and endless days of sun."

* * * *

Frontier Days dawned clear and bitterly cold. "You have all the gear you need?" I asked Benita.

"Yes." She stowed some field lights in the truck. "Where do we start?"

"According to Dwayne's schedule, we're to start at the Old West Museum, then hoof it over to catch the drum and dance group in the Indian village. We'll have to hurry to get you over to Tobin's weather shot at noon."

The Indians weren't dancing on Dwayne's schedule so we were race-walking back to the remote truck. Benita huffed, "You heard the news about Dwayne?"

"No, did he get fired yet?" I gulped in the frigid air.

"I wish," she said. "Dwayne's been putting out his resume for months now. He got an interview down in Colorado Springs with the Fox bunch. He didn't get the job. He's telling everyone 'working here has taken the edge off my skills.' I'm guessing that's why he's in such a snotty mood." She threw back her head and laughed. "We're pulling down his job performance."

We rounded the back of the truck and found Tobin staring at the small monitor at his feet. "Get ready, Tobin." Dwayne barked. "You have a forty-five second window. It's live. Don't screw it up. Benita, get over here. Move your camera. Your angle is off."

I quit listening to Dwayne give orders when I noticed Hunter and Tom Walker having an animated conversation on the footpath to the parking lot. Tom's right hand made an angry jab in the air in front of Hunter's face. Hunter reached up and swatted down the offending hand. Tom bunched up both shoulders and fisted his hands at his sides. Hunter leaned into Tom's face and spat out some quick words. *I can't hear a damned thing over Dwayne.* Hunter stalked around the corner out of sight. I hurried after Walker. "Tom, Tom Walker," I called to his back. He turned, looking none too happy to see me. "You and Hunter didn't look like you're on very good terms. You have some problem?" Walker's face furrowed and his shoulders rolled forward. He didn't lock eyes with me or speak. He hurried away, waving his arm at me in a "go away" gesture. *What upset Walker?*

"And out," Dwayne was saying when I got back to the truck. "Look more alive for the audience at your afternoon shot, Tobin. You two need to get to the Wild Gulch. Should be spot on for you girls, shopping and all." He sniffed in my direction.

Wild Horse Gulch was a replica of an old west town with boardwalks connecting the saloons with the shops. "Look." Benita held up a pair of frilly pantaloons to herself. "What do you think? Red ones under a denim skirt?"

With one pair of red frilly pantaloons in tow, we covered the Gulch. It looked like fun poking into tiny little shops and antique places.

"Meet you at the Balloon Glow this evening," I said to Benita when we dropped the footage at the remote truck.

* * * *

I speed-walked out to my Jeep. Now or never for Hunter's locked closet. Too damn bad he wasn't out of town. I'd feel a whole lot safer knowing he couldn't turn up at the house for a fresh shirt.

If I remembered correctly, his live-in housekeeper had her quarters back by the garage. With luck, she was watching TV with the volume cranked up high.

I parked in a pull-out on the highway and walked to Hunter's house, circling around the barn for cover from the front. Coming up behind the house, I peeked around at the driveway. No cars parked on the drive. Garage doors closed.

The thorns on the hedge under Hunter's office windows were a bitch to get through, snagging my sweater, tearing at my skin. Hunter's empty office glowed, lit by a single lamp throwing a weak circle of light into the empty hallway by the front door. I slipped on my gloves. Tried the window. Locked. Damned holly. I pushed back through the spiny leaves trying the windows along the side of the house. All closed and locked. She was a careful one, that housekeeper. On the north side, the laundry room window stood open a tiny slit. I could feel warm damp air pushing out and hear the washer and dryer noisily thumping. I tugged the window silently along the track and crawled on top of the washer. From the doorway, I heard a vacuum cleaner somewhere on the first floor.

I crept out of the laundry room into the empty kitchen, my rubber-soled boots squeaked on the freshly mopped tile floor. The vacuum stopped. I looked frantically for a place to hide. The walk-in pantry. I eased in and slipped off my boots. Over my thudding heart, I could hear scraping sounds. I could only see straight down to the wet tile through the slats of the pantry door. *Hunter's going to be livid if she scratches his hardwood floors with that vacuum.* The vacuum started up again, further away, coupled with an off-key rendition of some song I didn't recognize.

I eased into the hall, pausing at the staircase. She was vacuuming the dining room off to my right. I ran lightly up the stairs in my stocking feet, keeping to the sides of the treads to avoid the creaking middle. I flattened myself to the wall at the top. No one in the upstairs hall. The bedroom doors were all open, but the rooms were gloomy in the gathering evening. I hurried down the hall to Hunter's bedroom.

The lamp on the nightstand illuminated a pile of fresh towels dumped on the bed. The soft light filtered into the bathroom. I pulled my lock picks out of my fanny pack. Amazingly useful tools that I bought on the Internet along with DVD instructions. Asking the guy in the red vest at Home Depot about B&E was not an option.

I inserted the L-shaped tension wrench into the lock, applying pressure. I gently turned the lock counter clockwise. No movement. Turning the wrench clockwise, I felt the give. I held my breath. From inside the master bedroom with its thick carpet and drapes, I could barely hear the vacuum from downstairs.

I slipped the thin metal pin in the keyhole and felt for the individual lock pins. I pushed them up into the cylinder while increasing the torque on the wrench. The lock made a satisfying click when it popped.

In! I'm in. I pulled the solid closet door shut. Two low shelves lined the long walls of the closet. A corkboard hung on the back wall. Something smelled faintly like my high school chemistry lab.

I raked my flashlight along the length of one shelf. Floating eerily in a jar, illuminated by the harsh glow of light, was a buffalo testis. Large glass jars lined the shelf. Each jar had small whitish organs floating in a pale yellow liquid. My breathing was fast and shallow. *Relax. In and out.* On the shelf behind me was another row of jars filled with organs. I aimed the light at the corkboard. Snapshots of women. Newspaper stories. More pictures. Pinned in perfectly straight rows by size. I fingered the pictures, my heart pounding in my ears. *Pictures of me! Walking into the station, sitting with Julia outside the Albany. Unlocking my front door.* Sweat slicked my face. I yelped with fear, bumping the shelf, causing waves of yellow liquid to make the floating organs gently sway. He came in here to worship his bloody trophies. The primeval, reptilian part of my brain murmured, *Go now.*

Her singing was clearer and a lot closer. I killed the flashlight. Her song didn't cover her footsteps on the tile bathroom floor. I backed up to the corkboard. No place to hide. When she yanked open the other closet, I grew dizzy, steadying myself on the unused closet rod. In a few minutes, she snapped the door shut, her footsteps tapping out of the bathroom. I crept to the closet door and listened.

I waited five long, agonizing minutes in the dark. Silence. Only then, did I feel safe enough to shine the flashlight on the corkboard. I looked more closely at the other woman. *Emily.* A younger Emily with long hair. Emily posing with a dog, standing outside a house smiling and waving. Emily in a blue windbreaker on a trail in the mountains. The resemblance between us was uncanny. I wanted to jerk my pictures off and stuff them in my pack. *You can't have pictures of me!* Instead, I opened my phone and took a rapid set of photos, hoping the flashlight gave my camera phone the light it needed.

He came here to gloat and relive his glory, looking at the pictures of the woman he destroyed. And me, what is he planning for me? I shivered. *Now, go now.*

Silence from outside the closet. I opened the door and crept into the bedroom. The pile of towels weren't on the bed. At the door of Hunter's bedroom, I could hear a door close downstairs. No singing and no vacuuming. *She had to stop singing now? Where the hell was she?*

I tiptoed into the hallway, crouched down and peeked through the stair railing. No one. I raced down the stairs, and then slipped into the pantry for my boots. The washer and dryer were silent. I climbed up on the washer. My fingers were trembling so badly I fumbled the window lock. I grabbed with both hands and pulled harder, sliding the stubborn window on its track. I scrambled, ducking low, looking for anyone around me. No one was watching when I pulled the window shut.

I weaved my way through the brush to my Jeep. Nervous sweat poured down my face to drip onto my torn sweater. My hand shook so hard I could barely press the unlock button. I slipped into the car and rested my head on the wheel. I was exhausted and smelled of rancid sweat. I felt the first quiver of losing it. Hunter put the message on the car at the Albany. Thank god, he never hurt Julia. He sent the emails and the box. Oh my god, he sent the box to the station! His raging, twisted sense of reality sent shivers down my back. Did he pay Tom? Is Tom innocent? The answer coalesced in my fevered brain. Hunter saw the dust trail of Tom's truck coming toward the windmill. He left in a hurry leaving Tom to stumble on the scene and take the fall.

Now you just have to prove it.

* * * *

Teenage boys in yellow safety vests waved my car into the flat dirt field. Colorful hot air balloons ringed the field, hissing gas and penetrating the growing darkness with their colored orbs. The tailgaters were in full swing, the air smelling of grilled meat and wood smoke. I saw Benita waving to me from the northwest corner of the field. "Hey, Sawyer, Dwayne wants us to cover the awards ceremony after the Balloon Glow. Did he tell you? It's a live shot from the dance floor."

"No, he didn't." I said.

"You okay? You don't look like it."

"Yeah, I'm fine." I lied. Get yourself together. You have to see Hunter at the ceremony.

Benita and I walked to the remote truck backed in by the soundstage. "Hey, Sawyer, over here," Harold called. The chief engineer for CBS3 was peering at a vectorscope that monitored the video signal. "We've good signal coverage from out where the balloons are. We're set for your first live shot. When Mr. Kane presents the awards on the dance floor, you'll be live, too. Both times I'll cue you from your headset."

"Thanks for your help." I grabbed my headset on the way out.

My crews were in position on three sides of the field. I gave a few last minute directions over my headset, then watched the footage of the glowing balloons and happy tailgaters on the field monitor. My hands were trembling when I adjusted my earpiece. Crowding my tenuous hold on control was my revulsion for Hunter's depravity. Two children passed me, chatting happily and pulling spun sugar from their cones of cotton candy. Keeping time to the beat of their skipping steps was my mantra: *They all look so normal. They all look so normal. They don't know who walks among them.*

"Good job everyone. Let's set up for the awards ceremony." I stripped off my head set and stuffed it in my bag, breathing a sigh of relief.

Over by the soundstage, the mayor and Hunter were in position and wired for sound. Benita counted down the crew. I gave the signal to roll when the mayor began to talk about the importance of Frontier Days. Hunter was smiling and nodding his enthusiastic approval at the mayor's side. Hunter awarded the trophies to the top three racers and ended with, "A special thanks to CBS3 for hosting the Balloon Race for the fifth year."

"And in five we'll be out—five, four, three, two, one— and we're out," I called. "Good show, everyone. Enjoy the evening." I took out my earpiece and ran for the nearest exit.

The first few bars of Sugarland's latest hit boomed from the speakers. I rounded the soundstage crossing into the darkness. My adrenaline was still amped. Where was Jake?

An arm reached out of the darkness grabbing my right arm. "You save a dance for me?"

"Shit," I croaked. I whirled around, my left fist ready for an upper cut.

He snaked out his other arm, powerfully pulling down my left fist. "Sawyer, it's me. Jake."

My strength crumbled and I sagged into him.

"What the hell is going on?"

"Get away from the stage! I want to get away from the stage." I frantically pulled away.

He cinched his arm around my waist, half dragging me to the dark parking lot.

"I broke into Hunter's locked closet," I panted.

"You what?" He hissed into my ear. "Are you crazy? He could have walked in on you!"

"He was here all day playing big important person." I could see the dark form of my Jeep looming in the shadows.

In the gloom, I saw the raw emotions of love, anger and fear cross his face.

"I can hardly wait to hear this one, Ms. Cahill." He opened the Jeep's door "Drive to the edge of the parking lot and wait until I get there. Lock your doors." He tapped on the Jeep's roof and was gone.

Chapter 28

Jake strode up the porch, flung open the door and flipped on the hall lights. I followed his snapping boot heels back to the den. He turned on two lamps and looked at me. "You want something to drink? I want you to be comfortable when you tell me about your breaking and entering."

"Jake, it was an acceptable risk." I slumped in the chair. "Hunter told me all the events he was involved in today with Frontier Days when he asked me to join him."

"What?" Jake interrupted. "That's a sentence chock full of information. He asked you for a date? After that scene at the barbecue?"

"Jake, stop it." I was standing now an inch off his nose. "Hunter's nothing to me and you know it. You're just pissed and yeah, maybe afraid for me because I broke into his house. The useful information was that Hunter was going to be busy in Cheyenne all day." I pushed his shoulders and he fell back into the deep sofa cushions. "Now that you're seated, we can talk about the jars full of animal parts in Hunter's closet. He has pictures of Emily and me on a corkboard in there, too. Look," I demanded, pulling up the pictures on my phone.

"Hell yes, I'm angry and worried." He snatched the phone from my hand and scrolled through the pictures. "Jesus, you've lost your mind." Jake looked over at me. "Do you have any idea how dangerous this was? He could have walked in and surprised you in there."

"But he didn't." I reached over and put my hand on Jake's. "I took a chance. I was lucky. I admit it." I took the phone back from him.

"You scared the hell out of me."

"I'm sorry."

"Now what?" He demanded. "These pictures can't be used against him."

"He's an animal mutilator. He killed Emily and now he's so crazy he calls me by her name."

"He's obsessed with you. Look at the pictures he has of both of you. Calling him crazy is an understatement," Jake said. "Plus you publicly humiliated him by telling him you were with me."

"Hunter's stressed now and he'll make a mistake."

"Lousy idea..." Jake began.

"You'll be with me," I said.

He reached over and began to stroke my hair. He massaged my shoulders. "I'm going to be stuck to you until this is over."

"I know. I trust you." I surprised myself with the statement, then surprised myself again by *feeling* the trust in Jake.

"Damn well should." He slid his finger down to the hollow of my throat, lowered his head, and kissed me.

I got comfortable that the storm had passed too soon. Jake challenged, "How did you get into his house? I want to hear it all." His hands had quit massaging.

"Over the top of his washing machine. From there, I had clear path to his closet." I omitted the obstacles of Hunter's housekeeper folding laundry two feet from me.

"You didn't break the lock on that closet did you? How did you get in the closet Sawyer?" he asked, suspiciously.

"The closet looks exactly like it did when I walked in there."

"You didn't answer the question," he shot back.

"I know." I sighed. "I own a set of lock picks."

"Did you leave any trace in there? Anyway you can be put in his house?" The lawyer was talking now.

"I had to leave the laundry room window unlocked. The cleaning lady will think she forgot to lock up after she finished running the wash."

"Tell me you wore gloves." Jake shook his head.

"Of course, I wore gloves. No one can tell I was in there and nothing is missing. Why would Hunter call the cops to fingerprint? He has a closet full evidence to hide. If he did call the cops, I was in his house and his bathroom during the barbecue, leaving prints everywhere. Stop worrying," I reasoned.

"I have the vaguest feeling this is not your first time to do something like this," Jake replied.

If the sphinx could smile, Jake was looking at her.

"I need a scotch." Jake headed for the kitchen. "What do you want?"

"A vodka martini, please." I followed him into the kitchen, wrapping my arms around his back. God, he felt solid.

"You less tense?" He poured my martini into the icy glass.

"Some. And it's about to get better still." I took the martini from him.

"I figure my heart rate will settle down in a couple of days, Ms Cahill," he said, squeezing the nape of my neck.

"Come here." He sat next to me on the sofa. That single dimple made his mouth look delicious. I kissed that adorable lower lip. His response was quick and urgent.

He did the Groucho Marx leer. "I think you might need a shower after all your hard work today."

We never made it to the shower. I slipped my arms around his neck while his gentle kisses skimmed along my nose and cheeks. His lips glided across mine, lingering a moment. Deeply aroused, I tingled from his touch. His hands on my bottom caused an aching want in my belly.

"Come upstairs." I whispered. He picked me up and carried me up the stairs, laying me on the bed. He unbuttoned my blouse and ran his index finger over the mounds of my breasts spilling out of my bra. My breasts burned under the lazy attention of his circling fingers. His hand trailed down to the zipper on my jeans. He tantalizingly drew them off, kissing my thighs, my calves, my foot. I reached for his belt and pulled his jeans off his hips. He kicked them to the foot of the bed and quickly shrugged his shirt off his shoulders, tossing it to the floor.

"I love seeing you naked." His huge gray eyes were level with mine.

"Wrap your legs around me tightly." His lips closed on my eager mouth. His hands found mine, linking my fingers. He pulled our hands above my head. I opened my eyes when he broke the kiss. "Watch us become one," he whispered huskily, rising up to bear his weight on his arms. I arched to join with him watching him slowly enter me, making me quiver with anticipation for him to drive into me, filling me. Then he plundered fast and hard, pouring himself into me, carrying me over the edge of reason. I lay sated, feeling the warm glow of great sex. Jake rolled to his side and I stared into his eyes, still dilated with desire. *The urgency and pleasure of sex magnifies with danger.*

He pulled me into the curve of his body. "You are a beautiful lover. So giving."

"I may not move until morning," I murmured, closing my eyes.

But sleep twisted into weird dreams of Hunter holding a knife over Emily, and then her face morphed into mine. When I awoke, I was tired and restless.

* * * *

Weak sunshine did little to warm the brittle cold when Jake and I walked into the midway on Saturday. The carnival was doing a brisk business. Kids jumped up and down and clung to their less enthusiastic parents while standing in line for the Zipper and the Sky Flyer.

I looked up at Jake. "Hey, they're selling fried beer on the midway. Want to get some and go for a ride on the Tilt-a-Wheel?"

"No and no. How do you fry beer?"

"Dough. Texans fry anything. You can fry ice cream, beer, even butter. The trick is wrapping it in dough and frying it very quickly in extremely hot oil."

Jake slowed his step. "Look who's coming this way."

"Sawyer, I see you made it here to our town's little celebration." Hunter rocked on the balls of his feet, approving my attendance. "Could I interest you in joining me for a drink? I'd like to make up for my behavior at the barbecue. There's a nice wine bar. Shall we?"

I grabbed Jake's hand, pulling him close. "*Jake* and I will join you in about an hour. I promised myself a little shopping." I didn't look back at Hunter when we walked away. I wanted some time to think about taking any opportunity with Hunter.

"What's going on in your head? Because I like a little warning," Jake said.

"What are you talking about?"

Jake stopped abruptly. "Do I have to say be careful? If I put my hand on your leg under the table, I mean for you to stop talking right then. Do you understand?" The lawyer had reappeared and was lecturing his client.

"I completely understand what you just said."

Unmoved, Jake continued patiently, "I meant what I said." His eyes drilled into mine. "Fear keeps you safe. Start feeling it."

I listlessly traipsed through a couple of shops, killing time, not in the mood now for browsing. Jake followed behind me, not faring much better. "We better start toward the wine bar if we're going to have a drink with Hunter before the rodeo starts."

Hunter was sitting at a table in the back of the bar with a nearly empty bottle of red wine. He beckoned us over. "What will you have? The merlot is excellent. I was about to order another bottle. Sawyer, they have the great Riesling we enjoyed at our dinner at the Albany." He tapped his fingertips together in front of his flushed face.

"I'll get the next bottle of merlot and a glass of white for Sawyer." Jake headed for the bar, leaving me alone with Hunter.

"Enjoy your shopping?" Hunter asked me. "Jake buy you something special?"

"We enjoyed—"

Hunter cut me off. "I have box seats for the rodeo this afternoon. Would you like to join me?"

Jake returned, saving me from explaining again to the narcissist that we were not a couple. Cold shuttered through me. Hunter's eyes were overly bright in his pale face. Jake refilled Hunter's glass. "Thanks, but we'll be in my box right on top of the chutes."

Fury darkened his face for a nanosecond until he mastered his reaction and his face became neutral. "I see. You've heard, I suppose, the DA is worried about not having enough evidence to take Tom Walker to trial?"

He was a changeling, his face oozing amiability, his body relaxed as he baited his trap.

"I heard something about that," Jake replied.

"Not like you, is it Jake? When you were in the DA's office? You weren't ever too bothered by the lack of evidence."

"Evidence, there's an interesting word," I said.

Jake squeezed my thigh and interrupted me. "Walker's case has no similarity to any of my cases."

"Oh, yes, it's very similar." Hunter's smile looked so out of sync with his words. "You tried to pin a murder charge on me after my wife's death. You and that dimwitted Sheriff of Summit County called in the feds. You investigated Emily's death for over a year, twisting the facts. But you couldn't touch me," Hunter leaned back expansively in his chair, folding his hands behind his head.

"The DA's office didn't investigate Emily's death to harass you. We were Emily's advocates." Jake was leaning forward. His hand had forgotten my thigh.

"And you found nothing to hang on me, her grieving husband."

I interrupted him in a low voice. "I know how she died." Jake's hand was back tapping a frantic beat on my thigh. "You killed her." Instantly, dark fury clouded his face, all trace of charisma erased.

"You're a liar." He hissed. "A bitch." He jabbed his finger at Jake. "His bitch. No one knows how she died but me! *We* were the only two people on the mountain. *I* saw her die. Me! Me!" he shrilled.

"Did you know, Hunter," I said softly, "they ran a tox screen on her body? She was loaded with Oxycodone and alcohol. A dangerous mix at eleven thousand feet, but I assume with your medical background, you knew that. You didn't pay Barstow enough to keep silent."

"You." He pounded the table in front of Jake, slopping wine on the table. "You lied to her. You wanted her for yourself!" Mottled purple rage colored his face.

Jake's hand squeezed my leg.

Hunter stood up, pushing his chair back nosily. The air crackled with the stench of his wrath. He taunted me. "You lying slut. You disappoint me. After all I did for you! Pity, you don't have the ability to know what you've lost." Both his hands were flat on the table, his face inches from mine. "I'm not going into that darkness, you little tramp." He kicked his chair under the table and strode out the side door.

Jake's lips formed a grim smile. "You surprise me at how deftly you can enrage a man. He's not that drunk. What are you going to do if he checks and finds out there wasn't a scan?"

"You think he's going to call Dr. Barstow and ask him? Hunter doesn't want to remind Barstow he's still alive." I placed my glass carefully on the table and looked up at Jake.

"Dangerous gamble," Jake said. "You make it difficult for me to keep you safe."

"I trust you for the job. Now, do we lose the afternoon or enjoy the rodeo?"

"I'm in. Nothing can happen to you in front of hundreds of people." Jake scooted back his chair.

A whisper in my ear hoped he was right.

The view from Jake's box was perfect. I could look down

into the chutes, see the bulls penned in by thick pipes and a long legged cowboy standing on the outside of the gate, ready to swing it open on the announcer's call. "Do you know where Hunter's box is?"

"No, but the private boxes are on this side and near the center of the arena. Why? You want to go at him again?" Jake asked.

"Nope." I laughed. "I want to see if anyone joins him."

I scanned the private boxes looking for Hunter's box. No sign of him, but there was a large empty private box above the chutes.

Jake caught me staring at the empty box and rolled his head on his shoulders. He squeezed my hand. "Let's enjoy the rodeo. Moratorium on Hunter. What are your favorite events?"

"Bull riding." I went along with Jake's intent to enjoy the present. "Nothing beats the excitement." The music started and the grand entry parade began. "You have a favorite?"

"Bronc busting. Breaking a yearling to a cutting horse is an art."

The bull was shifting his weight from side to side, banging into the sides of the chutes, building up anxiety and snorting when the rider stepped off the rails to mount him. The cowboy gripped the rope. The emcee announced, "The first competitor is 2011 PBR World Finals Winner, Joe Palermo, riding Twister." Cowboys opened the gate and Twister charged into the arena, bucking and spinning to his right. Palermo gripped the long braided rope with his right hand keeping his left hand high in the air for the judges to see. The emcee continued, "And this, ladies and gentlemen, is why bull riding is called the most dangerous eight seconds in the sports world. Look at that bull spin." The arena clock buzzed. Palermo flew to the dirt. The rodeo clowns distracted the bull while he ran to the rails. "Eight seconds," the emcee shouted in glee. "Great ride. Exceptional. This is gonna be the ride to beat!"

The next bull stormed onto the arena floor. "Here's B.H. Fields, the 2009 PBR World Finals winner riding Payback." I leaned over to Jake's ear so he could hear me over the emcee, "You think that empty box up there is Hunter's? It's the only empty private box."

"Can you live in the present, babe? We may have precious few times to relax until this is over. This is one of them."

"Sorry."

"I know you're over there worrying like a cat with a mouse."

"Ladies and Gentlemen, the next event is a rodeo classic, Saddle Bronc Bustin.' Keep your toes turned out and a smooth action going."

"Watch how this horse comes out of the chute," Jake said, leaning forward enthusiastically.

The horse bolted out of the chute, twisting and shaking the cowboy who rode him with a smooth rhythm while keeping his right hand high in the air. Widowmaker appeared to slow and the crowd surged to their feet stomping and clapping. Suddenly, Widowmaker charged to the middle of the arena, his head frantically bowing and his rear end bucking. His head arched back so far that his mane was tangled in the cowboy's rope hand.

"He's hyper-extending his neck!" Jake yelled.

Widowmaker went down in a heap, collapsing on the rider. I stood up covering my mouth in horror. "Oh my god. Look Jake. Both his legs are pinned under the horse!" The rider's feet and lower legs begin to convulse under the weight of the downed horse.

Rodeo clowns and the paramedics rushed to the scene. They lifted enough of the horse's weight to pull the cowboy to the safety of a litter. The rider gave a weak one-arm salute to the crowd and they roared their support. The vet examined the horse while a front-end loader idled at the edge of the arena floor. The vet motioned the loader to come, and it slowly churned across the dirt to scoop up Widowmaker's body.

Benita was capturing the unfolding scene. Two rodeo officials were striding toward her. Benita swung the camera to follow the ambulance rumble out.

"I have to get down there." I was scrambling over the people around us. "The rodeo officials will want to take the footage."

We ran into Dwayne on the stairs where Benita had hurriedly retreated. "You take the footage to the station and cut it," Dwayne ordered me.

"Dwayne, I'm not working crew tonight."

"I got this Dwayne. No problem," Benita said.

"I'm the producer, it's a sports event, for Christ's sake. I'm the sports guy! Not you. You're not giving orders. You're taking them," Dwayne snapped.

"Why don't you take the footage?" I asked.

"My job is to stay here with the rest of our folks and produce this event. I'm directly telling you, as *your* producer, to go to the station and cut that footage. Hurry up. We can make the ten o'clock with your voice under it." Dwayne's head jutted forward. "Well?"

I gritted my teeth. "I'm sorry Jake. This isn't the way I wanted it to be."

He gave me quick smile. "Want me to go to the station with you two?"

"No, we'll be fine together. Can you meet me at my house when I finish? I want to get some clothes." My face flushed with embarrassment to be arranging my personal life in front of Dwayne.

"Absolutely," he answered seriously. "Call me when you leave the station. I'll meet you on your back drive." He stepped aside to let Benita and I pass. "Take care," he called softly.

Chapter 29

Dusk was falling when I turned into my back driveway. No sign of Jake. Light snow and sleet peppered my windshield faster than the wipers could clear it. I pulled the Jeep into my detached garage, betting he'd be here by the time I got into the backyard. Icy patches had formed on the back sidewalk. The house loomed ahead, partially hidden by the stinging sleet. Suddenly, clouds of smoke and dust swirled through the sleet and the air was sucked from my lungs. I felt the explosion before I heard it. Shock waves tossed me to the icy sidewalk, triggering a show of white-hot dots of pain that grayed into darkness.

I stirred, groaning at the pounding pain in my head. Blood dripped into my right eye. Black oily smoke swirled around me. The heat and stench of burning rubber made me gag. Painstakingly, I twisted to see flames shooting through the garage roof into the evening sky. I tried to get up, but my legs shuffled pitifully on the frozen sidewalk, unwilling to support me. I pulled myself by my arms along the walk. *You have to get away from the garage before the gas tank explodes.* Greasy smoke shrouded the porch. I skinned my knuckles on the rough steps, wrapped my arm around the column and heaved myself up. Pain reeled through my head, dizzying me. With a huge whoosh, there was a second explosion. Bits of wood and burning sparks rained down on me. Hot fetid smoke billowed across the yard. I curled into the fetal position pulling my coat up over my head.

"Sawyer." Someone was gently shaking my shoulder. I touched him to make sure he was real. "Jake."

"Are you hurt bad? My god, if you'd waited for me in the Jeep you would have died."

"My head…"

"Shh, lay still. The fire department and ambulance are on their way." He took off his heavy coat and draped it over me. "I got here just after the gas tank went." He tucked his heavy coat around me. Flames licked the exposed garage rafters that collapsed moments later with a tumbling crash to the floor.

The pounding of feet echoed in my aching head. A medic leaned over me and began to feel my arms and legs. "Did you lose consciousness?" I started to nod but the pain was too great. "Yes," I croaked.

"She has a large lump here." Jake cupped the side of my head.

The medic gingerly touched the lump and then shined a pen light into my eyes. "Concussion most likely." The medic's face hovered over mine. "Nothing seems broken though. Try to relax. We're going to get you up." He snapped open the gurney. Hands tucked blankets around me.

My head hurt. Jumbled thoughts pinged in my head like errant beams of light appearing and disappearing. Barton was here now. He and Jake were talking. I wanted to join them, but strong binders around my torso and legs held me to the gurney.

"I'm going in the ambulance. We can finish this at the hospital," Jake said to Barton.

I drifted in and out. Jake was holding my hand each time I swam up to consciousness. Finally, my mind formed a question and I rasped, "Was anyone in the garage?"

"Not that we know. Can you tell me what you remember?"

One nod of my head and I was enveloped in pain. I squeezed my eyes shut and willed my mind to sharpen. "Some. The first blast knocked me down and I hit my head. When I came to, I dragged myself to the porch. Then you were there."

"I was crazy with fear. My god, I thought you were dead." He laid his head close to my ear. "I love you Sawyer. My god, I thought I'd lost you." His voice cracked.

My arms were bound to the stretcher; I couldn't touch him. My raw voice, layered with fear and rasped by smoke, told him all I could think, "I love you Jake. I love you." I sank back into painless sleep.

* * * *

The ER physician shined a bright light in my eyes and ordered x-rays. I lay quietly trying to summon up any reserve strength. "Severe concussion," he said. "I'll admit her upstairs and she'll stay the night. She can probably go home tomorrow," he told Jake.

Barton parted the curtains of the ER bay and asked the doctor, "Is she well enough to answer a few questions?"

"Few minutes, no more," the doctor said.

"Tell me what you remember." Barton stood by the bed.

Drugs eased the pain in my head. "I remember I left the overhead garage door open. I could look through the garage into the darkness on the other side of the fire before the Jeep blew."

"You store any explosives in the garage?" Barton asked.

"No, just books and stuff."

"Did you see anyone?" Barton persisted.

"No, and I didn't hear anything but the explosions."

"Think you were followed?"

"I didn't pay any attention." I sighed quietly. "I just drove home."

Barton looked at Jake. "We'll get the Cheyenne police out there too. They have a forensics investigator and a good technician. According to her, the car didn't blow first so probably the car didn't malfunction. She going home?"

"She's staying the night," Jake replied.

"I'll put an officer on her door," Barton said.

"I'll be here too," Jake said quietly. "Step out in the hall with me, Barton."

* * * *

The next morning I lay still in the bed with my eyes closed, trying to put some order to the jumbled events and burning snapshots in my mind. *Someone tried to kill me.*

I heard movement off to my right and gingerly turned my head. Jake was sprawled in a recliner. His eyes were open. "Morning, sunshine. How're you feeling?"

"Better, but I have the mother of all headaches."

"You have a concussion," Jake soothed, "but the doctor says you are going to be all right." He lowered the rails on the bed and sat down, smoothing my hair and caressing my check. "Barton put a cop on your door. And I'm not going anywhere. You're safe," he finished emphatically.

"But when I leave the hospital…?"

"We're going to the ranch. Your job is to heal. My job is to keep you safe."

I gathered strength from his calm, sure manner.

"The forensic investigator will be out to sift through the garage. Do you remember anything else?"

"No, I left the station and drove to the house." I shivered. "I nearly stayed in the garage in the Jeep to wait for you."

"Shh. You didn't. Your instincts kept you alive."

"Did Barton tell you anything else?"

"Not about last night. He did tell me no truck has turned up in a body shop for front end repairs."

Barton knocked and poked his head in. "How she's doing this morning?

"Much better." I struggled to sit up.

Barton came to the side of the bed. "How about a few more questions? See anybody, any cars around your place last evening?"

"No, but I wasn't really paying any attention. I was just thinking of meeting Jake and getting my things."

"You remember seeing any headlights on Horse Creek Road?" Barton asked.

"No."

"You go out to the house often?"

"Yeah, sometimes." I admitted.

"Wouldn't be hard for someone to know then," he said, scratching his head.

"You think he followed her?" Jake asked Barton.

"Could have. He could have already been within sight of the house and just waiting. He could have rigged the garage anytime before last night and then just waited for the right minute. We'll know more in a couple of days."

"She'll be dismissed this afternoon and we're going out to the ranch," Jake said.

"You gonna want any help out at your place?" Barton asked

"You offering?" Jake countered.

"I can have a patrol go by your house a couple of times on each shift. I can't spare a man twenty-four hours a day."

"I'd appreciate the patrols. We'll all be armed."

As they talked, I eased back into sleep, their voices getting further and further away.

* * * *

Jake drove slowly when we left the hospital. He had never left my side, feeding me ice chips and soothing my fears. I hurt like hell and looked worse than that, but he was still by me. We reached the turn-off to our houses. "Please, drive by my house. I just want to see it," I croaked.

"You sure?"

"Yes." Anger slinked back in on silent little feet.

The garage was a heap of twisted metal and black wood. The charred frame of my Laredo sat squarely in the middle of it. Two men were sifting through the remains, occasionally picking something up and then discarding it or bagging it.

"I guess I need to rent a car," I said, a bit too glibly. Too afraid to say the obvious. *I could have died here.*

"Yeah, right. A rental car is the first thing I thought of when I saw your Jeep. You want to get out? Please say no."

"No, I just needed to see it."

He held my hand on the short drive to his house.

Jake opened my car door. "Easy does it. Let's get you upstairs to bed."

After a day of rest and pampering, I dressed and came downstairs. Julia was in the kitchen chatting easily with Jake. She took a wonderful-smelling casserole out of the oven. I was surprised at how hungry I was.

"Hey there. You're awake." She hugged me. "Let's get some food in you." She busied herself making a plate for me. Julia tried to cheer me by telling funny anecdotes about her students and bits of gossip from town, but I had a hard time focusing on her stories. She helped clean up the kitchen and kissed me goodbye. I waited anxiously. Barton was supposed to come this afternoon.

Barton rang the doorbell and Jake showed in a grim looking Barton. "It wasn't an accident," Barton said. "The garage was destroyed by dynamite."

"Dynamite?" Jake reacted. Did you recover any fragments of the detonator?"

"Yeah, several fragments. Built out of common materials you can buy at any Radio Shack. He coulda parked down the road right out of sight, waiting for you." Barton nodded to me. "Then, when you drove into the garage, he pulled into range to detonate it. His having to move his car is what may have saved your life. You had time to get out of the garage into the yard. He didn't count on that."

I didn't store much in the garage. "Where did he hide dynamite in there?"

"The blast pattern is midway into the garage, on the right side." Barton looked at me. "It's not a big package. Did you store anything in that spot?"

"Yes." I felt chilled. "I would have never noticed another

box or bag there." Pure unadulterated anger cleansed the fear and the pain.

"I've got men talking to the Radio Shack stores in Laramie and Cheyenne. Don't mean it couldn't have been bought elsewhere, but those are the closest two."

"Can Radio Shack do a regional search if nothing turns up in Laramie and Cheyenne?" I asked.

"Already checked. They can." Barton crossed his leg over his knee and leaned back. "Also, the dynamite appears to be old and had been wet. Makes it very unstable. Someone had been storing this dynamite for a while. Maybe in a barn, but it had gotten wet all right. He could have blown himself up carrying the box and putting it down in the garage. We find the rest of the dynamite, it's a break for us."

"A lot of ranchers have a stick or two of old dynamite around their place," Jake said. "Handy to have around."

"The dynamite may not be the break we need." Barton looked proud. "We found a place where a heavy vehicle was parked. Right around the curve from Sawyer's place. Got a cast of a tire print and a shoe print out of the mud. Probably our guy." Barton was pleased with himself.

"Anything special about them?" I asked.

"Yeah, those tires were Goodyear crossovers. The front left tire has a cut in it shaped like a Y with a short tail. It'll be easy to match the tire track to the vehicle when we find it. That'll be a good break for us. The shoe print is a man's boot, size thirteen. So, he's probably a good size man."

"Hunter has an old ranch truck with crossover tires. He wanted me to buy some for my Jeep. He's a big man—could be a size thirteen boot. Take a look at his truck."

Chapter 30

A night of howling winds and bone-freezing temperatures transformed eastern Wyoming into a bitterly cold landscape. Blowing drifts made soft mounds of the fence lines that marked the boundary between Hunter's and Jake's pastures. Where there was no windbreak, the screaming winds had scoured the snow from the land. Jake's house had lost power twice, but he had a generator. Modern life continued. When I called the station, Clay said, "We're just running off the network feed. Just me and an engineer made it in so far and we walked. I'll take the network news feed at six and ten. I don't think the crew's coming in. You stay put out there. The real punch of the storm is going to wallop us this afternoon."

Jake walked into the den and I gave him the weather report. "Clay says the snow is going to get a lot worse. With the storm blowing in we're going to be isolated out here until the weather passes through." I paced a trail into the rug in front of the fireplace. "I can't stand doing nothing."

"We've got everything we need here even if we're cut off from town for a couple of days. You stay put in the house this morning. Keep your cell phone handy and don't answer the door. Any problems, you call Barton and me. Got it?"

"Where are you going?"

"We've got to put out hay and crack the ice in the windmill tanks for the herd. Most of us will be out until dark. I'm leaving a good man with you. He's out in the barn cleaning stalls and feeding the horses. He's armed."

"We'll fine here, Jake."

"Yeah, I know you will. Take this." He handed me a

sawed-off shotgun. "Not much different from the .410 you hunted dove with as a kid. Just point it and pull the trigger. And don't shoot my man with it either. You remember Terry, don't you?"

"Yeah, tall red-headed guy." I took the shotgun and opened the breach. "Be better if you'd give me some shells."

"Here's a box," Jake said grimly. "Lock up behind me. I'm leaving Chet with you. He'll bark if anyone comes near the house. I'll try and check on you during the day, but cell service is crap on parts of the ranch." He kissed me goodbye, then stopped at the door. "Remember, the house has an intercom system out to the barn. Punch talk on the box in the kitchen and you'll be able to call Terry out there. Take your finger off the talk button to hear."

Within two hours, I was bored witless. I tried reading a book. I tried watching television. I finally gave up and paced the den, musing about life's irony. As soon as you can't get out, that's when all you can think about is going somewhere. The intercom crackled to life. "Sawyer, it's Terry. I'm coming over to the house in about thirty minutes for some food. Could you make a fresh pot of coffee? I'll call you on the intercom before I start toward the house. I know the boss left you that shotgun. Don't get excited and shoot me."

I pushed the talk button. "Sure thing on the coffee, Terry. I'll have some sandwich stuff out. And I promise not to shoot you."

I headed toward the kitchen grateful for something to do even if it did involve preparing a meal. My cell phone hummed in my jeans pocket. Jake. He must be on some high ground to get a signal. "Hey, I'm slowly going nuts. How's it going out there?"

"Slow. The wind is ferocious. I'm breaking off from the boys. They're going to be awhile chipping ice and dropping this load of hay out in the west pastures."

"Are you sure you'll be all right out there by yourself?"

"All in a day's work. I need to check fence lines over on the north side. You probably won't hear from me—there's no cell service out there. Everything quiet at home?"

"We're fine here."

"I'll see you later. Love you."

"Love you more."

I rummaged in the refrigerator for cold cuts and cheese and popped some bread in the toaster. I was pouring water in the back of the coffee pot when I heard the cold hard crack of rifle fire coming from Jake's back pasture. Chet and I rushed to the den windows. He was barking wildly and jumping on the back door. Smoke drifted off the barrel of a scoped rifle.

I dropped to the floor. Reached up and pulled the shotgun out of the rack. The shells clattered on the floor. I grabbed a handful and stuffed them in my pockets. My hands were shaking so hard I could barely open the breach and shove in a shell. Chet clawed the back door and danced wildly back to me. I pulled the squirming dog to me. "Down," I hissed.

I crawled over to the kitchen wall, dragging the shotgun and Chet with me. Without getting my head above the window, I reached up and pushed the talk button. Crack. Crack. Damn, he had a high-powered rifle and some big targets.

"Terry, Terry! It's Sawyer. Don't come out of the barn. Can you hear it? Someone's shooting the buffalo." I let go of the talk button. No answer. Pushed it again, "Terry? Terry, answer me!" I squirmed along the floor back to the den windows, raised my head and scanned the pasture. A horse stood almost belly deep in the snow. A man's back was turned to me and he seemed to be hunched over, reloading the rifle. *Who is he?* He was too small a figure for me to tell.

I called Barton. The connection was poor, but I shouted what was happening over Chet's frenzied barks to the dispatcher. She hemmed and hawed. "Jesus, woman this is an emergency! Are you coming or not?"

"The storm's isolated the city. I don't know if we can get out there," she said.

"Do the best you can!" I clicked off and dialed Jake's phone. A tinny voice announced the user had shut the phone off or was out of cellular service. *Out of cell range, out of cell range* circled in my brain.

Terry. I need Terry to stop this madness. I belly-crawled back to the kitchen window. Pushed the talk button. "Terry, can you hear me?" No answer. I raised my head enough to see the barn door swing slowly open. The wind banged it on the side of the barn. Where was Terry? With the door open, he couldn't miss hearing that rifle fire. I eased open the kitchen door and pushed a scrambling Chet back into the house. The barn was no more than thirty yards away and the side of Jake's house shielded me from the rifleman.

I ran to the barn, gulping in the frigid air. *Damn I wish I had a coat.* My fingers were freezing to the stock of the shotgun. I stepped in the gloomy barn and dropped low behind a wall of hay bales. No noise but the creak of the door swinging gently into the side of the barn. My eyes grew accustomed to the gloom. Nothing but bales of hay and horse stalls. A horse nickered softly. I whirled toward the sound, pointing the shotgun, then eased it back to my side. I worked my way into the barn, keeping the hay bales between me and the open area. "Terry? You here?" I asked quietly. My breath was a white vapor cloud in the still air. Not even a rustle in the loose hay. I moved farther into the barn, my footsteps muted by the layer of dried grass. What was I going to do when I ran out of cover from the wall of hay bales? "Terry?"

The last stall door was open. A pair of booted feet stuck out the open stall gate. "Terry! Can you hear me?" The horse in the stall adjacent snorted and reared up. "Shh, boy. Shh."

Another rifle shot from the pasture broke the silence in the barn. I shouldered the shotgun and stepped out from behind the bales. Turned a three-sixty. No one else in the filtered light. I crept up to the figure lying in the hay. Terry was lying on his back, blood slowly freezing into the hay. A bloody slash circled his neck. I put my trembling fingers on his pulse and jerked my fingers off his cooling body. The horse in the adjacent stall snorted and kicked at the wall. "Shush, boy," I soothed, moving instinctively back behind the sheltering wall of hay. Terry, redheaded fun loving Terry, was dead. I was alone, isolated in a world of bone-freezing wind and snow punctuated with rifle fire. What if no one came?

I had to get back to the house. I couldn't—wouldn't—stay here with Terry's body. I opened the barn door and made a run for the house. I crashed into Chet as I careened into the kitchen. We crawled over to the den window, staying low. Another rifle shot pierced the cold air. I found Jake's binoculars jumbled in with the overshoes under the coat rack and rested them on the windowsill. A buffalo crashed to the snow. Clouds of steamy breath surrounded the bull's huge head when he struggled to rise. The rifleman shot him again. *Barton isn't going to get here before he kills them all.* The rifleman turned around, peering into the den windows through the riflescope. His face was huge in my binoculars. Hunter! My god. The frigid wind blew his blond hair over his forehead. He wasn't wearing a coat or a hat, only jeans and a shirt. The wind chill was well below zero. He couldn't bear the freezing temps much longer. If I waited for help, Hunter would kill the entire herd before he died. *Damn you, Hunter, for putting in me in this position.*

I wiggled into a pair of Jake's insulated coveralls while staying well below the window and quietly opened the back door. The low stone wall around the back porch gave me cover. "Hunter," I screamed. "Hunter, it's Sawyer."

Hunter carefully aimed his rifle at a yearling and squeezed off a shot. The calf toppled over, blood spurting from his shoulder, staining the snow around him.

Maybe the keening wind had shifted and blown my yelling away from him. I raised the shotgun and fired into the air. The spent shell clattered down the porch step. "Hunter, stop!"

Hunter swung the rifle around and fired erratically toward me, spraying me with glass from the transom window above me.

"Put the rifle down Hunter. Sheriff Barton is on his way."

"Jake's animals are on my land." Another crack of his rifle. "You comin' for me? I'm ready for you. This is my land," Hunter yelled.

"Put it *down*! Snowdrifts are covering the fence line between your ranch and his."

"No," he screamed. He erratically squeezed off a shot missing a buffalo cow. "Nothing's moving in this storm. Barton isn't coming. It's just you and me."

"You're going to die of exposure. Go home."

"Nooo," he raged. Hunter's voice was high-pitched and spine-chilling. His contorted face in my binoculars was barely recognizable. He swung the rifle toward the house.

I ducked behind the wall and yelled into the wind, "Hunter, you're going to freeze to death. Put the rifle down before Barton gets here."

"You lying bitch." I heard the lead slam into the wood column, splintering slivers around me. "I'm in control here. I lost Emily to the bottle and I'm not going to lose you to that bastard, Spooner."

"You're freezing your ass off!" The wind snatched my words and whirled them toward Hunter. "You're not losing me. You never had me. Put the rifle down. You're gonna die out there."

"No!" The wind carried his scream.

"Put it down now! Barton's seen inside your locked closet." I yelled from behind the wall, embellishing the truth. Anything to stop him and get him out of the storm. "I saw the jars, and the pictures of Emily and me."

Damn it. Barton get here!

"You lying cunt," he screeched into the wind. "I'll kill you before I let you ruin me."

"You're through killing."

"No Emily, you never understood what the darkness is." His moan whistled over the wind. "The darkness comes over me. The warm blood in my hands. The power. I'm powerful now."

"For god's sake, shut up your psychobabble about darkness and go the hell home to freeze to death! I've called Jake. He's on his way. Don't let him come up on you with that rifle."

Hunter's arms sagged and the rifle hung at his side. He stumbled to his horse screeching, "Nothing I'd like better than Jake Spooner to come up to me right now so I could kill the son of a bitch. Leave me alone Emily. It's dark. It's dark…" After mounting, he whipped the horse with the reins and they plowed through the drifts.

I kept low as I went into the warm house. *Where the hell was Barton?* Hunter would die of exposure. A quiet voice from my darker side answered, *So what? He's a crazy bastard with nothing to live for.* I watched his retreat through the den window with the binocs. He pulled up his horse in the tree line, reined him to the right and spurred him north. *North! Nooo!* Jake was out there alone somewhere riding fence. I fumbled my phone out of the cumbersome coveralls and dialed Jake's cell. No service. I rolled over on my back, tears running down my cheeks. Chet snuggled next to me and licked them off my face. His head nudged my shoulder until I threw one arm over his head, hugging him to me. The screaming wind would silence Hunter's approach. Jake wouldn't hear him until Hunter had him sighted in the damn rifle. "Jake's not gonna die boy." I rolled to my feet, grabbed a fur hat and gloves from the rack in the den and stuffed more shells in the coverall's deep pockets. Chet and I raced each other to the kitchen door. He was prancing and barking wildly. "You stay, boy. No one is killing my love."

The barn was silent except for the soft nickering sounds of horses. I threw a fleece saddle blanket over a mare, cinching the girth strap tightly. She nervously shifted her weight when I stuffed a spare blanket in the saddlebag and the shotgun in the scabbard. The mare shuffled through the loose snow around the barn and then labored past the dead buffalo. Six bodies bled red rivulets into the snow.

I followed the trail left by Hunter's horse into a stand of trees. The wind howled, shaking the dry snow from the branches. The horse struggled through the rocks and snow, great clouds of steam swirling around her head. I bent over the saddle, scanning a trail scoured smooth in places by the wind. Barely visible tracks headed up a ridgeline moving north. He'd never make it far in the storm, but he might run into Jake. Hunter and that rifle would be on top of him before he realized Hunter was there and armed.

The subzero wind battered snow into my nose and eyes. Even with the heavy down coveralls, my body ached from the wind chill. The mare picked her way around a switchback. Boulders lined the trail. Hunter couldn't have made it much farther. The mare was breathing heavily and slick with sweat. I slid off. "It's okay girl." I slipped the shotgun out of the scabbard. I didn't want to round the corner making a damn big target on a horse if Hunter were lying in wait.

I led the mare up the trail. She shielded me from the wind chill and warmth rolled off her body. I fumbled out my cell. No service. Could Barton get here or was he stuck in Cheyenne? The wind was dying down and the snow became heavier, muffling sounds. Great drifts softly tumbled off the tree limbs. No sound of a jingling bridle or snorting horse laboring up the trail in front of me. The trail widened into the clearing, bordered by a stand of trees.

I kept the mare to the edge of the tree line. Her velvety nose snuffled my neck. Moving silently toward the clearing, I was careful to stay behind the trees. I dropped to my stomach, unable to see the entire clearing from my vantage point. No sign of Hunter from what I could make out. I flattened myself in the snow. He could be just ahead in the clearing on the other side of the tree line. Waiting for me to step out. I'd make a perfect target in the blinding whiteness around me. No sign of Jake. No shots rang out. The forest was supernaturally silent with the heavy snow deadening any sound. I moved forward on my belly, taking shelter behind any cover I could find, wiggling to find a spot where I could see the entire clearing. I burrowed into the snow behind a small boulder and raised my head. Hunter leaned heavily on the stock of his rifle. His horse's foreleg canted at a crazy angle. The animal snorted, wild-eyed as he struggled to stand. Hunter put the rifle to its head and the crack reverberated through the snow.

I crouched behind the boulder. "Throw the rifle away from you. I've got a horse and a saddle blanket for you. You know you're freezing. You have a ranch that needs you, the auction house—George needs you." I hoped to heaven Jake hadn't heard the shot and us screaming.

Hunter made a half spin and simultaneously shot from his hip. The blast deafened me. Chips from the rock drew blood on my face. Pine needles rained down on my shoulders.

He dove over the back of the dead horse and took cover. "Get away from me Emily. I killed you." His head rested on the horse's belly. "Go away, Emily. Take the darkness with you."

The wind was quiet, big flakes floating down. Damn, I was tired and Hunter was crazy-talking, maybe so nuts he wasn't suffering from the bitter cold. As much as I hated him, I couldn't leave him out here to die. I just couldn't do it. "You're going to freeze to death if you don't get moving."

"Can't walk. My ankle's broken." He pulled himself up on one leg with surprising speed and braced himself over the dead horse's back. He tucked the rifle under his chin, pad to his shoulder and turned the scope on me. "You left me for Spooner." He elevated the rifle barrel slightly.

"Don't do it," I cried.

Time slowed. My head barely above the rocks, I watched as his finger slipped from the guard to the trigger. I flattened myself behind the boulders before the shot screamed through the snowy silence.

I stayed flat on the ground, peering around the rock. The recoil and his broken ankle had made Hunter lose his balance and fall, twisting his leg under him. He screamed in agony, "My leg. Emily, I'm hurting bad." The rifle now lay far from his reach.

"I'm coming out to help you! Lie flat." His head eased back in the snow. I reached the rifle first and threw it aside. His leg was canted at an unnatural angle under him and his jeans were dark with blood. The snow under his leg was stained pink. His breathing was shallow and breathy. "I can feel my leg bone sticking out." Blood was everywhere—seeping into the frozen ground. I stayed out of reach. No telling what he had in his pockets.

"Kill me Emily..." His eyes tracked me. "Please," he mumbled.

"No." I slipped closer to him.

Hunter's eyes fluttered closed. He was still. "You're going to have to help me get you closer to the dead horse. Its body warmth can save your life."

"Kill me now, Emily," he begged in a hoarse whisper.

"I'm not your executioner! I'm going for help. Hurry up! We're both going to freeze!" He tried to pull himself through the snow to the horse and fell into blessed unconsciousness.

I dragged him the rest of the way until he lay against the belly of the horse, then returned to my own to retrieve the spare blanket. I covered him, tucking the ends around his torso and legs. Gave him a chance, at least. Not much, but as much as I could do.

I was breathing heavily, dizzy from the effort and sweating profusely when I walked out of the clearing without looking back. He couldn't harm Jake now.

.

Chapter 31

I wrapped my arms around the mare's neck, my head bobbing in time with her gait. She found her way back to the ranch. When she broke through the trees into Jake's pasture, he grabbed her reins. "My god, I missed your calls. I've been crazy."

I raised my head from the mare's sweating neck. "I couldn't get you on the cell. I was afraid he'd killed you too." Relief surged through me, but I was so exhausted my head dropped back on the horse's neck. I clung to her while Jake led her to the porch. I slid off into his arms and he carried me in the house.

"Where are you hurt?"

The world darkened at the edges of my vision. I sank boneless to the floor.

When I came to, I was on the sofa, out of the stinking coveralls and smothered in blankets. I still smelled of blood and filth. "Drink this. It'll help warm you up," Jake said, handing me some hot coffee. "I don't see any wounds, except the scratches on your check."

I reached up and touched the bandage on my right check.

He held me gently. "Tell me. I know Terry's dead and someone shot the buffalo." He stroked back my hair.

I sat up and jerked off the blankets. "We have to get to Hunter. I left him out there by his dead horse." I pulled on Jake's sleeve. "Get up! Get up, he'll die. He doesn't have a coat. We have to go back up there!"

Jake gently pulled me down holding me close. "It's been too long since you left him. He couldn't survive this long in the storm. Shush. Shush. You're all right now," he murmured in my hair.

I wrenched away from Jake wailing, "Nooo. What time is it? How long since you found me?"

"I found you in the pasture over an hour ago. The thermometer on the porch shows minus fifteen, which puts the wind chill at minus thirty at a minimum. You did what you could. He's dead," Jake ended softly.

I held myself very still. Tears rolled down my cheeks. I sank down on the sofa and buried my face in Jake's neck.

"What happened, babe?" He rocked me as he would a child. "You're safe, tell me."

"I was afraid Hunter would find you out there. You said you were going north. When Hunter turned north, I was terrified he would kill you. He had already killed Terry and the buffalo. Oh my god," I snuffled.

Jake made soothing noises. I took a couple of deep breaths and straightened up to look in his eyes. "I could go on living without you because I'm complete within myself. You are too. It's one of the many things I love about you. But I'm a better person with you than without you. I wasn't going to let him ambush you." Jake opened his mouth to speak and I put a finger over his lips. "You damn well better take good care of yourself. I'm depending on you."

"Babe, you can bet I'll take care of both of us." He crushed me to him. "I love you and I don't want to lose you."

We clung to each other. I broke the embrace. "You asked me what happened. When the firing started, I called Terry on the intercom. He didn't answer so I took the shotgun out to the barn and found him dead. Hunter thought I was Emily, called me over and over by her name." Rhythmic shudders started at my shoulders and passed down to my legs. First one and then the next tremor wracked my body.

Coffee sloshed out of my cup. Jake took the mug out of my hands and held it to my lips. "Drink, you're going to be okay." He shifted his weight to hold my shuddering body tightly.

The shaking faded away. "I followed Hunter..." My teeth were chattering out the short sentences. "When I found him, his horse was lame and he shot her. He called me Emily, begged me to shoot him. Then he pointed the rifle at me saying *I* left him and he fired.

"When he thought I was Emily, he said he had killed me." My voice rose higher and higher. ". He begged Emily—me—to kill him." I sobbed. "I left him with all I could, a blanket and a body of a horse and he was *freezing to death*."

"Listen to me, Sawyer. You tried to save him. You did everything you could to save him. You called Barton and me. No one could have reached you in this storm." Jake's voice filled the room. "It's a wonder you didn't die, too." He cupped my chin and turned my face to him. "Hunter committed suicide by Emily. He *made* Emily leave him. Hunter was done with living. He used you. And you could have died out there."

Jake called Barton, canceling his and my calls for help. I heard him tell Barton that Hunter was dead. They talked for a few minutes. "Barton says nothing's moving out of Cheyenne. When the weather breaks and plows are running, they'll get out here and go by horseback to retrieve Hunter's body." Jake touched squeezed my shoulder. "He feels guilty he couldn't get here to help you. But he's damn relieved you're all right."

I was haunted by the memory of Hunter lying by the horse, the snow sifting down around him. "Are you sure? Jake, what if he's *alive*?"

"He's dead and anyone who goes out in the dark in this storm after him is a dead man, too." Jake walked over to me, "The bastard used you and he's gone, Sawyer."

I scrubbed my body until my skin was raw and stinging in the hot water, then fell into bed, finally drifting to sleep when a weak dawn streamed in the windows. When I awoke, Jake was already gone. I went downstairs and found him perched high on a front-end loader scooping out the snow and earth to make a pit. I grabbed my coat and joined him in the back pasture. He loaded each buffalo in the bucket and placed the body gently in the pit. When he dropped the calf in, he turned the loader, using the scoop to push the dirt over them. Jake turned off the heavy diesel engine and stepped down into my arms.

I dropped my hand around his waist. "I'm so sorry they were killed…"

"I can breed another herd." He slipped his arms around my shoulders. "You feeling any better?"

"Yeah. Thanks for last night." I kissed him. "I still can't believe he killed Terry."

"You went out to the barn to help Terry. I'm proud of you. He wanted to stay yesterday and guard you. He volunteered to help you."

"I'm grateful. If he hadn't stayed, he would be alive, but I probably wouldn't. I still can't believe they're both gone."

* * * *

Jake and I cuddled on the sofa under a soft cashmere throw before a crackling fire. I only felt secure close to Jake and the life-giving warmth from the fire. We both felt the bone-deep exhaustion that comes after hours of coursing adrenaline. Jake refilled my coffee from the pot on the table. I added a shot of Bailey's, fearing I would never feel warm again.

Chet jumped up, barking ferociously. Satisfied that Jake would do the heavy fighting once alerted, he settled back down by the hearth with a sigh, his guard dog duties accomplished.

Jake brought Barton back to the den. "Afternoon, Sawyer. I'm real sorry I couldn't get out here yesterday. Plows cleared the county road early this morning."

I poured Barton some coffee and set the mug in front of him. He fingered his sweat stained felt hat. "I'm real sorry for what you went through. We recovered Hunter's body this morning. Hell of a sight up there."

Jake put a reassuring hand on my shoulder.

"I don't think Hunter would have let any of us save him," I said.

"'Spect your right about that," he said. "Before the storm blew in, we took a look at that old truck of Hunter's. Had the Y cut in the tire and front-end damage too. We got a judge to give us a search warrant for Hunter's place this morning and we went over there." Barton's eyes darted around the room and settled uncomfortably on a spot on the floor.

"What did you find?" I asked.

He twisted his hat in his hands and cleared his throat. "He had boots up in his closet that made those prints out on the side of the road."

"Anything else?"

"Yeah." He shifted. "See, he had a second closet up there in his bathroom. I've never seen anything like it. Never."

I waited patiently.

Barton put his hat down on the lamp table and scrubbed his hand across his face. "Jars. Big jars with animal parts in them. Looked like buffalo tits and balls." He looked stricken. "Sorry."

"It's okay." I waved his words away.

"Had a buffalo tail coiled up in a jar full of yellow liquid. Faint, nasty smell in there."

He tweaked at the sharp edges of his khaki pants, worn white in the pleats. "Hunter had pictures of you on the walls of his closet. Pictures of another woman, too. Turns out, she's his dead wife. He had the two of you up there, side by side looking like twins." He stared hard at me. "You're not acting real surprised about the animal parts and the stuff in the closet. Be normal to be asking a lot of questions right now. How much of this you already know?"

"Only what I thought might be possible. You did the hard work."

"Do you think anyone was helping Hunter?" Jake asked. "Walker?"

"His prints weren't on anything. Got nothing to charge him with. Got no prints but Hunter's in the truck and the closet. I know we got enough to put Hunter in prison if he'd lived. His closet was set up like a shrine with those body parts and the pictures of you two."

"Did you find a knife? Jake asked.

"There was a little kit. Had a bunch of scalpels in different sizes and even a pair of bone shears. Hunter's prints were on them, too."

Both Jake and I watched him silently.

"Well," he said awkwardly. "Wanted you to know. He put his hat on and shook my hand and then Jake's.

"Thank you and your deputies for all you've done." I shook his hand.

"You're welcome," he said gruffly. "You did some good work."

Jake walked him to the door and I heard him thank Barton. The door softly closed. He walked back into the den, hands on his hips.

I patted the sofa beside me and Jake slid in next to me, wrapping his arms around me. "It's over. I hope Emily is at rest and maybe the ranchers can find some peace, too. Most folks will want to put a little distance between themselves and Hunter."

He stroked my hair back from my forehead. "Gonna take a little time to process all this. You did real well, Ms. Cahill. I'm proud of you." He kissed me gently. "Come with me," he said, pulling me to my feet. He reached for my parka and held it for me. "I have something I want you to see."

"Outside? It's freezing outside. Can't we see it from the window?"

"Nope, you can't." He stuffed a hat on my head and pulled one on his own.

Chet bounded out into the cold sunshine, sniffing a trail

and barking for Jake to follow him. "Come here, boy," Jake called to him and rubbed his head. We stepped off the porch by the gnarled cottonwood tree. Jake took my hand and we walked around the ancient tree. "My granddad carved this over eighty years ago when he bought this place." He ran his fingers over the old carving, EH. Chet sat and obediently listened, turning his head from Jake to me.

"Who's the SH?" I asked.

"My Grandmother, Sarah. Granddad carved her initials when they married. Look around here."

On the other side of the tree, he ran his fingers over his crudely carved initials. "I was out here the summer I turned twelve and I carved JS right here." He rested his hand below the childish carving. "When this place became mine, I added my Lazy E brand. Shut your eyes." He took my index finger, tracing my fingertip over the rough bark. I opened my eyes and saw a freshly cut SC. His gray eyes were full of warmth, a smile tugging at his lips. He wrapped his arms around my waist. "I think an S would finish that perfectly. What do you think?"

I kissed his full mouth, "Yes. Perfectly." Chet wriggled between us, bumping my legs and nosing my hand with his excitement.

Jake's gray eyes crinkled with happiness as he held me close. "We belong to each other, Ms. Cahill. Now. Tomorrow. Forever. So get used to it."

Teaching and shooting news and documentaries took me to work on the East and West coasts, the Midwest and an island in the Gulf of Mexico. Born a fourth generation Texan, I live in Denver with an energetic mutt that waits patiently every day for me to come home and write.